THE TROUB

I heard a shot behind me ~~and then~~ ... st have aged a year in the next few seconds, trying to guess who was running after me, but I kept going.

Another gunshot echoed through the halls and I turned down the first hall I came to, this one still dark. I was completely lost now, disoriented by running in the darkness.

I stopped in front of a closed door, opened it, then hurried into a classroom. I moved away from the door and put my back against the wall.

Suddenly a light came on in the hall outside the door. "I know you're in there," a soft voice said. "There's nowhere for you to go."

A figure passed by the door, its shadow brushing against the translucent glass on the door.

I hardly dared breathe . . .

**

Praise for TROUBLE LOOKING FOR A PLACE TO HAPPEN:

Books by Toni L.P. Kelner

DOWN HOME MURDER

DEAD RINGER

TROUBLE LOOKING FOR A
PLACE TO HAPPEN

Published by Zebra Books

Toni L.P. Kelner

TROUBLE LOOKING FOR A PLACE TO HAPPEN

KENSINGTON BOOKS
KENSINGTON PUBLISHING CORP.

KENSINGTON BOOKS are published by

Kensington Publishing Corp.
850 Third Avenue
New York, NY 10022

First Kensington Hardcover Printing: March, 1995
First Kensington Paperback Printing: March, 1996

Printed in the United States of America

To paraphrase *Henry IV, Part Two*, Act IV, Scene 5:

'Tis prize enough to be their daughter.

This book is dedicated to my parents:
William Everett Perry and Peggy Reece Perry.

Acknowledgments

I want to thank:

- Stephen P. Kelner, Jr., for all the obvious reasons, and some that aren't so obvious.
- Robin P. Schnabel and Paul Briggs for helping me research odd things like country music and how long it takes a body to start smelling.
- Elizabeth Shaw for proofreading. (Or does that have a hyphen?)

Chapter 1

I don't come home to Byerly to rest. Especially not this time, when my husband Richard and I were in town for Aunt Ruby Lee and Roger's wedding and all the accompanying festivities. Still, I had expected to get *some* time to relax. I certainly didn't expect Aunt Ruby Lee to call and wake me up three mornings in a row, each time with a different emergency.

The first morning we were in town, Aunt Ruby Lee called to ask me to watch out for her daughter Ilene at the country music Jamboree in Rocky Shoals. Ilene was fighting with her father Roger, and it was likely to be worse if he saw her there. The next morning, she called because Ilene hadn't shown up the night before and she was sure that she had run away. By the third morning, she was in a panic because Ilene's boyfriend had been shot, and the police were on her doorstep.

I had to wonder what would have happened if we hadn't come into town over a week early, because otherwise, we wouldn't have been there when the trouble started.

Chapter 2

It was dark as all get-out in the room, enough to disorient me, and I reached out and held on to the couch to anchor myself while I stared at the door. I heard a key turning in the lock, and then the door swung open. The woman at the door hadn't had enough time to reach for the light switch when my cousin Vasti leapt up and hollered, "Surprise!"

Aunt Ruby Lee jumped, of course, but she was giggling as the lights came on. The rest of us yelled "Surprise!" then but it wasn't much of a surprise anymore. Vasti had made us promise to wait for the count of three, but she hadn't been able to contain herself. Which is just like Vasti.

Aunt Ruby Lee was in the middle of hugging Aunt Daphine and Aunt Nora when she saw me. "Laurie Anne! I didn't think you'd be here until next week. You come right over here and let me hug your neck."

"Richard and I snuck into town early so I could come to the shower," I explained as we hugged. In fact, our flight had landed in Hickory a few minutes late, and I had barely made it to Aunt Ruby Lee's house in time to hide and surprise her.

"This is so nice of y'all," Aunt Ruby Lee said. "I never expected it." She turned to look at the big man standing out on the porch behind her. "Roger, did you know what they were planning?"

He grinned widely, which was answer enough.

"I was wondering why he was in such a rush to get back here after dinner," Aunt Ruby Lee said to me. "And why Clifford and Earl wanted to go see Thaddeous tonight."

Richard liked to call Roger my once-and-future uncle, because he had been Aunt Ruby Lee's third husband and was going to become her fifth in a little over a week. The whole family was hoping that this time the marriage would take.

Roger peered over Aunt Ruby Lee's head at the pastel crepe paper strung everywhere, the dainty sandwiches and punch on the table, and of course, the giggling women. "I can see this ain't no place for me. Slim's going to pick me up in a minute so we can rehearse over at Al's place. I'll be back later." He gave Aunt Ruby Lee a quick kiss, and beat a hasty retreat.

Aunt Ruby Lee smiled after him in the sweetest way, and I wished Richard were there to quote something appropriate from Shakespeare. I know taste in feminine beauty has changed since Elizabethan times, but surely buxom blondes with dimples and sparkling eyes were appreciated even then. Especially one with a personality as lovable as Aunt Ruby Lee's. After Roger drove out of sight, she came on into the living room and looked around. "Is Ilene not here?"

Vasti assumed the same expression she used to use when she was about to tell on somebody. "I don't know where she is, Aunt Ruby Lee. I *told* her when we were going to be here and I *thought* she'd be here to let us in. As it was, I had to use the key hidden under the flowerpot."

Neither Aunt Ruby Lee nor I asked how Vasti knew where the spare key was. Vasti just has a way of finding these things out.

Vasti went on, "When I spoke to Ilene about helping with the shower, she said she didn't have time to help fix party favors or make cookies or *anything*."

"She's been awfully busy getting ready for the Jamboree," Aunt Ruby Lee explained.

"I had forgotten the Jamboree is this weekend," I said. The Rocky Shoals Memorial Country Music Jamboree included a serious competition for new musicians, and I hadn't realized that Ilene had inherited her father's musical interests. "Then no wonder she lost track of time. I'm sure she'll be along shortly." Actually, I couldn't imagine how Ilene could be late for her own mother's bridal shower, Jamboree or no Jamboree. I could tell that Aunt Ruby Lee's feelings were hurt.

"I'm sure she will be," Aunt Ruby Lee said, but then sighed so faintly that I think I was the only one to hear it. Then she seemed to gather herself together and went to hug Aunt Nellie, Aunt Edna, and anybody else who came within reach.

Even with Ilene missing, there was plenty of family for me to catch up with. All five of my late mother's sisters and their daughters and daughters-in-law were there: Aunt Edna and her daughter-in-law Sue; Aunt Nora; Aunt Nellie and her three daughters Carlelle, Idelle, and Odelle; Aunt Daphine and Vasti; and of course Aunt Ruby Lee. There were even a few people who weren't related to us Burnettes. Of course, one of those was well on her way. Liz Sanderson, a pretty nurse at the Byerly Nursing Home, had been dating my cousin Clifford for over a year, and everybody knew it was only a matter of time before we would be throwing a bridal shower for her.

Manners said that I should start with my great-aunt Maggie. She had rarely attended family gatherings when I was growing up, but since my grandfather Paw died, she had been doing her best to take his place as the head of the family, even when she'd rather be somewhere else. I could tell she wasn't much interested in the shower from the I'm-going-to-do-the-right-thing-if-it-kills-me expression on her face. She had even dressed for the occasion. Not in a dress, of course, but she had worn a nice pair of black slacks and a fuchsia blouse. True, she was wearing sneakers with the outfit, but at least they were the same color as the blouse.

After the obligatory hug, I asked, "How's the flea market business?"

"Doing pretty well. I paid fifteen dollars for a box of glassware at an auction the other week, and I've already made seventy dollars off of it. And I saved the best piece in the box for Ruby Lee and Roger's wedding present." She looked around to make sure that neither Aunt Ruby Lee nor Vasti was in earshot. "It's a platter in her china pattern," she whispered.

"Desert Rose?" I whispered back. Aunt Ruby Lee had inherited my grandmother's china.

Aunt Maggie nodded.

"She'll love that."

"Do you know what that china goes for these days? I priced it, and I'd eat off of paper plates for the rest of my life before I'd pay any such price for dishes."

"What are you two whispering about?" Vasti said, suddenly appearing right next to us.

"Nothing much," Aunt Maggie said, but I could tell that Vasti wasn't fooled.

"That's a gorgeous necklace, Vasti," I said, by way of distraction. I knew that if Vasti found out what Aunt Maggie had bought for Aunt Ruby Lee, the surprise would be ruined in a matter of hours. Maybe minutes.

"Don't you love it," Vasti said, holding the pendant out on its chain so I could admire it more thoroughly. "Those are diamonds all around the star sapphire."

"Really?" I said.

Vasti nodded, and let it fall back onto her chest. "It weighs a ton. I told Arthur he shouldn't have gotten me something so *big*, but you know how he is. He says I've got to have the best."

Actually Arthur said that Vasti had to have what she wanted, which meant the same thing.

"Do you think it looks all right with this dress?" Vasti said with patently false anxiety.

"It looks wonderful," I said politely. Actually, it did look pretty good. The dress was the same blue as the stone in the pendant, and though the ruffles along the hem were a bit much for my taste, they somehow went along with Vasti's thick, brown curls and big brown eyes.

"How can you stand to wear those shoes?" Aunt Maggie said. "Don't you know they're bad for your feet?"

Vasti and I looked down at her patent leather pumps, which of course matched her dress. The heels were twice as high as anything I would wear, which meant that they were normal for Vasti. "They do hurt my feet sometimes," Vasti admitted, "but with Arthur on the City Council, I've got to keep up appearances."

That was baloney, of course. Having a husband on the

Byerly City Council did not require Vasti to cripple herself. Besides which, I knew for a fact that she had been wearing high heels ever since she talked her mother into buying her the first pair when she was ten years old.

"You ought to try wearing heels, Laurie Anne," Vasti said to me. "They'd make your calves look thinner."

I couldn't help looking down, but my calves looked all right to me.

"Laurie Anne's legs are fine the way they are," Aunt Maggie said.

"What about you, Aunt Maggie?" Vasti persisted. "High heels would make you look taller."

"Vasti, I've lived in Byerly my whole life. People already know how tall I am."

"But Aunt Maggie . . ." she began. Then she was caught by another concern. "Aunt Maggie, you are going to wear dress shoes to the wedding, aren't you?"

"I don't know what I'm wearing to the wedding yet," Aunt Maggie said airily, but I could tell from the twinkle in her eyes that she was pulling Vasti's leg. "I'll make sure my shoes go with my outfit. These I'm wearing match my shirt, don't they?"

Vasti looked at the sneakers and winced. "Yes, but—"

"Depending on what I wear, people might not even notice my shoes," Aunt Maggie said. "I saw some real cute pantsuits the other day."

Vasti gasped. "Aunt Maggie, you aren't going to wear pants to the wedding, are you?"

"Why not? That way I won't have to shave my legs."

"But Aunt Maggie, Hank Parker from the *Gazette* is going to be there taking pictures. What if they put a picture of you in the paper and said that you were Arthur's great-aunt by marriage?"

"Vasti, I've been living in this town a lot longer than Arthur has been city councilor. Maybe he should ask me what to wear." Before Vasti could finish her gasp, Aunt Maggie said, "Excuse me, girls, I want to speak to Ruby Lee for a minute."

Vasti shook her head after her. "Maybe if I bought her some shoes . . ."

"You know she's going to wear what she wants to, no matter what anybody else thinks," I said.

Vasti nodded sadly.

"And she dresses nicely when it's called for, doesn't she?"

"I suppose so. *You've* got something decent to wear, don't you?"

I was tempted to say something like, 'No, I'm going to wear a tank top and shorts,' but what I said was, "Yes, Vasti."

"Thank goodness for that. You know, Laurie Anne, I'm glad you came into town early."

For a minute I was touched.

Then she added, "I've got so much to do to get ready for the wedding, and I can put you to work right away."

Great. Running errands was just how I wanted to spend my vacation. "Richard and I do have some plans," I said.

"That's all right. I've got things for him to do, too. I *was* expecting to have Ilene's help, but she's been too busy."

"I'm kind of surprised that she isn't here," I admitted. "Aunt Nora wrote me that she's been hard to get along with lately." Aunt Nora had been particularly upset when Ilene quit the Girl Scouts, after having been a member for so long, but I hadn't taken that too seriously.

Vasti snorted. "Too big for her britches, is more like it. Never lets anybody know where she's going or when she'll be back, and never has a pleasant word for anybody. I hear from Clifford and Earl that she's just *impossible* to live with."

Clifford and Earl were Ilene's older half-brothers. Clifford's daddy was Fred Collins, Aunt Ruby Lee's first husband, and Earl's father was Alton Brown, her second. Ilene was Roger's daughter.

Vasti was starting to say something else when I saw headlights in the driveway.

"Maybe that's her now," I said, and went to look out the window. A silver Camaro with half a dozen small dents and two great big ones had pulled into the driveway, and I thought I recognized Ilene in the front seat.

"Who's that she's with?" I asked Vasti, who had joined me at the window.

Vasti shook her head disgustedly. "That's her new boyfriend. You know Tom Honeywell, don't you?"

I knew him by sight and by reputation, and that was plenty enough for me. I did some fast mental calculations. "He's at least seven years older than she is."

"Eight, as a matter of fact," Vasti said, "but if you ask me, his age is the least of his faults."

That was true enough, if half of the tales I had heard about him were true. He had been a behavior problem since the day he was born: skipping school, smoking and drinking at an early age, vandalism, petty theft. Even Aunt Nora, known for liking just about everybody, had sadly described him as trouble looking for a place to happen. And that was *before* the big scandal over what he did to his father.

Though Sid Honeywell had never filed charges against his only child, everybody in Byerly knew how Tom had run off with every bit of money he could find at the family's filling station. Sid had nearly gone bankrupt, and the strain took its toll on his health, too. Afterward, he was so nervous about trusting anybody that he had converted the station to self-service so he could run it by himself.

"Is Ilene coming inside or not?" Vasti said. "Maybe I should go out and get her."

"I'll go," I said hurriedly. "You tend to the party." If Vasti went barreling out there, she was likely to say something to get Ilene mad, and I didn't want Aunt Ruby Lee's shower spoiled.

"All right," Vasti said. "I probably should make sure that the punch turned out all right."

I took my time going out onto the front porch. From there, I could see that Ilene and Tom were kissing good-bye, so I just waited a few minutes. Then I started humming, and tapping my foot, and clearing my throat. I had about decided that they wouldn't notice a marching band going past them when the car doors opened.

"Ilene?" I said. "Is that you?"

"Of course it's me," she said. "Who did you think you were spying on?"

Tom laughed at that, and I decided to hold off saying anything else until I finished counting to ten. In binary. Twice.

The two of them went to the trunk of the car and pulled out something on a hanger wrapped in plastic, and several big bags.

"Do you need any help?" I asked politely.

They didn't answer, so I assumed that they didn't and waited for them on the porch.

"Hi," I said. "I'm Laura Fleming, Ilene's cousin."

"I know who you are," Tom said. He was dark-haired, with that vaguely pouty look you see in male models. I might have considered him good-looking if I hadn't known so much about him. He said, "I thought you went up to Yankee land."

"I came back to town for Aunt Ruby Lee's wedding." As a reminder to Ilene, I added, "And for the shower, of course."

Tom didn't answer, just looked me up and down like he was considering how much money to offer for my services. "You sure don't look much like Ilene."

Ilene giggled, and I felt my face go red. Admittedly Ilene had her mother's blond hair and blue eyes, which made my own brown hair and hazel eyes seem a bit drab by comparison. And Ilene's figure had been spectacular since she was thirteen, while mine was no more than average. In all honesty, I had been jealous of Ilene's looks for years, but I had never encountered anybody but Tom Honeywell rude enough to make the comparisons I occasionally made to myself.

There wasn't anything I could politely say to him, so I turned to Ilene instead. "The shower's already started. Aunt Ruby Lee's been looking for you."

"I *told* her I had to go shopping," she said. Then, to Tom she said, "I better go in before Mama has a hissy fit." She leaned toward him, and they kissed for what seemed like an awfully long time when somebody else was standing there.

Then Tom pushed the bags he was carrying at me. "Here you go, cousin."

I wanted to tell him that I sure as shooting wasn't his

cousin, but politeness won out and I just took the bags and went inside.

"Ilene's here," I said as brightly as I could manage.

"There you are," Aunt Ruby Lee said with evident relief. "I was afraid that nobody had told you about the shower."

"Of *course* I told her about it," Vasti said.

"Sorry I'm late," Ilene said unconvincingly. "Tom and I had things to do to get ready for the Jamboree."

"That's all right, baby," Aunt Ruby Lee said, and she did sound sincere. "Why don't you put those things away and come join the party?"

"All right. I'll be back in a minute," Ilene said and headed for the stairs. I followed along with her bags.

The door to Ilene's room was the only one on the hall that was shut, and there was a KEEP OUT sign on it. She opened it without turning on the light, and carefully hung whatever it was she was carrying in the closet.

"Is that your bridesmaid dress?" I asked, following along behind her.

"No," she said and reached for her bags.

If this was the way Ilene had been acting, it looked like Vasti had avoided exaggeration for once in her life. But then again, I said to myself, maybe Ilene was feeling left out of all the wedding plans. "You did know about the shower, didn't you?" Ignoring Ilene would have been pretty thoughtless, even for Vasti.

"Vasti told me she was going to throw one, but I didn't know when it was going to be. I think it's silly to have a shower anyway. It's not like Mama hasn't been married before."

Ouch! True, this was Aunt Ruby Lee's fifth marriage, but what harm would it do to throw her another shower. "It has been a long time since that first wedding," I said. "And any excuse for a party is a good one."

Ilene said, "Just what this family needs, another chance for them to stick their noses in everybody else's business."

I honestly wasn't sure if she meant me, too, or not.

"You can go back downstairs now," she said.

I guess I was halfway expecting a hug, despite the way she had been treating me, and I hesitated.

"Do you mind if I brush my hair by myself?" she snapped.

"Sorry," I mumbled, and fled down the stairs to be with people who wanted me around.

Chapter 3

Carlelle, another one of my cousins, must have seen from the look on my face what had happened, because when I got downstairs, she came right over and gave me a big hug.

"Hey there, Laurie Anne. You're looking good."

"Thank you. You look pretty sharp yourself." Carlelle and her sisters could come up with the most elaborate systems of curls and twists for their hair that I had ever seen, and make it stay up no matter what the weather was like. "I'm glad that somebody wants to see me," I said, glancing upstairs.

"Teenagers," she said, shaking her head. "There's nothing you can do with them other than wait for them to grow up."

"If Ilene keeps acting like that," I said, "she's not going to get a chance to grow up." Then I grinned, "Of course, I seem to remember that you, Idelle, and Odelle were pretty obnoxious at that age, too."

Surprisingly, Carlelle stiffened at the mention of her sisters. "At least one of us grew out of it," she said sharply.

"What's that supposed to mean?"

"Let's just say that you can't always trust people the way you think you can, even if they are your sisters." She glared across the room to where Idelle was chatting with her mother, my Aunt Nellie, and then over to another corner where Odelle was talking to our cousin-in-law Sue. "You'd think that growing up with people would mean something, but when push comes to shove, it's everybody for herself."

I was so surprised you could have knocked me over with a feather. "You three aren't fighting, are you?" I had never known the triplets to quarrel, not ever. Every other woman I know who has sisters has had at least short-lived feuds, but not these three. Sure, there had been tiffs over whose turn it was to set the table or who left the clothes in the washer, but nothing serious.

I realized that while the three of them still had the same hairstyle, Carlelle was wearing a dress with violet stripes, Idelle was wearing a peach blouse and white skirt, and Odelle was in slacks and a long tunic. I had never seen them dressed that way before. The three had worn matching outfits since they were babies.

"What's the matter?" I said.

"I don't want to go into it here, Laurie Anne. Let's us get something to eat, and we'll talk about it later." Again she glanced darkly at her sisters. "I want to make sure that you hear the *real* story of what's been going on around here."

I was starting to feel like I was at the wrong shower. First Ilene acting as ill as a hornet, and now the triplets fighting. At least I was pretty sure that I could count on the food.

As usual, Vasti had done an excellent job of supervising the cooking. Carlelle and I picked up paper plates and quickly filled them with Aunt Edna's ginger snaps, apple pie from Aunt Daphine, and tiny versions of the biscuits that are Aunt Nora's specialty, filled with country ham. While I was getting a glass of punch, Odelle came over to say hello, and Carlelle pointedly went to the other end of the room.

"When did all this with your sisters happen?" I asked Odelle.

She sniffed. "I just recently noticed what kind of people I've been living with."

"Odelle—"

"I don't want to ruin Aunt Ruby Lee's party, Laurie Anne. Let's us get together while you're in town and I'll tell you the whole story. The *real* story." She raised her eyebrows meaningfully, and went to get some pie.

Or maybe she was just trying to avoid Idelle, who gestured to me at that moment. I had a good idea of what it was she was going to say, but I went anyway.

"Idelle, what on Earth is going on with you three?"

Idelle shook her head sadly and said, "Laurie Anne, I never would have guessed that it would come to this. My own sisters turning on me the way they have."

"What did they *do?*"

Again that mournful shake. "I just can't talk about it right now."

Before she could add what I knew was coming, I said, "Why don't you call me later this week and you can tell me about it then? The *real* story."

"I'll just do that." Then she headed for the refreshments, which meant that Odelle had to rush away, and Carlelle had to move off the couch to stay as far as possible from both of them. It was a good thing that Aunt Ruby Lee had such a big living room, or the three of them might have actually had to come within arm's reach.

There was a snort from behind me. "If those three aren't the silliest things I've ever seen."

"Hi, Aunt Edna." I tried to figure out a way to hug her with a plate in one hand and a cup of punch in the other, but couldn't quite manage it. "What are they fighting about?"

"A man, of course."

"He must be something special to get them stirred up like this," I said.

Aunt Maggie joined in then, and said, "It's Slim Grady, the guitar player who joined Roger's band. He didn't seem like that much of a much to me, but then I've never met any man worth fighting over."

That attitude was probably why she was still single. The women in my family had always thought it was a shame because Aunt Maggie was a handsome woman, but I guess her penchant for wearing T-shirts with sayings like LEAVE ME ALONE! and I'VE GOT P.M.S. (PUTTING UP WITH MEN'S STUPID-ITY) made her feelings on the subject of romance pretty clear.

"Not all men are bad," Aunt Edna said with a little giggle. She had rekindled her romance with old flame Caleb Wilkins last Christmas, and judging from how happy she looked, things were going very well. I couldn't have imagined her giggling a year ago.

"Most of them are," Aunt Maggie insisted. "Look at Ilene. Barely out of diapers and she's already making a fool of herself over that Honeywell boy."

"Seventeen is a long way out of diapers," I reminded Aunt Maggie, but couldn't help asking, "How did she get hooked up with him?"

Aunt Edna shrugged. "She's got it into her head that he can help her with a music career. As if he knew a bit more about the music business than I do. Ruby Lee isn't doing

Ilene any favors by letting her run around with somebody like him."

I was about to ask for more details when Vasti raised her voice and said, "All right, ladies, go ahead and get settled down so Aunt Ruby Lee can open her presents." She pulled a chair into the middle of the room. "Aunt Ruby Lee, you sit right here."

As Aunt Ruby Lee obeyed, Vasti pulled out a complicated-looking camera and said, "Who wants to take pictures?"

"I will," Sue said.

"Are you sure you know how to use it?" Vasti said doubtfully.

"Sure I'm sure," Sue said. Vasti gave it to her, and Sue examined it and peered through the viewfinder. "Just aim and shoot, right?"

"I guess," Vasti said. "Arthur just bought it for me this week, and I haven't had a chance to practice with it. Try to do a good job. If the pictures come out right, Hank Parker said he'd run one in the paper."

Sue said, "What's the worst that could happen? Hank Parker can print a picture of my thumb." Vasti looked appalled, and Sue picked that moment to snap a picture.

I shouldn't have laughed, but Sue does have a knack for deflating Vasti. Lord knows that somebody has to once in awhile.

Anyway, Vasti heard me and said, "Laurie Anne, you're done eating, aren't you?"

I hadn't realized that I was, but since Vasti took my plate away, apparently I was. She said, "You sit here and keep track of the bows." She put a folding chair next to Aunt Ruby Lee's. "Where's Ilene?"

"Right here," Ilene said without a bit of enthusiasm as she came down the stairs.

"Ilene, I want you to write down everything your mama says while she's opening the presents," Vasti said, thrusting a pad of paper and a ballpoint pen at her.

"What for?"

"Just do it," Vasti said and went to supervise something else.

"It's a shower game," I explained to Ilene, hoping that her disposition had improved.

Ilene didn't look amused, but this was probably her first bridal shower.

I said, "Would you rather I did it?" and she handed me the pen and paper. What Vasti had in mind was crude and embarrassing, but it was awfully funny. Besides, Aunt Ruby Lee had been the one to take down my remarks at my bridal shower, so I owed her one.

"You can keep up with the bows from the gifts," I told Ilene.

"What for?" she asked again.

"To make a pretend bouquet for Aunt Ruby Lee to carry at the wedding rehearsal. For good luck." Actually I wasn't sure why this particular tradition was supposed to be carried out, but I figured that it had to be for good luck.

"I don't know what they're having a rehearsal for anyway," Ilene muttered. "You'd think she could walk down the aisle blindfolded by now."

I checked to make sure that Aunt Ruby Lee hadn't heard, and fortunately she hadn't. Bringing up Aunt Ruby Lee's other marriages at her bridal shower was pretty tactless.

Vasti finally corralled and arranged everybody to her

liking, and handed Aunt Ruby Lee the first package. I immediately got busy writing down what she said. Aunt Ruby Lee knew what I was up to, so she didn't say too much as she opened the first couple of gifts, but it didn't take long for her to forget about me. By the fourth gift, she was squealing and giggling and saying all kinds of potentially hilarious things.

I guess Vasti had decided on a lingerie shower because after her other marriages, Aunt Ruby Lee probably had all of the toasters and place mats that she needed. Nightgowns and such were something she could always use, and she did get some pretty things. She seemed to especially like the red satin robe I gave her, but then Aunt Ruby Lee has a way of making everybody think that she's special.

The last and nicest gift was from Aunt Nora and Aunt Daphine. They had bought their sister the laciest, most delicate negligee I had ever seen. We all oooed and ahhhed over it, and I nearly forgot to write down what Aunt Ruby Lee said. We made her pass around the box so we could all take a closer look.

Aunt Maggie was the last one to look at it. "That's right pretty," she said. "But Ruby Lee, you need to get Carlelle to sew you some fur around the hem."

"Fur? What on Earth for?" Vasti said.

"To keep her nose warm," Aunt Maggie said innocently.

It took a couple of seconds for her meaning to sink in, and then the room exploded in giggles. The only one who didn't laugh was Ilene. She just rolled her eyes and looked disgusted.

Despite Ilene's reaction, I knew that this was a great time for me to do my part. Once the laughter subsided, I cleared my throat and announced, "I'm going to read you what Aunt Ruby Lee is going to say on her wedding night."

Now, Aunt Ruby Lee hadn't made any untoward remarks, but there's no way anybody can open presents without saying things that sound risqué, if read the right way.

"I didn't say anything bad, did I?" Aunt Ruby Lee said, trying to remember.

I just grinned, and started reading out my notes, pausing between each to let the others react. "Isn't that nice? I've always wanted one of those. Feel how soft it is. I hope it's big enough. It's stuck. Can you give me a hand?" All innocent remarks, unless you're in a room filled with giggling women.

I read through them all, finally ending with what Aunt Ruby Lee had said when she got a look at the negligee. "My goodness, I've never seen anything so pretty in my entire life." That brought the house down again. My mama had always told me that women's sense of humor is much lower than men's, but it wasn't until my own bridal shower that I really believed her.

Chapter 4

Vasti had some shower games for us to play after that, and of course we munched some more, but eventually people started to leave. Richard and I were staying with Aunt Maggie, so while I was waiting for her to get out of the bathroom so we could drive over to her house together, I listened in as Vasti gave Aunt Ruby Lee some last-minute instructions.

"You checked with the florist like I told you to, didn't you?"

"Yes, Vasti," Aunt Ruby Lee said.

"And you made sure that Aunt Daphine can fix your hair the morning before the wedding, haven't you?"

"Yes, Vasti."

"Good. Now I got a call from the lady at the dress shop this afternoon. Your dress is all ready, but she said that Ilene hasn't come in for her final fitting."

Aunt Ruby Lee turned to her daughter, who had put on a Walkman, and said, "Ilene, I thought you had an appointment yesterday."

Ilene didn't answer.

"Ilene? Ilene!"

There was still no reaction.

Finally Vasti called out in her shrillest voice. *"Ilene!"*

Even a sullen teenager couldn't pretend not to have heard that, and Ilene looked in our direction. "What?"

Aunt Ruby Lee said, "Honey, can you turn that down a minute?"

Ilene made a show of doing so.

"Vasti said you haven't gone for the final fitting of your dress for the wedding. I thought that's where you were heading when you took the car yesterday."

"I guess I forgot," Ilene said.

Vasti sighed theatrically. "You forgot? Ilene, the wedding is *only* eight days away. Don't you want everything to be perfect?"

Ilene shrugged. "Tom and I had to go down to Rocky Shoals and register for the Jamboree, and it took longer than we expected. I don't see what the big deal is—I'll go the first of next week."

"I should hope so," Vasti said.

Ilene turned the Walkman back on and closed her eyes, making it plain that she was finished with us.

"Aunt Ruby Lee," Vasti said, "doesn't Ilene realize how important the appearance of an attendant is to the beauty of the wedding? Especially when she's the only bridesmaid. I *told* you we should have had more."

"Vasti, you know I wanted to keep the wedding simple," Aunt Ruby Lee protested. "Having Ilene and the boys stand up with me and Roger is a plenty."

Vasti did not look convinced. "I suppose it's too late to ask anybody else now, anyway. Unless I had a seamstress make the dresses special . . ."

"Who are you getting dresses for now, Vasti?" Aunt Maggie said as she came out of the bathroom. "I thought you had one already."

"Of course I do. I ordered my dress ages ago. Only I had to have it altered just this week because I've lost weight." She put her hands on her waist. "I think I'm even tinier than I was when I got married." She waited a minute for compliments, but when none came, she said, "Where's your mail, Aunt Ruby Lee? I want to check and see if you got any more RSVPs today."

Now that Aunt Maggie was ready, I thought that we were finally going to get out the door, but just then the groom-to-be Roger came in, followed by Clifford, Earl, and a tall man I didn't recognize. Of course that meant taking a few minutes to hug Roger, Clifford, and Earl, which normally I don't mind, but it was getting late.

I didn't know if I was supposed to hug the stranger or not, so I said, "Hi. I'm Laura Fleming, one of Ruby Lee's nieces. Which makes me Roger's niece-to-be, I suppose. Most people call me Laurie Anne."

The man took this explanation in stride, which made me think that he was a Southerner. When he spoke, I was sure of it.

"Pleased to meet you, Laura. I'm Slim Grady. I play in the Ramblers with Roger."

The Ramblers were Roger's country music band, and that meant that this fellow was the object of Carlelle's, Idelle's, and Odelle's affections. "Slim" was a pretty good name for him, because he wasn't plump, but he wasn't skinny. His hair was dark and his eyes even darker. He had big, strong-looking hands, which were good for a musician and reminded me of a tale about male anatomy I had heard in junior high school.

I shook that thought right out of my head. I was more tired than I had realized.

With the formalities over with, Clifford and Earl headed for the kitchen to dig into the leftover goodies and Roger asked, "Did y'all ladies have yourselves a good time?"

"We sure did," Aunt Ruby Lee said. "Everybody gave me the prettiest things."

"Well, haul them out and let me see."

"Roger, I can't show you those things," Aunt Ruby Lee said, and darned if she wasn't blushing.

Vasti explained, "It was a lingerie shower."

"Is that so?" Roger said with a gleam in his eye. "I'll be looking forward to seeing just what you got in a week or so."

He put his arms around Aunt Ruby Lee and gave her a big hug. They were a handsome couple. Roger was blond, too, but his hair was sandy-colored and wavy. Roger's the only country musician I've ever heard of who dresses flashier offstage than on. He was wearing a bright blue Western shirt that would have looked gaudy on anybody else, and of course had on his trademark turquoise and bear claw bracelet, ring, and belt buckle.

They looked so cute standing there that I had to smile, and even Aunt Maggie looked indulgent. Then I heard a loud snort from the couch. It had been so long since Ilene had spoken to anybody that I had nigh about forgotten she was there.

Aunt Ruby Lee pulled away from Roger, and Roger said to Ilene, "Hey there, pumpkin. I didn't see you over there. Did you enjoy your mama's party?"

Ilene shrugged. "It was all right."

"She's just tired," Aunt Ruby Lee said. "All these wedding activities are getting to her."

"What about me?" Vasti wailed. "I spent all day putting

the shower together, and I've still got to get the plates and punch bowl set I borrowed into the car."

"Clifford and Earl can take care of that for you," Roger said, right on cue. He called them out of the kitchen, and when Slim volunteered to help, Vasti put them all to work. She made a couple of pointed hints for Ilene to help, too, but Ilene ignored her just as pointedly.

While the fellows loaded the car, Roger added, "Speaking of wedding activities, Vasti, you don't have anything for me to do this weekend, do you?"

Vasti pulled a tiny leather-bound notebook from her pocketbook and consulted it. "I don't think so."

"Good. I got a call from Forrest Jefferson over in Rocky Shoals. One of the judges she had lined up for the Jamboree backed out, and she asked me to take his place. Since me and the Ramblers were already going to play a couple of sets there, I told her I would."

"Without checking with me first?" Vasti said in a shocked tone.

"Vasti, have you ever tried to say no to Forrest Jefferson?"

"She is awfully pushy," Vasti agreed, which was the pot calling the kettle black as far as I was concerned. "I guess it's all right."

Ilene snorted again. "A person would think it was you getting married, instead of Mama and Daddy. Haven't you got something else you need to do?"

Vasti smiled in a way that told me trouble was coming, and said, "I guess I get carried away. So Roger, are you going to be judging the novice competition?"

"No, just the semi-pros," he answered.

"That's good. I was afraid that your being a judge might

be a problem with Ilene being in the competition," Vasti said, far too innocently. Clearly she knew something that I didn't.

"Since when is Ilene in the competition?" Roger said. "I don't remember being asked about it."

"Mama said I could," Ilene said quickly.

"Is that right? Ruby Lee, don't you think that you and I should have talked about something like this?"

Aunt Ruby Lee looked distinctly uncomfortable. "I didn't think it was necessary, Roger. Ilene's been in contests before, in school and all."

"The Jamboree isn't just a school talent contest, honey," Roger said. "It's for people who are planning to become professionals. Our little Ilene would be way out of her league."

I swear I saw the blood rushing to Ilene's face.

Aunt Ruby Lee must have seen it too, because she said, "But Clifford and Earl were in it last year, and they did good enough to move up to intermediate."

"That's different. Clifford and Earl are working toward careers in music."

"So am I!" Ilene said. "I'm as good as they are."

"Honey, you know that's not so," Roger said. "I'm just thinking of you. You don't want to go out there and embarrass yourself, now do you."

"Daddy, I'm good. I am!"

"She does have a pretty voice," Aunt Ruby Lee said.

"A pretty voice isn't enough," Roger said, and the patronizing tone in his voice was raising even my hackles. "The Jamboree is for serious musicians, not for little girls."

"I'm not a little girl," Ilene said.

"Ilene, I'm afraid you're just not ready for something like this. Maybe next year."

Ilene must have been able to see from his face that talking to her father was like talking to a stone wall, so she turned to her mother. "Mama, you said I could. I've been practicing for ages. Tom helped me work out an act, and I've got my costume all ready."

Aunt Ruby Lee looked at Ilene, then at Roger, then back at Ilene. "Well, baby, if your daddy says you're not ready, maybe it would be better to wait a year."

"But Mama! Tom and I paid my money yesterday. You can't change your mind now."

"That's another thing I don't like," Roger said. "I don't know that Tom Honeywell is a good influence on you. Ever since you started running with him, you've been talking back to me and your mama, being out at all hours, dressing like a— Like you've been dressing. You never used to act like that before Honeywell came sniffing around."

"How would you know?" Ilene shot back. "You were never around."

Even Roger had to realize that Ilene had a point there. After he split up with Aunt Ruby Lee, he hadn't spent as much time with Ilene as he should have.

He said, "Well I'm here now, and I think it's high time you found somebody else to spend your time with instead of that—"

"Don't you dare say anything about Tom," Ilene said. "You've got no right to talk about him like that, and you've got no right to tell me who I can see."

"The hell I don't! Just who do you think you're talking to?"

Ilene didn't bother to answer that. Instead she looked at Aunt Ruby Lee again and said, "Please, Mama. You said I could be in the Jamboree."

"I know I did, honey, but if your father feels this strongly about it, maybe you shouldn't."

"If *he* feels this strongly? What about how I feel?"

"Don't talk back to your mother," Roger warned.

"But it's not fair!"

"You watch your tone!"

"You watch yours!" Ilene yelled at him. "We were doing just fine, Mama and me and the boys. Why did you have to come back? You don't own this house, and you don't own me. I'm going to be in that Jamboree and I'm going to win, too. You just watch me!"

Before anybody could respond, she spun around and ran up the stairs.

"Just wait one minute!" Roger started, but Aunt Ruby Lee took hold of his arm.

"You better let her be for now, Roger," she said. "I'll talk to her later."

He relented, but he didn't look happy about it. Seconds later, we heard a door slam hard enough to shake the rest of the house.

That's when the two of them remembered that Slim, Aunt Maggie, Vasti, and I were still there, just as embarrassed to have seen that as they were. At least, Slim, Aunt Maggie, and I were embarrassed. Aunt Ruby Lee murmured an apology, and we said something equally meaningless in return. Then we all left, with Aunt Maggie making sure that Vasti went, too. Slim was too polite to say anything about the fight. He just walked us to our cars before leaving himself.

Chapter 5

As soon as Aunt Maggie and I got into her car, I took a deep breath and said, "That was unpleasant."

"Folks ought to keep their arguments to themselves," Aunt Maggie said.

"I imagine that they would have if Vasti hadn't been there to egg them on."

"That's true. Sometimes Vasti is enough to try a saint."

"Don't you think Roger was being unreasonable about Ilene? If Clifford and Earl were in the contest last year, why can't Ilene give it a shot?"

"That's between Ruby Lee and Roger."

"Is Ilene any good? I don't think I've heard her sing in years."

"I wouldn't know."

"I felt so sorry for her. Roger was so condescending. She is seventeen after all. Nearly eighteen."

Aunt Maggie didn't say anything.

I said, "Have Ilene and Roger been fighting much before now? It seemed to me like this wasn't the first time."

"Laurie Anne, I'd just as soon not talk about this. There isn't a thing I can do about their problems, and even if there was, I wouldn't stick my nose in somebody else's business. I'm not one for giving advice when it's not asked for."

"You're probably right," I said. Even though her words had been mild enough, it still felt like a rebuke. "I guess I was starting to sound like Vasti."

Aunt Maggie chuckled. "Not hardly. I don't think you could sound like Vasti if you tried."

That made me feel better, and I steered the conversation toward other topics for the rest of the drive back to the house.

"I'll bet that Richard has gone on to bed," Aunt Maggie said as we pulled into the driveway. "I didn't have any idea that we'd be out so late."

"I'm sure he waited up to say hello to you." Sure enough, he was sitting in the living room reading a paperback copy of *A Midsummer Night's Dream.* After four years of marriage, I still wasn't sure what it was about my husband's lanky frame and ill-behaved mop of hair that appealed to me so much, but I knew that they did. As for his big brown eyes with long lashes that could have been effeminate had his features not been so strong, I knew just why it was I loved looking at them.

Hugs were exchanged, and then we all got bottles of Coke and went downstairs to the den in the basement, where it was cooler to sit on a warm June evening.

I felt that odd mix of familiarity and unfamiliarity that I always did when staying with Aunt Maggie. Her house was the Burnette home place, and I had spent a lot of time there as a child. Only then, my grandfather Paw lived there. When my parents died, I moved in with Paw, and lived there until I went to college in Boston and decided to stay there. When

Paw died, he left the house to Aunt Maggie, his sister and the last of their generation.

Aunt Maggie wasn't one for changing things just for the sake of change, but after two years, it just wasn't Paw's house anymore. She had covered the paneling with antique advertising signs in place of the family photos, and had filled all the bookshelves with an impressive collection of knick-knacks.

"What happened to the fiddle bottles?" Richard asked. Now that he mentioned it, I saw that they were gone, though there was no longer any space for them.

"I got tired of looking at them, so I sold them," Aunt Maggie said. "Got a good price for them, too."

"What are you collecting now?" I asked.

"Heads."

I didn't dare look at Richard, because I knew that I'd start laughing. "Oh?"

Aunt Maggie grinned. "Not the shrunken kind, Laurie Anne. This kind." She got up and brought over a ceramic piece shaped like a woman in a sun bonnet, and another that was a woman in a wide-brimmed hat. Both were hollow, with big holes on top. "They were made as planters, but I don't have time to mess with plants. Besides, they're collectible and I want to keep them clean."

She pulled out another that was an Indian maiden, complete with feather pointing proudly up. "Edna's boyfriend Caleb found this one for me. It's a rare one, too. Most of them like this have lost their feathers."

"I didn't get a chance to ask Aunt Edna at the shower. Are she and he getting along all right?" I asked cautiously. After our conversation in the car, I wasn't sure if asking would be considered nosy or not.

Apparently it wasn't. "Well, they're together all the time, so I guess they're getting along. He's talking about opening up a store in Byerly."

"No kidding." There hadn't been a grocery store in Byerly for years. The IGA in Granite Falls was the closest. "Would he close the store in Greensboro?"

"Edna says not. I guess he can afford to run both places."

"He must be richer than God." I turned to Richard. "Well?"

" 'The force of his own merit makes his way.' *Henry IV, Part Two*, Act IV, Scene 3."

"You call that colorful? I win that one hands down."

"No argument." He pulled a small spiral notebook from his pocket, and made a mark on my page.

"What are you two up to now?" Aunt Maggie wanted to know.

"We're having a contest," I said. "I told him that Southern expressions are more colorful than Shakespearean quotes, and he said that they aren't. So we're keeping track."

"I'm winning," Richard said.

"Only by two points. Excuse me, by one point now."

"And how long do you intend to keep this foolishness up?"

Richard said, "Until the wedding. Though I think I'm awfully generous to give Laura the home court advantage."

"But you're around people talking about Shakespeare all the time," I said. As an instructor at Boston College, one would think that he'd get sick of the Bard, but Richard never seemed to run out of quotes.

Aunt Maggie was shaking her head at the two of us. "For two people with as much schooling as y'all have, sometimes I think y'all don't have enough sense to come in out of the rain." Then she raised a finger at Richard. "And don't you put that in your little book."

"No, ma'am," he said in mock alarm and jammed it back into his pocket.

She had to grin at that. "Well, I'm about ready to head for bed. How about y'all?"

We thought it sounded like a good idea, and we shut out the lights and went upstairs.

When Richard and I were alone in my old bedroom, the room Aunt Maggie now used as a guest room, Richard gave me a real hug and kiss. Then he said, "I forgot to ask. How went the festivities?"

"Pretty well, but with a couple of rough spots." I told him about the triplets' feud and the even worse feud between Ilene and Roger.

"It sounds nasty," he said. "With which of the warring factions are you planning to open diplomatic relations first?"

"What makes you think I'm planning to get involved?"

"Past experience."

I stuck my tongue out at him, but then said, "Seriously, do you think I've been meddling?"

"You haven't had a chance to, yet," he said with a grin.

"Seriously."

This time he sat down on the bed and leaned back against the headboard before replying. "That's a tough question, Laura. The line between meddling and caring is a thin one. But no, I don't think you've crossed it. What you did for Paw, and for Aunt Daphine, and for Aunt Edna were all very good things. I just don't want you thinking that it's your responsibility to solve all of your family's problems."

"You're right," I said. "No more being the official Burnette troubleshooter."

"Let them solve your problems for a change."

"What problems? With a husband like you, how could I have problems?" I know it was sappy, but Richard appreciated it, and showed his appreciation in a way that precluded any more conversation that night.

Chapter 6

After the trip from Boston, Aunt Ruby Lee's shower, and the fight between Ilene and Roger, I really needed a good night's sleep, but I didn't get it. Oh, the sleep I got was good. I just didn't get enough of it. The phone woke me at seven o'clock.

I reached for the phone at the side of the bed, only it wasn't there. After another ring and some useless groping, I remembered that we weren't in our bedroom in Boston. Richard, the world's soundest sleeper, didn't even stir while I stumbled around the dark room to find my bathrobe, and stubbed my big toe on the way out the door.

Either Aunt Maggie hadn't heard the phone, or she had already left for the day. Both phones were downstairs, of course, and I promised myself that if Aunt Maggie hadn't put one in upstairs by the next time I visited, I'd put one in myself.

The caller was determined to get through. The phone must have rung more than ten times before I got to the kitchen and picked up the receiver. "Burnette residence."

"Laurie Anne?"

"Aunt Ruby Lee? What's wrong?"

"Ilene's gone."

"She didn't run away, did she?"

"Oh no, I don't think so. I think she's gone to the Jamboree, and Roger's going to be awfully mad if he finds out. After last night and all. Both of them are still real upset." There was a small silence. "Were you and Richard planning to go to the Jamboree?"

"We hadn't decided yet," I said, which was more or less true. The fact was that we hadn't even discussed it. "Are you?"

"I want to, but Vasti has me scheduled for the photographer to get my picture made in my wedding gown. Then we have to pick out the shots we want at the wedding. I think we have to see the videographer, too, to pick out background music or something. She says it's going to take most of the day." There was another pause. "Ilene probably doesn't know Roger is going to be there all day today. He wasn't supposed to be going until later on, because he and the Ramblers don't have to play until tonight and he doesn't have to judge anybody until tomorrow afternoon. But I just found out that Forrest Jefferson called him this morning, wanting him to come early so she can make sure he knows how he's supposed to judge." Another pause.

I knew I shouldn't say anything, but I couldn't resist that pause. "So you're wondering if Richard and I could go to the Jamboree and keep an eye out for Ilene?"

"If you don't mind. I'd send Clifford and Earl, but they're competing tomorrow morning so they were planning to practice most of the day. But if y'all were going anyway . . ."

"I'd be glad to," I said. "It's so nice out that I think it would be a perfect day for the Jamboree." Actually, it was already hot and hazy, even at this hour of the morning, but it was the best I could come up with.

"I sure would appreciate it, Laurie Anne." I heard a strident voice in the background. "Vasti just got here, so I better go. Bye."

After I hung up, I got a glass of water and drank it slowly, stalling while I tried to think of a way to tell Richard I had let myself be talked into going to a country music Jamboree when neither of us cared for country music. I like it in small doses, of course. It would have been hard growing up in Byerly if I hadn't. And I had always liked listening to Paw play gospel on his guitar, and I liked Roger's stuff. Still, I wasn't exactly a fan, and Richard liked country music even less than I did.

I finished the water, thought about drinking a second glass, but decided that there was no answer but to go right up there and tell him. " 'Twere well it were done quickly,' " I said to myself, but couldn't remember which act of *Macbeth* it came from.

Richard was still asleep, and though he looked pretty darned tempting, I shook his arm a bit to try and wake him. "Richard?"

"Mmmm?"

"Richard, that was Aunt Ruby Lee on the phone."

"Mmm mm?"

"Ilene is gone, and Aunt Ruby Lee thinks she's gone to the Jamboree. She wants to know if we can check on her. She'd go herself, but Vasti has her tied up all day."

"Hmmm?"

"You know, the country music Jamboree. It's supposed to be a lot of fun."

Dead silence.

"I know, you hate the idea. And I know I'm supposed to

be butting out of family stuff, but Aunt Ruby Lee asked me to."

"Mmmm!"

"I know it's not my responsibility, but I still want to help out. If you don't want to go, that's all right. I'll go by myself."

"Mmmm."

"You will?" I kissed his forehead. "You're wonderful! I'll take the first shower so you can sleep a little more."

It didn't take long for us to get dressed, and then stop by Hardee's to get sausage biscuits for breakfast.

"How far away is the Jamboree?" Richard asked as I pulled out onto the highway.

"About half an hour, forty-five minute drive," I said. "It's at the Rocky Shoals High School." I had never been to the Jamboree before, but knew that there would be signs along the highway. We saw the first one about a mile before the Rocky Shoals exit.

"It says 'Rocky Shoals Memorial Country Music Jamboree,'" Richard said. "Who are we memorializing?"

"The Rocky Shoals High School Class of 1980," I said. "Or at least, a good part of it."

"Aren't memorials usually for the departed?"

"Most of the Class of '80 died a month before graduation."

"You're kidding."

"Nope," I said. "It was a bus crash. They were on their way back from an Allman Brothers concert in Charlotte. This was before the highway went to Rocky Shoals, so they had to go down Mountain View Road, which is only two lanes and one curve after another. A Volkswagen was trying to pass them, and an eighteen-wheeler came around a curve and saw this car headed right for him. The truck swerved to keep from hitting the Volkswagen, and hit the bus hard enough to knock it right off the road. It fell twenty feet down a hillside. The bus had thirty-something kids on it. Only the driver and seven of the kids survived."

"Death lies on them like an untimely frost," Richard said softly, "to paraphrase *Romeo and Juliet*. Act IV, Scene 5."

"The whole town of Rocky Shoals was devastated, of course. Plus Rocky Shoals is close enough that folks there had relatives in Byerly, and the two high schools had group dances and such, so it hit us pretty hard, too. People talked about it for weeks and weeks. They even canceled school the Monday afterward. I was in junior high school at the time, but I remember how horrified everybody was. It was probably the worst thing to ever happen around here, short of the Civil War. Everybody remembers where they were when they heard about the Rocky Shoals bus crash. Kind of like when Kennedy got shot, on a local level."

"I can imagine."

"Then it got dredged up again when what was left of the class graduated. These kids were up there trying to be happy about graduating, when they had lost so many of their friends. I remember the picture in the paper of those ten kids."

"You said there were only seven survivors."

"Not everybody went to the concert. A couple of kids were sick, and one girl's parents wouldn't let her go."

"I bet she was grateful afterward."

"Yes and no," I said. "I remember hearing that her best friend and her boyfriend died on the bus."

"Oh."

"Talk about survivor guilt. Anyway, that's why they started the Jamboree."

"I don't follow."

"The kids went to the concert because there wasn't ever anything like that around here, and this wasn't the first time kids got hurt on their way somewhere else. The folks in Rocky Shoals started thinking that if there was something for kids to do nearby, they wouldn't be on the roads so much. So the next year, they put together the Jamboree so the Class of '81 wouldn't have to go anywhere else to celebrate graduation. They invited the kids from Byerly and from a couple of other schools, too. It was pretty dinky at first, just a bunch of garage bands playing and the one who got the most applause got a trophy. But it got bigger, and better organized. Now people come from all over this part of the country to participate."

Richard looked at the road. "I think they all got here ahead of us."

From the way traffic was beginning to build, he could have been right. I knew that we were still a mile from the high school, but we had come to a standstill.

"Don't you know any shortcuts?" Richard asked.

"I grew up in Byerly, not Rocky Shoals," I said, but I thought about it for a minute. "There is a back way I used once or twice . . . Now I remember. I should have gone that way in the first place. All I have to do is figure out how to get turned around."

The other direction was pretty clear, so I waited for the car in front to inch up another few feet, then made a three-point road turn that confused the heck out of the other drivers. "This will work," I said to Richard as we sped off in the direction from which we had come.

"If you say so," he said doubtfully.

"You said you wanted a shortcut." I got a little confused about where to turn, because they had built a new Hardee's, but finally found the tiny road that led to the back parking lot of the school. There were a few other cars going that way, satisfying me that it was the right road, but not nearly so many as there had been going the other way.

"See?" I told Richard. "I didn't just roll into town on a head of lettuce."

He thought for a minute. "You mean, 'I know a hawk from a handsaw.' *Hamlet*, Act II, Scene 2."

I pulled into a parking place and said, "You call that colorful? Anybody can tell a bird from a saw."

"Ah, but a hawk is a kind of ax, and the word 'handsaw' calls to mind the Old French word for a young heron. So it's really very clever."

"Maybe it was to the Elizabethans, but if you have to explain it, it can't be all that colorful."

Richard shrugged. "It was worth a shot." He pulled out the notebook and added in my score. "That makes us even."

"Ha!"

"A temporary setback only."

"We'll see."

Parking in the back lot meant that we had to walk all the way around the school to get to the entrance. There was a ridiculously long line at the ticket booth, and I couldn't help but compare this setup with what Vasti could have put together with just one clipboard and a telephone with call waiting. Eventually we were allowed to pay our money for a three-day pass and go in. I was hoping that we'd find Ilene long before that, of course, but as I told Richard, we might want to come back the next day and hear Clifford and Earl perform.

The signs posted directed us to the football field, where the stages were set up. There was a flea market in the other direction, and all kinds of food booths were scattered everywhere.

"Where should we look?" Richard asked, looking at the crowds surging around us. "I don't think just standing here and yelling 'Ilene' is going to help."

"How about asking there?" I said, pointing at a tent just inside the entrance with a large INFORMATION sign.

There was a considerable line in front of the tent, and the lady answering questions looked more than a little harried. The most common question I heard was, "Where's the rest room?" which was closely followed in popularity by, "When are the rest rooms going to be fixed?" I decided that I'd better watch what I drank.

When Richard and I finally got to the head of the line, I said, "Excuse me," to the lady at the table. "I'm trying to find one of the participants."

"We've got programs right here," she said, handing copies to me and Richard. "They're listed in the order in which they'll be performing."

Richard flipped through his and almost immediately said, "Here she is." His being such a fast reader does come in handy sometimes.

"What time does she perform?" I asked.

"Not until two," he said.

"Rats! I don't want to hang around here that long. And I want to warn her that Roger is going to be here. Maybe we can catch her before she goes on stage." I turned back to the information lady. "Can you tell me where the dressing rooms are?"

"They're in the west wing of the school, but you can't go back there," the woman said. "Only performers and staff are allowed in there."

"This is a special case," I said, not wanting to tell the whole story in public. "She's my cousin, and I *really* need to talk to her."

The lady shook her head. "I'm sorry, but there's nothing I can do. You'll just have to wait until she's finished performing."

"But this is kind of an emergency," I said.

"Is it life or death?"

"Not exactly, but—"

"If it's not life or death, you can't go back there."

Now I wished that I had claimed a death in the family or the need for a blood transfusion.

"Do you think we could speak to somebody else about this?" Richard said. "We can see you've got enough to deal with already."

"Well, if you find Forrest, you can ask her, but I don't think it's going to make any difference."

"Forrest?" he asked.

"Forrest Jefferson," she said. "About my height, light hair, wearing a blue and gold skirt suit. She's probably somewhere near the stage."

"Thank you," Richard said, and we made way for the next person in search of the rest room.

Even though the show hadn't started yet, there were swarms of people all around the stage. It took us fifteen minutes of concentrated searching to find Forrest, and even then we would have missed her if Richard hadn't been tall enough to see over most of the other people.

Forrest Jefferson had what I call a matronly figure, with an imposing bosom and hips but no waist to speak of. Her hair was pulled up into an efficient chignon, and the only makeup she was wearing was dark red lipstick. She wasn't pretty by any stretch of the imagination, but she had the look and air of command.

If it had been anything less than a family problem, I probably wouldn't have bothered Forrest. She already looked like she was under siege, yelling orders and constantly flipping through a huge sheaf of papers that she had in a death grip. One sheet dared to come loose just as we got to her, and Richard quickly bent down to grab it and hand it back to her.

"Thank you," she said.

"Excuse me, ma'am, but are you Forrest Jefferson?" I asked.

"I am."

"The lady at information sent us to you."

"Are you from Party-Potty?" she asked doubtfully.

"I'm afraid not. My name's Laura Fleming, and this is my husband Richard." We would have shaken hands, but at that moment somebody yelled a question about speakers and Forrest had to check a piece of paper and yell back an answer. Then I continued. "We're trying to track down my cousin, Ilene Bailey."

Forrest consulted a piece of paper. "She's scheduled for two o'clock." She looked pointedly at the program I was holding. "That should be in your program. Of course, I have no way of knowing where she is now." She started to turn away.

"Yes, ma'am, I know that, but I need to talk to her. Would it be all right if we went backstage and looked for her there?"

"Absolutely not. Only performers and staff can go backstage."

"We wouldn't bother any of the other performers," I assured her. "We just need to look for my cousin."

"No, I'm sorry. This is a serious competition, and I don't want the performers disturbed."

"But—"

Just then a man in a green coverall with the words PARTY-POTTY embroidered on his shoulder came up. "Ma'am? Are you in charge here?"

"I certainly am," Forrest said. "I called your people over an hour ago!"

"Sorry, ma'am, but the traffic was pretty bad."

"I don't know why you didn't have somebody here on duty," she retorted. "As much money as we're paying you, that's the least you can do." She seemed to forget Richard and me completely in her eagerness to tell the man what the problem was. The crowd surged around us, and carried her and the Party-Potty man away.

"Aren't there bathrooms in the school?" Richard asked.

"Of course there are," I said, "but God forbid that the performers be disturbed!"

"So what do we do now? Wait for this afternoon?" Richard said.

"Not on your life. We're going to look for Ilene."

"But Forrest said—"

"I heard what she said, but we're going backstage anyway. I can talk my way past any volunteer."

Richard looked doubtful, but said, " 'I am a kind of burr; I shall stick.' *Measure for Measure*, Act IV, Scene 3."

"If that means that I'm as stubborn as a mule, then you're right," I said, and didn't even bother to see who he gave the point to.

I considered climbing onto the stage and getting back that way, but decided that it would be a bit too obvious. Instead I led Richard toward the gym door, where a multitude of people seemed to be coming and going. The banner over the door proclaimed JAMBOREE PARTICIPANTS ONLY, so I was fairly sure that was the right place.

As we got closer to the door, I sped into my best imitation of Vasti's get-out-of-my-way-because-I'm-more-important-than-you-are walk. It worked long enough to get us through the door, but as we stepped onto the gym floor, a deep voice called out, "Excuse me! Can I see your pass?"

I turned with a smile, expecting to find an easily cowed volunteer. What I saw was a police officer with sharp creases in his pants, a cap that was on perfectly straight, and shoes that were polished so thoroughly that should a contestant need to touch up her makeup, she wouldn't need a mirror. Even though it was quite warm in the gym, there wasn't the hint of a perspiration stain under his arms, and his cheek was so carefully shaved as to make *me* feel like I had a five o'clock shadow.

I could tell that I wasn't going to be able to sweet-talk this man, but like I had just told Richard, I'm as stubborn as a mule. So I tried anyway. "Actually, we aren't participants."

"Then I'm afraid you can't come in here."

"The problem is that we need to find my cousin, and she is a participant. It's a family emergency."

He looked concerned, but not convinced. "And what is the nature of the emergency?"

I could have made something up on the spot, but even though I was in Rocky Shoals, I knew that anything I said would eventually get back to Byerly. Besides which, I just couldn't bring myself to lie outright to a police officer. At the same time, I really didn't want to air my family's dirty laundry in public. With those two constraints, there wasn't a whole lot I could say.

I took a look at the name tag pinned to his shirt. "You see, Officer Monroe, my cousin's mother sent me down with a message for her, and it's very personal. Couldn't I just slip into her dressing room? It won't take but a second, and I'll be sure not to bother anybody."

Monroe shook his head. "I am sorry, but rules are rules."

"Isn't there some way we can get a message to her?" Richard asked.

"Only in case of emergency."

"This *is* an emergency," I insisted.

Monroe just kept shaking his head, and Richard pulled me away from him before I could explode.

Chapter 7

"I'm so mad I could just spit!" I said, not caring if we were out of earshot or not.

" 'My heart is turned to stone; I strike it, and it hurts my hand.' *Othello*, Act IV, Scene 1," Richard said.

"Richard, I am not playing right now."

"Sorry. I'll give the point to you."

I was not appeased. "Can you believe that police officer?"

"Police chief," Richard said.

I looked back over at the man, and saw the word CHIEF on his hat. "Whatever. We may as well go outside."

Richard followed me as I stomped outside, not an easy thing to do in sandals. "Rocky Shoals must be pretty hard up if that's the best they can do for a chief of police!" I said.

"Extremely hard up," Richard agreed.

"Somebody with an attitude like that wouldn't last a minute in Byerly."

"Not even a second."

I went on in that vein for several minutes before I realized that while Richard kept agreeing, he was giving a lot more of his attention to his Jamboree program than to me. "Richard, are you listening to me?"

"Of course I am. You just finished accusing Chief Monroe of being Jack the Ripper."

"I said no such thing!"

"Didn't you? I'm sure you were working up to it."

I had to grin. "Okay, maybe I was getting carried away, but you'd think he could make an exception for a family emergency. What do I have to do to get in there? Bleed?"

"Maybe we could cover you with ketchup—"

"Okay, okay. I said I was getting carried away."

"Speaking of getting carried away," Richard said, "did you read the poem in the program?"

"What poem?"

He handed me his program, opened to the inside front cover. It was a set of rhyming couplets, more or less, describing the Rocky Shoals bus crash. All of the stanzas were awful, but the final one was perhaps the worse.

> *The road was dire and dark that night*
> *But not so dark as to hide the sight*
> *Of the many who in that bus did die.*
> *Listen now, to hear Rocky Shoals cry.*

The byline was Forrest Jefferson.

"That's really bad," I said, which was a mighty understatement. "If she's going to be so picky about rules, you would think she'd follow the rules of poetry."

" 'This is a very false gallop of verses; why do you infect yourselves with them?' " Richard said. "*As You Like It*, Act III, Scene 2."

"She can't write her way out of a wet paper bag," I replied.

He considered it. "That's a tough one. I think we need an impartial judge."

I looked around. "How about him?" I said, pointing to a man in a straw cowboy hat. "That's Slim Grady, the newest Rambler."

"And he's rambling our way," Richard said.

Slim saw us, smiled, and came over. "Hey there, Laura."

"Hi. Slim, this is my husband Richard Fleming. Richard, this is Slim Grady."

They shook hands and said their pleased-to-meet-you's.

"How are y'all doing today?" Slim asked.

"Not too good," I said, and explained how I had been trying to get in to see Ilene. Since he had been there during the argument last night, it didn't seem necessary to be particularly discreet with him now.

"That's a shame," Slim said. "Did you try the back door to the gym?"

"I didn't know there was one." I was tempted to try it, and obviously Richard could tell.

"It's probably locked," he said quickly. Then, no doubt as a distraction, he said, "Slim, we need you to be a judge for a little competition we're having. Which is the more colorful way to skewer a bad piece of poetry? Shakespeare's quote, 'This is a very false gallop of verses; why do you infect yourselves with them?' or the folksy, 'She can't write her way out of a wet paper bag'?"

Most people would have asked for more explanation than that, but Slim just took it in stride. No wonder the triplets liked him.

He said, "I hate to badmouth the Bard, but this time I'd have to go with the more modern insult."

"Ha!" I said. "Mark it down."

Richard dutifully pulled out his notebook and added a hash mark to my score.

Slim asked, "What poem were y'all talking about? It must have been a real stinker."

I handed him Richard's program. "Read it and weep."

His reaction, if anything, was even more perturbed than Richard's. Obviously he appreciated good poetry, or at least, hated bad verse.

"What is this doing in here?" he asked.

"I imagine Forrest Jefferson didn't want people to forget the reason behind the Jamboree," I said.

"I don't understand," he said.

"Did you not know?" I pointed out the word MEMORIAL on the program cover. "The Jamboree is to commemorate the Rocky Shoals bus wreck. That's right—you're not from around here." I took a deep breath, meaning to tell him the same story I had told Richard, but before I could, we heard a shriek.

We all looked up, and saw a fifteen- or sixteen-year-old girl with light brown hair and glasses pointing at Slim.

"It's him!" she trilled.

Slim stiffened.

"It's him!" the girl repeated. "It's Slim from the Ramblers."

She ran over to us, program clutched in her hand. "It *is* you, isn't it?"

"It sure is, sweet thing," Slim said with a warm smile. I noticed that his accent had suddenly gotten thicker.

"I just *knew* it was." She thrust the program at him. "Can I have your autograph?"

He smiled. "I'd be right pleased to give it to you. Now who should I make it out to? Should I call you Sweet Thing?"

She blushed. "My name's Karen."

Slim found the picture of the Ramblers in the program, and wrote, "I'll be singing my heart out over Karen, my own Sweet Thing." Then he signed it, "Rambling Slim Grady."

"Thank you *so* much," she said. "I think you're better than Jimmie Dale Gilmore or Billy Ray Cyrus, and almost as good as Clint Black."

"Well, I'm mighty proud you think so."

"Do you know Wynonna Judd?" she asked.

"No, but I sure wish I did. Maybe you could introduce us someday."

She giggled. "Oh, I don't know her, either. I better be going. I can't wait to tell my sister." She started to run off, then stopped and ran back, looking distraught.

"Oh! I should have had you make it out to me *and* Kristi. She's as big a fan of yours as I am."

"Why don't you sign that one for her?" Richard said, since Slim was still holding his copy of the program.

"That would be wonderful," Karen said, probably noticing Richard and me for the first time. "Her name is Kristi, K-r-i-s-t-i."

"Is she as pretty as you are?" Slim asked.

Karen just giggled again as he wrote out another message.

"Here you go," he said, handing it to her. "Now I'll be looking for y'all when we play this evening. Y'all be sure and wave."

"We will," she said, and ran away again.

"Does that kind of thing happen often in your line of work?" Richard asked.

"Oh, now and again. I suppose I'd get sick of it if I was a real big star, but for me it's all right."

"That little girl sure thinks you're a big star," I said.

"No, it's not me. It's the Ramblers."

"It's funny, but with Roger being part of the family, at least almost, I never realized how popular y'all were getting."

"I was real lucky to be invited into the group," Slim said.

"Slim just joined this year," I explained to Richard. "Were you in a band before?"

Slim nodded. "I've been in a couple of other bands, as a matter of fact, but none of them had the sound the Ramblers have. The money's a lot better, too. Before this, I had to work full-time and play at night."

"What did you do?" Richard said.

"Just about anything that would give me enough time for my music," Slim said. "Most of the time, I worked on cars. Which came in handy when we had problems with the bus awhile back. What do y'all two do?"

"Laura is a computer programmer," Richard said, "and I teach literature at Boston College."

"Specializing in Shakespeare," I added, though I probably didn't need to bother.

"Is that a fact? No wonder Roger talks about how smart y'all are."

I hadn't realized that Roger spoke well of me.

Slim went on, "And your cousins think a lot of y'all, too."

"Is that the triplets you're talking about?" I asked. Okay, it wasn't any of my business, but I wanted to know what he thought about the triple threat. "I hear you've been seeing a lot of them. Or is it just one of them?"

Slim just smiled. "Those three are something else, aren't they?" Which was a polite way of not telling me what it was I had no business asking. Then, probably to change the subject, he said, "Tell me something, if you would. Last night, you introduced yourself as Laura, but Roger always calls you Laurie Anne. Which do you go by?"

"Both," I said. "Most of the folks in Byerly call me Laurie Anne, but up North, everybody calls me Laura." I looked sideways at Richard, and added, "You can call me anything, just don't call me late for supper."

"Is that a Southern expression?" Richard asked.

"It has to be. Yankees don't eat supper."

"Good enough. 'What's in a name? That which we call a rose, by any other word would smell as sweet.' "

Slim said, *"Romeo and Juliet."*

Richard nodded in approval. "Act II, Scene 2. What do you think?"

Slim considered it. "This time, I think Shakespeare has the edge."

Richard and I agreed, and Richard added the point to his score.

Then Slim looked at his watch and said, "This has been nice, but I better see if Roger's gotten here with the bus yet. We've got to get set up." He tipped his hat to me, and said, "I'll see y'all later."

"I'll be sure to wave," I said in an imitation of Slim's adoring fan.

He just grinned, and dove into the crowd.

"I'll be sure to wave?" Richard asked with one eyebrow raised.

"It was just a joke."

"Uh-huh. I better keep an eye on you with all these musicians around, or you'll turn into a groupie."

"Musicians don't do a thing for me," I said airily. "It's

English professors that really turn me on. Especially assist-ant professors."

"Is that so?" He waggled his eyebrows in an exaggerated leer. "Maybe I can arrange a private lecture."

Not that that wasn't a distracting thought, but when I saw a couple of performers walk by carrying guitar cases, I remembered why we were at the Jamboree. "Maybe later. Right now, what I'd really like is a chance to get inside those dressing rooms."

"Musicians again?" Richard said with a sigh.

"Cut that out. You know I'm just trying to find Ilene." Then I said, "I wonder if the triplets are here."

"With Slim here, I don't think they'd be far behind, but I don't think they'd be able to get past that police chief, ei-ther," Richard said.

"They might if they could confuse him enough."

"Perhaps, but that would probably require more cooper-ation than they can bring themselves to provide at this point."

"You're probably right," I admitted. "I'm not used to their not getting along."

"It were a good motion if they leave their pribbles and prabbles. That's a paraphrase of *The Merry Wives of Wind-sor*, Act I, Scene 1."

"They're fighting like cats and dogs," I said.

"I think that one's mine," Richard said. I nodded, and he added it to his score.

Since we couldn't go where I wanted to go, Richard and I wandered around the Jamboree instead, hoping that Ilene would venture out where we could see her.

It wasn't a badly put together event, even if Vasti could have done it better. In addition to the music, which you could hear over speakers no matter where you were, there was a good-sized flea market on the lawn in front of the school. Dealers were selling records and CDs, guitars and harmonicas, sheet music, and posters of country musicians. I bought a signed photo of Garth Brooks as a gift for Michelle, the secretary at my office, even though it gave Richard a chance to make more groupie jokes.

By the time we had been all through the flea market, it was getting awfully hot, so we bought an iced tea for me and a Coke for Richard and found a shady spot to sit on the grass and watch the crowd go by.

" 'The many-headed multitude.' *Coriolanus*, Act II, Scene 3," Richard said.

I thought for a minute, but then said, "It's too hot to think. You can have the point."

"Poor Laura," Richard said sympathetically, but he added it to his score. "Do you want to head back to Aunt Maggie's house?"

"No," I said peevishly. "I came out here to find Ilene, and that's what I'm going to do."

Then I heard a voice calling, "Laurie Anne! Richard!"

Carlelle was coming our way. Since she hadn't seen Richard yet this trip, that meant she had to hug him, and she hugged me, too, just for good measure.

"Isn't this heat something?" she asked, once she joined us on the grass.

"Hotter than the hinges of hell," I said.

Richard hesitated, then quoted, " 'Hot blood begets hot thoughts.' *Troilus and Cressida*, Act III, Scene 1."

I shook my head and pointed to myself. He nodded and pulled out the notebook to add to my score.

To Carlelle I said, "Your outfit is great, but isn't it warm for a day like this?" I was only wearing shorts and a loose T-shirt and I was still about to burn up. Carlelle was dressed in tight blue jeans and a long-sleeved, red cowboy shirt with silver piping. Make that cowgirl shirt, because she was filling it in ways that no cowboy ever could. Plus she was wearing red and black boots that made me hotter just to look at them.

"I'm fine," she said, not too convincingly. "There's going to be a dance tonight, and I knew I wouldn't have a chance to go back home and change."

"Why not?" I asked. "It's not that far."

She looked at Richard out of the corner of her eyes, and shrugged.

Richard is smart enough to know when somebody wants a little privacy, and he said, "I think I could use another Coke. Carlelle, can I get you something?"

"That would be wonderful," she said. "I'd love a Diet Coke, but anything is fine, as long as it's cold and wet."

"Since you're going, can I have some more iced tea?" I asked.

"You bet," he said, and loped off in search of a concession stand. He knew that with the crowd and the heat, Carlelle and I would have enough time to recite *Hamlet* before he returned.

"The truth is, Laurie Anne," Carlelle said, "if I go home to change, Idelle and Odelle will be on Slim like white on rice. I tried to set it up so we'd all go back together, but *they* wouldn't agree to a time." She sighed. "My own sisters. I thought I knew them better than anybody on Earth, and I'd have trusted either one of them with my life."

"I can't believe that the three of you are fighting over a man," I said.

"Not just *any* man," Carlelle said. "Slim fits everything I have on my list for a man, to a T. Idelle always *said* she wanted a blonde, and Odelle swore me up and down that she preferred a man with more meat on his bones, but they've sure changed their tunes. It just goes to show, doesn't it?"

I wasn't sure what it went to show, but I nodded anyway. "What about Slim's preferences? Which one of you does he like best?"

Carlelle sighed again. "I wish I knew. I can't tell if he likes me and is only being polite to the other two, or if it's the other way around."

My first thought was that he wasn't interested in any of them, but I didn't know if I could say that without hurting her feelings. Then I spotted another familiar face in the crowd. "Speaking of your sisters, here comes one now."

Carlelle sniffed loudly, and looked in every direction other than the one Idelle was coming from. Idelle was dressed just as inappropriately for the weather as Carlelle was. Her wide skirt was probably cooler than Carlelle's jeans, but it was made of heavy denim. The low-cut, ruffled cotton blouse wouldn't have been too bad if it hadn't been for the heavy turquoise necklace that covered just about every bit of skin left bare by the blouse. Idelle was wearing cowboy boots, too, and I didn't know how she could stand it.

"Hey there, Laurie Anne," she said to me, but didn't say anything to Carlelle as she sat down on the other side of me. "What are you sitting here alone for?"

I started to remind her that I wasn't alone, but decided it wasn't worth it. "Just waiting for Richard to bring me something to drink. That's a gorgeous necklace, Idelle."

"It's not hers," Carlelle said. "Roger gave it to Aunt Ruby Lee for Christmas, and *she* borrowed it from her."

"Somebody's just mad because I thought of it first."

That didn't leave me a whole lot of room for pleasant conversation, but fortunately Richard returned just then. He hugged Idelle, and handed out drinks to me and Carlelle.

"I wish I had brought myself something to drink," Idelle said wistfully.

Carlelle slurped hers loudly and said, "Ahhhh."

"Take mine," Richard said. "I'll go get another."

"Are you sure?" Idelle said.

"Absolutely," he said. "I'll be right back." He disappeared into the crowd once again.

"That's awfully nice of him," Idelle said.

I nodded. It really was beyond the call of duty. "I'll reward him somehow."

Both of my cousins giggled, but each stopped upon realizing that the other one was giggling, too.

"I wouldn't have let him do it," Carlelle said to nobody in particular. *"Some* women try to run men ragged, instead of making them happy."

Idelle said, *"Some* women are worth waiting on once in awhile, without having to beg and scrape."

"Look," I said, before the discussion could escalate. "There's Odelle."

Since her sisters had laid claim to western attire, Odelle had dressed in country. She was wearing a flower print dress and a straw hat with a matching ribbon. Though she looked cooler than the other two, I wouldn't have worn panty hose on a day like that for love or money.

"Hey, Laurie Anne, don't you look nice and cool," Odelle said.

"You look very pretty, Odelle," I said. "Why don't you have a seat?"

"I better not. I don't want to get any grass stains on this dress."

Carlelle snorted. "You'd think a person would have more sense than to wear something so delicate at a Jamboree. That dress is going to pure wilt in an hour."

"Better that than a pair of jeans so tight that the person wearing them could barely sit down to get in the car," Odelle said.

"At least I didn't spend fifteen minutes arranging my skirt so it wouldn't wrinkle," Carlelle retorted.

"Wait a minute," I said before Idelle could get involved. "Did the three of you ride over here together?"

"Of course we did," Idelle said. "You know we don't have but the one car."

I just couldn't picture three women in one car not talking, especially not three women who were related to me. I also couldn't picture myself having three separate conversations with my cousins when they were all right there. Fortunately, Richard returned once again, carrying cans of Coke.

He hugged Odelle, and handed drinks to everybody.

"Why did you get so many?" I asked. He had gone to get himself one, and came back with five.

"Just a hunch," he said, opened a can, and took a swallow with an expression of pure satisfaction.

"Have any of you seen Ilene?" I asked the triplets.

They all shook their heads.

"I didn't know she was here," Idelle said.

I said, "She's supposed to compete, but Roger doesn't want her to."

"So I heard," Odelle said. I didn't have to ask—I knew that they must have found out about last night's fight from Vasti.

"Aunt Ruby Lee called this morning because she found out Roger was going to be here today," I said, "and Ilene doesn't know it."

"I hope he doesn't see her," Carlelle said. "He'll be awful mad if he does."

"Mad as a wet hen," I said without thinking, which meant that Richard had to come up with a Shakespearean counterpart.

" 'Anger is like a full-hot horse, who being allow'd his way, self-mettle tires him,' " he said. "*King Henry VIII*, Act I, Scene 1."

The triplets looked confused, and I shook my head firmly. Richard shrugged and added a mark to my score.

Still, his quote gave me an idea. "Maybe we can get Roger over his mad," I said speculatively. "He keeps saying that Ilene isn't good enough to compete. Have y'all heard her?"

"Not in years," Odelle said, "but she used to have a real nice voice. I know she's performed at school, but only in the chorus, so I don't know how she'd sound by herself."

I waved a dismissing hand at the nearest speaker, from which was coming an unimpressive warbling. "Well, even if she's not good enough to win, she's got to be better than that clown. I bet if Roger heard her sing, he'd be so tickled that he'd stop being mad and start being proud."

"Do you think so?" Idelle asked.

"It's a wonderful idea!" Carlelle said, probably just to be contrary to her sister.

"It won't work," Odelle said flatly.

"Richard, what do you think?" I asked.

"It might work," he said doubtfully.

"I hate to see them fighting like they have been." I

looked over at the triplets. "I hate to see *any* of the family fighting."

"Unless it's for a good reason," Carlelle said, and the other two nodded. Of all of the issues possible, this was the one they agreed on.

"Don't you think it's worth a shot?" I asked Richard again.

He sighed, but said, "What do you have in mind?"

"Ilene is supposed to go on at two o'clock." I checked my watch. "It's just shy of one now, so we've got one hour to find Roger and get him into position. The trick is to lure him over to the stage so he can see her singing."

"With the speakers, he'll be able to hear her anywhere," Richard said.

"But if he hasn't looked at a program and he doesn't hear her being introduced, he won't know who it is." To the triplets, I said, "Are you three going to help?"

Carlelle nodded right away and Idelle looked like she was thinking about it, but Odelle was shaking her head until I said, "Slim said they had to set up, so he and Roger will probably be somewhere around the stage." Then they all nodded.

Mentioning Slim was a dirty trick, but I wanted their help, and I knew that none of them would risk one of the others getting near Slim without a chaperone.

Richard and I went in one direction, and the triplets took off separately. I could tell that Richard still had his doubts. "Do you not think this is a good idea?" I asked him.

"It might work," he said again. "I'm just concerned about what could happen if Roger gets mad when he sees her."

"I told you. He'll be so tickled at how good she is—"

"That he'll forget being mad. Maybe. If she is good."

"She's got to be good," I said firmly. "Clifford and Earl are good, and she's their sister. And Roger is good, and she's his daughter."

"You're her cousin, too, and while you have many gifts, singing is not among them," he pointed out.

I ignored the last comment, and said, "But I thought you'd like enacting a Shakespearean conceit."

"How's that?"

"Wasn't there something like this in *King Lear?* That man who got his eyes poked out?"

"The Earl of Gloucester."

"Right. He didn't trust his good son—"

"Edgar."

"Whatever. Gloucester didn't trust Edgar until after he was blinded, and then Edgar came and took care of him, and then Gloucester realized what a great son Edgar really was all along."

"What does this have to do with Ilene and Roger?"

"Roger is the father who hasn't been appreciating his good daughter Ilene. In this case, good in the sense of talented, because goodness knows Ilene hasn't been all that good a daughter lately. Anyway, he'll hear her voice and realize how good she is. It's perfect."

"Except that Roger isn't deaf," Richard said.

"Okay, it's not a perfect analog to *King Lear.*"

"I think it's more of an analog for *I Love Lucy*, when Ricky wouldn't let Lucy into his show."

"Well, it worked for Lucy, and it's going to work for Ilene. I know it is."

"Okay," he said. "We'll give it a try." But I thought I heard him whisper, "The task she undertakes is numbering sands and drinking oceans dry," which wasn't exactly a quote of confidence.

As it turned out, I should have listened to Richard and Shakespeare. Oh, the first part of the plan went perfectly. Richard and I checked the back parking lot and found the Ramblers' bus, a converted school bus that had been painted royal blue with musical notes on the windows and their logo on the side. Then we only had to wait a few minutes for Roger and Slim to appear, the triplets following after Slim like a trio of lost puppies. Except that lost puppies don't keep trying to push each other out of the way.

"Hey there, Roger," I said, happy to see that he didn't have a program in hand. "How's it going?"

"Just perfect," he said in a tone that meant the opposite. "Cotton and Al aren't here yet, so Slim and I have been trying to set up by ourselves, only that fool woman in charge of this mess says that we can't run a sound check until after the last performance. Except that we're supposed to start playing then, while the judges come up with the winners from the beginner class."

After last night, I guess I shouldn't have expected him to be in a good mood. "What a pain," I said sympathetically. "Tell you what. Why don't you come rest a spell and listen to the performers? Some of them sound pretty good."

At that moment, the kid singing hit a particularly flat note, and Roger rolled his eyes in disgust.

"They're saving the good ones for later," I said quickly. "Let's us go find a good spot and relax, get something cold to drink."

"That's another thing," Roger said. "They aren't selling anything but Coke and iced tea. You'd think a man could buy himself a beer, but Forrest Jefferson said that it's illegal to sell alcoholic beverages on school property. School's been out for two weeks!"

"Richard was about to make a beer run anyway," I said, not looking at my husband. "Want him to get you some?"

That won him over. Richard wasn't happy about being volunteered, but with a little sweet-talking, he agreed to go to the convenience store a couple of blocks away.

So, at two o'clock, Richard, Roger, Slim, the triplets, and I were sitting on beach towels the triplets had brought, comfortably installed on the school football field with an excellent view of the outdoor stage. Roger had a beer in his hand and, as Paw would have said, felt more like himself than he had when he came in. I had hidden my program from him, and made sure that he hadn't seen Ilene's name listed anywhere. Slim was being polite to all three triplets, though of course they still weren't talking to one another. Richard had forgiven me for making him go after beer, partially because he was a wonderful husband, and partially because he had gotten himself an ice cream sandwich at the store and he loves ice cream sandwiches.

I was *so* proud of myself when the announcer called out "Ilene Bailey," even though Roger was talking to Slim right then and didn't hear it. I just knew that as soon as Ilene started singing, Roger would be so impressed that he'd beg her to forgive him. I wasn't even watching the stage—I was watching Roger's face to see his expression of amazement and delight.

The problem was, the only expression on Roger's face as the music started was polite interest. I looked at the stage myself, and at first I thought I had made one heck of a mistake. That blond bimbo with the sprayed-on black leather miniskirt and the fringed top that pushed her bosom out and left her midriff bare wasn't Ilene. That vixen prancing around in thigh-high spike-heeled boots wasn't my young cousin. Then I looked again, and realized that under all that makeup and hair spray, it was her after all.

I took a quick look at Roger, and he was starting to frown. Then Ilene started to sing, and that only made it worse. Her voice was good enough, but it was hard to make out for all the squeals and deep breathing that went along with the lyrics, which were something about lust and leather.

From the wolf whistles and whoops from the crowd, it was obvious that somebody liked the performance, but now Roger's frown had changed into a look of pure horror. Seconds later, it evolved into fury. He stood up, and at the top of his lungs, he hollered, *"Ilene!"*

I don't know if she heard him or not, but she didn't react, just kept going with her number. Now she was wriggling right up to the edge of the stage, bending over in case anybody hadn't got a good look at her cleavage yet.

"Ilene!" Roger yelled again. *"Get off of that stage!"*

This time she did look up and saw her father, but she kept on singing.

Roger stood up and strode toward the stage, carrying the towel he had been sitting on. I looked at Richard, but all he had to offer was a shrug.

By then Roger was halfway to the stage, and Ilene was starting to lose her concentration and mumble the words to her song. She looked offstage, and I guessed that that was where Tom Honeywell was standing. Apparently he gave her no comfort, because she gave up singing entirely, and watched as her father approached. A tape was still blaring forth the instrumentals.

The stage was several feet off the ground, but when he got there, Roger climbed right up and grabbed the microphone from Ilene and threw it to the stage. Then he wrapped the towel around her, and started pushing her off the stage.

I couldn't hear what the two of them were saying because of the tape and the boos from the crowd, but I could make a pretty good guess. Ilene struggled against her father, pulled the towel off, and flung it away, all the while yelling something. Roger said something that required the use of a wagging finger, and then Ilene stamped her boots. When Roger reached for the towel again, Ilene burst into tears and ran offstage. Roger calmly picked up the towel, then walked offstage himself.

Finally, somebody in back noticed that the singing had stopped, and turned off the tape.

Chapter 8

One time, not long after I got my driver's license, I wasn't paying close enough attention as I backed into a parking place, and I backed right into a light pole. It didn't hurt the pole, and it didn't even damage the bumper much, just enough to show immediately. I remember standing next to the car, staring at the dent in horror because Paw was going to be so disappointed in me, and knowing I had no excuse but out-and-out stupidity. I wanted to pinch myself, wake up, and start the day all over again.

That was about a one-hundredth of how I felt when Roger followed Ilene off the stage.

"Oh my goodness," the triplets said in unison, forgetting for a moment that they weren't supposed to be doing that anymore, and Carlelle added, "I've never seen Roger so mad before."

"Maybe we better go find him," Slim said. "He is awfully upset."

We gathered up the towels and headed for the gym. None of us was saying a whole lot, but Richard could tell that my silence was more than just embarrassment.

"It's not your fault," he whispered to me, squeezing my hand.

I loved him for saying that, but I had to say, "Yes, it is."

"You were only trying to help."

"And I've made things worse." Why hadn't I listened to Richard and whichever triplet it was who had been against the idea? Why did I have to make such a mess of things?

Richard squeezed my hand again.

When we reached the gym, Roger was there talking to Monroe, the chief of police who had kept me and Richard at bay before. I think I'd have been happier if Roger had been yelling, waving his hands, making a big show. Instead, he was talking in a low, deadly calm voice.

Still, Monroe was clearly disagreeing with him, shaking his head and making it plain that he wasn't letting Roger go into the back. A second later, Forrest Jefferson joined the two of them and she was much louder.

Slim said something about stepping in before things got out of hand, and he and the triplets went into the middle of it.

I held Richard back. "While they're all occupied, I'm going to try to sneak into the back and find Ilene."

"Are you sure that that's a good idea?"

"Since it's my idea, it's probably a terrible idea," I said bitterly, "but why stop doing stupid things now?"

I know he wanted to argue with that last part, but all he did was kiss me quickly and say, "I'll distract them."

I didn't know that they needed any more distraction, but he provided a dandy one anyway. He swaggered up and started talking in the most exaggerated Harvard accent I had ever heard, referring to rights and laws and policies and I don't know what all. I'd have enjoyed staying to watch, but I didn't want his efforts to be in vain.

I don't think a single head turned in my direction as I

casually walked past the group of combatants, and through the door marked DRESSING ROOMS. They were all watching Richard.

I hadn't had a chance to wonder how I was going to find Ilene, but as it turned out, I didn't need to worry. There was a chart just inside the door with names and dressing room assignments, and a map next to it to show me where the dressing room was. I took off in that direction, hoping that nobody would challenge me.

Nobody did, and in fact, I was fairly sure that the Boston Red Sox could have strolled through in their uniforms without anybody noticing them. I had never been involved in plays or any kind of performance before, and had no idea of what confusion lurked backstage. Did all backstages have people running around half-dressed, young men with guitars begging for the loan of a string or a pick, and the occasional musician leaning against the wall with eyes closed, either meditating in preparation for a performance or petrified from stage fright? And Forrest had been concerned about *me* disturbing the performers?

Despite all the noise, I heard the commotion from Ilene's dressing room before I saw the door with her name taped on it. The dressing rooms were actually classrooms, emptied for the summer. I looked inside and saw Ilene sitting on a chair in front of a school desk covered with makeup bottles and compacts, and a large mirror. Tears were still running down her face, making a mess of her mascara and eye shadow.

Tom was pacing back and forth across the room, hands clenched into fists. "Jesus fucking Christ, I can't believe this! All that time and money right down the damned drain!" He stopped and banged his fist on a desk. Ilene jerked at the sound. "Why in hell didn't you keep singing? Why did you just stop and stand there like a damned idiot?" Again he banged his fist.

I didn't like him getting that physical with his anger, so I stepped far enough inside to be between him and Ilene, and said, "Ilene, can I talk to you?"

"What do you want?" Tom demanded.

Ilene said, "Did Daddy send you after me?"

"No, I just wanted to see if you're all right."

"Oh she's fine!" Tom said. "She's just dandy. I spend *months* putting that routine together and picking out her costume and developing her style, and her damned fool of a father comes in and ruins it." He turned to glare at Ilene. "What did you stop singing for, anyway?" he asked again. "If you had kept at it, we might have been able to get a few sympathy votes anyway."

"Tom! I couldn't. I just couldn't, not with Daddy acting like that. You saw him get onto the stage." She reached out her hand toward him. "I'm as sorry as you are, you know I am."

He either didn't see her hand, or didn't want to. "There can't be anybody who's as sorry as I am. I needed that prize money, damn it!"

"Tom—" Ilene began.

"I'm going to find that woman who's running this thing," Tom said, "and see if I can get us another performance time."

"I don't think I could try again," Ilene said. "Not now."

"You'll sing, all right! And if your father tries to mess it up again . . . Well, he better not even try." Tom stomped off down the hall.

I didn't like the sound of that, and I didn't like the way he was treating Ilene or the way he was planning to spend her prize money, but this wasn't the time to bring up Ilene's boyfriend's failings. "Ilene, I'm so sorry," I said.

She turned to the mirror and started wiping off smudges of mascara. "I didn't think Daddy would be here so early today, and I sure didn't think he'd be listening to the beginner class. It's just my luck that he happened to be there when I went on stage."

I've never been able to hide my feelings, and I guess Ilene saw my face in the mirror, because she turned around to glare at me. "It wasn't just bad luck, was it?"

I couldn't very well deny it. "No, it was my fault. I knew when you were going to perform."

"So you couldn't wait to get Daddy out there to get me in trouble. I know you don't like me, but I sure didn't know that you'd pull a stunt like that. You must really hate me!"

Now I was willing to apologize, but that was going too far. "That's not true! I only got Roger out there because I thought that he'd like your singing."

"Sure you did."

"I'm sorry," was all I could say.

"Sorry? Sorry! You ruin my entire life, and all you can say is that you're sorry. You're pretty damned sorry, all right."

"Ilene—"

"I don't want to hear anything you've got to say, *cousin*. You've said and done enough today to last a lifetime." She turned back to the mirror.

I hesitated for a minute.

"Go on and get out of here," she said.

I went. She wasn't going to listen to me now, and I couldn't very well blame her.

I suppose it was just as noisy backstage when I went back through as it had been a few minutes earlier, but I didn't really notice it. I didn't know whether I was madder at Ilene for yelling at me, or at Roger for picking on Ilene, or at Aunt Ruby Lee for getting me into this when she should have come herself. No, that's not true. I knew that the person I was really angry at was myself, both for sticking my nose in where it didn't belong and for making such a mess of it.

Richard, Slim, and the triplets weren't there in the gym when I got there, and I figured that they had finally talked Roger out of storming into the dressing rooms.

The police chief was still there, looking more than a little strained, and for good reason. He had survived one confrontation, but was in the middle of another. Forrest Jefferson was still there, too, and now she was face-to-face, nearly nose-to-nose, with Tom Honeywell.

"I tell you it ain't right!" Tom said. "It's not her fault that her fool of a father ruined her performance. The *least* you could do is to give her another time slot."

"How many times do I have to explain this, young man? Every time slot is filled. The rules allow for one try and one try only. She had her chance, the same as everybody else."

"If you had decent security around here, this wouldn't have happened." Tom turned to glare at the police chief. "Why didn't you put Dudley Do-Right outside by the stage instead of back here?"

The chief started to speak, but Forrest held up a hand. "My security arrangements are none of your affair."

"There ain't no security arrangements, that's the problem. You owe Ilene another chance, and you damned well better let her have it!"

Forrest took a deep breath. "She's entitled to nothing! As a matter of fact, even had she finished her performance and won, she would have been disqualified."

"What are you talking about!"

Forrest pulled a piece of paper from the stack she was still carrying and waved it in front of Tom's face. "Surely you remember the rules, Mr. Honeywell. Miss Bailey signed a disclaimer to confirm that she had read them. The rules state clearly that minors must have the consent of their parents to perform. And Miss Bailey is a minor."

"She had her mama's permission. You just call and ask her."

"Be that as it may, the rule says 'parents.' Plural. Obviously she did *not* have her father's permission."

"That's nuts!" Tom said, and I had to agree with him. Divorced parents seldom agree on anything. Requiring dual permission in this case was ridiculous. I thought about throwing in my two cents' worth, but didn't think Tom would appreciate my intrusion. Besides which, it was time for me to butt out.

"Call it what you will," Forrest said with a smug smile. "Those are the rules."

Tom said, "Then I want my money back. I paid for her to compete, and if she ain't eligible, I want my fifty bucks back."

Forrest's smile grew wider and more smug. "That's also not possible. Rule 14 states that entry fees are not refundable under any circumstances. Or to put it in a way you might understand, 'You pays your money, and you takes your chances.'"

"You're the one taking chances around here, lady!" He

stepped closer to Forrest, but the police chief got between them.

"That's enough of that," Monroe said. "Miss Jefferson has told you how it is, and that's how it's going to be. Now I think it's time for you to get on out of here."

Tom wasn't a complete fool, and he knew better than to tangle with a police officer. He moved back, and went toward the door, muttering profanities.

Forrest couldn't let well enough alone, either. "Chief Monroe," she said loudly, "make sure that Mr. Honeywell does not go backstage again. I'll not have him disrupting the Jamboree further."

Tom's face went dark red at that, but he didn't say anything, just stalked outside.

I decided it was time for me to get out of there, too, before I was noticed. As it was, Forrest glanced at me briefly as I hurried by, but she didn't say anything to me. I did hear her say, "It's their own fault, you know. If they had followed the rules, this wouldn't have happened."

No matter what she thought, I knew that it was all my fault, and I felt right sick to my stomach to think of it.

Richard was waiting for me outside, and took me in his arms as soon as he saw me. He didn't ask me what had happened or anything, just held me for a while. For a man who uses words so well, he sure knows when not to use them.

After awhile, when I was sure that I wasn't going to cry after all, I pulled away a little and asked, "What happened with Roger?"

"We managed to calm him down," Richard said. "That Jefferson woman looked pretty angry about the disruption, but she didn't say much."

"She was probably afraid that Roger and the Ramblers

would back out of performing tonight. Where did everybody go?"

"Back to the Ramblers' bus to unload equipment and set up."

"The triplets too? In their nice outfits?"

"Whoever it was in jeans offered first, and then the others had to join in."

"I hope they get over this feud soon." Then I added emphatically, "Not that *I'm* going to do anything about it, not after the mess I've made today."

"That's enough!" Richard said. "I'm not saying that we did the right thing, but we did it for the right reasons. Notice that I said 'we.' That's because I mean 'we.' You didn't twist my arm to get me to go along, or the triplets' arms, either. Plus we wouldn't be out here in the first place if Aunt Ruby Lee hadn't asked you to come look for Ilene. You have *nothing* to be sorry about."

"Are you sure?" I asked, wanting to believe him.

"Yes, Laura, I'm sure. If any fault lies with you, it's the fault of saying yes too easily when your family asks it."

"I have to say yes," I said.

"Why?"

I cocked my head at him. "Are you serious?"

He nodded. "Why do you have to say yes every time?"

"That's kind of my role in the family, isn't it? I take care of problems, I troubleshoot."

"You're more than the Burnette troubleshooter, Laura. Your family loves you for who you are, not what you do."

"I know that," I answered automatically, but then I thought about it. Did I know that? Not just with my head, but with my heart?

For many years, even before I went up North, I hadn't

felt like a part of my family at all. Then, after finishing college and staying in Boston, it seemed as if I was never going to fit in. Then Paw died, and in finding his killer, I had somehow found my way back into the fold. Since then, I had rescued Aunt Daphine from a blackmailer, and helped other family members with other problems.

That was fine; I didn't regret any of it. But how long was I going to have to keep on proving myself a loyal Burnette? Who was I proving myself to: my family or myself?

"What are you thinking?" Richard wanted to know.

"About what you said."

"Any conclusions?"

"Not yet, but I've got some interesting questions to chew on." I leaned up to give Richard a kiss. "Thank you, love."

"My pleasure." He returned the kiss, with interest. "Now what do you want to do?"

"Well, Roger and the Ramblers are going to be playing later, and there's going to be a dance," I said without a whole lot of enthusiasm.

"That's not what I asked. I asked you what you want to do. Do you want to go back to Aunt Maggie's?"

"Yes!"

He offered me his arm, and we headed for the car.

Chapter 9

When the ringing woke me the next morning, I had a profound sense of what Aunt Maggie calls déjà vu all over again. The time of day, Richard's uninterrupted slumber, everything was just like the day before. The only difference was that this time I was somewhat rested. After the Jamboree, Richard and I had gone to see Aunt Edna, Aunt Nellie and Uncle Ruben, and Aunt Daphine, then ended up over at Aunt Nora's for dinner. Despite all that, we got to bed at a decent hour.

Still, I would have preferred another half hour of sleep, but the phone kept ringing. This being Saturday, Aunt Maggie would have already been up and at the flea market for hours. Now anybody in the family would have known that, and only a family member who knew Richard and I were there would have let the phone ring for so long. Feeling very sorry for myself, I got out of the bed. At least this time I made it downstairs without stubbing my toe.

"Hello?"

"Laurie Anne! Thank goodness you're there."

I couldn't believe it was her again. "Aunt Ruby Lee? What's the matter?" I resisted adding the words "this time."

"It's Ilene! She's run away!"

"What?"

"She never came home last night, Laurie Anne. I found out about the mess at the Jamboree yesterday, so I sat up to wait for her. But she never got here, and she never called. She always calls. Laurie Anne, what am I going to do? I just can't bear the thought of my baby being out there alone somewhere."

I didn't have any idea that Ilene was alone—chances were that she was with Tom Honeywell. "Have you called around to see if anybody knows where she is?"

"Not yet. I thought maybe you could find her for me."

So much for my resignation from being the official Burnette troubleshooter, but I couldn't worry about that now. Especially not when I heard sniffling from the other end of the phone. "Richard and I will be over as quick as we can get there. You stay by the phone in case she calls."

"All right," she said.

It took me less than an hour to get Richard up, explain the situation to him, get the both of us dressed, and drive to Aunt Ruby Lee's.

Aunt Ruby Lee was sitting by the phone when we came in, and I had the awful feeling that she had been staring at it ever since she hung up from talking to me. Her eyes were red and swollen from crying, and she was still wearing a nightgown and bathrobe. For Aunt Ruby Lee not to be dressed with her hair fixed and face made up was a sure sign of trouble. I gave her a hug, and she just clung to me for a long time.

"Have you heard anything?" I asked.

Aunt Ruby Lee shook her head sadly.

"Then sit down and tell me what happened," I said, and took a seat on the couch.

Aunt Ruby Lee started to sit down next to me, but then said, "Let me get you two some coffee."

"I'll get it," Richard said, and was out of the room before Aunt Ruby Lee could object.

"That's so nice of him," she said. "You two are just wonderful for rushing over here."

"Don't you worry about that," I said. "Just tell me about Ilene."

She took a deep breath, and blew her nose before starting. "Well, I kind of expected her to come home last night for dinner. Especially when Roger told me what happened at the Jamboree. When she didn't, I figured she had stayed for the dance and I was hoping that she was feeling better. Clifford and Earl went, and when they came home, they said they had seen her there fighting with Tom Honeywell. Clifford tried to break it up, but she got mad at him, too, and ran off." She broke off long enough to blow her nose again. "I knew I should have gone to the dance, but Vasti kept me busy later than I thought she would and I just didn't feel like getting all dressed up."

"Your being there wouldn't have made a bit of difference," I said, hoping it was true. I was starting to feel guilty for not staying for the dance myself.

"Anyway, she ran off long before the dance was over, Clifford says, so she should have been home before him and Earl. But I stayed up all night and she never came. Laurie Anne, where can she be?"

She started to cry, but fortunately Richard came in right then with three cups of coffee, and that distracted her long enough for her to calm down a bit.

Once I thought that Aunt Ruby Lee was ready to go on, I

said briskly, "First things first. Where are Clifford and Earl?"

"They've gone out to the Jamboree. They're supposed to perform this afternoon."

"Do you think they'd know where she's gone?"

Aunt Ruby Lee shook her head. "Clifford said they didn't see her again last night. Besides, the boys and Ilene haven't been getting along too well lately. You know how kids can be, fighting over nothing."

"Then we don't need to tell them yet. With luck, we'll get Ilene back home before they get back from the Jamboree."

"Oh Lord, I hope so," Aunt Ruby Lee said.

Richard said, "When most kids run away, they don't go any further than their closest friend's house. I ran away when I was thirteen and hid at my friend Mike's. He had this big bedroom in the basement, and for some reason, I was sure that no one would think to look for me there."

"How long did it take for your parents to figure it out?" I asked.

"About ten minutes, but they let me stew for a day or so before coming after me. By then I had gotten so tired of eating leftovers and hiding under Mike's bed that I was glad to go back home."

Aunt Ruby Lee smiled at that, despite herself.

"Who's Ilene's best friend?" I asked.

"Cheryl Lender. You know the Lenders, Laurie Anne. Jennifer works at the mill, and Donald works at the Woolworth's. At least he used to, before it closed down."

"The Woolworth's closed?" I said, letting myself be distracted for a minute. That store had been the place where I had shopped for the first store-bought Christmas presents I ever gave my parents. And their lunch counter had wonderful food and huge ice cream sundaes.

"A month or so back," Aunt Ruby Lee said. "I hear they closed them down all over the country."

Richard cleared his throat, reminding us of the business at hand.

"Anyway," Aunt Ruby Lee said, "the Lenders live in that dark green house a couple of houses down from Linwood and Sue."

I did know the name, and I thought I remembered talking to members of the family once or twice. "Let's call Cheryl."

Aunt Ruby Lee dialed the number, then handed the phone to me. "I'm afraid I'll start crying," she explained, and I nodded.

"Lender residence," a young-sounding voice said on the other end of the line.

"May I speak to Cheryl Lender?"

"This is Cheryl."

"Cheryl, this is Laura Fleming. I'm one of Ilene Bailey's cousins."

There was no response.

"I think Ilene calls me Laurie Anne."

"Oh, the one who went to Boston. Ilene's told me about you."

"That's right. The reason I'm calling is that Ilene's run away."

"Did she have another fight with her daddy?"

Cheryl was a good friend, all right. "I'm afraid so. I don't want to make you break any confidences, but do you know where she is?"

"No, I sure don't. I haven't heard from her in over a week now."

That surprised me. With school being out, I would have expected that Ilene would spend a good part of every day talking to her best friend.

Cheryl must have guessed what I was thinking, because she went on, "To tell you the truth, Ilene and I haven't been spending that much time together lately. She started dating Tom Honeywell awhile back, and you know how it is when a girl gets a new boyfriend." She paused. "And I have to say that I don't like Tom all that well."

It sounded like Cheryl had more sense than Ilene, at least when it came to men. "You don't have any idea of where she'd go, do you?"

"I'd check with Tom, if I were you."

"I'll do that. If you hear from Ilene, I sure would appreciate your letting her mother know."

"I will," Cheryl said. "If you like, I'll call around and check with some of the other kids in town."

"That would be great. Thanks, Cheryl."

I hung up the phone and said, "Cheryl hasn't heard from her."

"Do you think Cheryl would be likely to tell us if she's stashed Ilene somewhere?" Richard asked. "My friend Mike kept my secret faithfully—he just wasn't very good at covering his tracks."

Aunt Ruby Lee shook her head. "I think Cheryl would tell me. She used to spend a lot of time over here, so I got to know her pretty well. She was spending the night here when she first got her period, and I was the one who got her situated. Something like that means a lot to a woman."

Richard looked doubtful, but I knew just what she was

talking about. "She sounded sincere to me," I said, "but we'll double-check just to be sure. With Sue and Linwood in eyesight, we can call them and see if they've seen anything."

Aunt Ruby Lee agreed, and I picked up the phone again. Sue answered the phone and I told her about Ilene's running away, then I ended with, "I'm pretty sure that Cheryl was telling me the truth, but I thought I'd check with you to see if you had seen Ilene around."

Sue said, "I sure haven't, Laurie Anne, and I think I would have. Linwood and I were out on the porch last night because it was so hot, and I saw Cheryl get dropped off from her date. Ilene wasn't with her then."

"Could Ilene have snuck in the back door?" I asked.

"Not without my seeing it," Sue said. "I didn't think she and Cheryl were friends anymore. She used to be over there all the time, but I haven't seen her there in a couple of months."

I thanked her and she promised to keep an eye out before we hung up.

"Sue says Ilene can't possibly be over at the Lenders'," I said. "If I had realized that Ilene and Cheryl weren't spending much time together these days, I wouldn't have bothered to check."

"What do you mean?" Aunt Ruby Lee said. "Ilene goes over there all the time. She spent the night over there earlier this week, and two times last week."

I didn't say a word, but my expression must have said something, because Aunt Ruby Lee said, "She's been lying to me, hasn't she? She hasn't been with Cheryl at all. She's been with Tom Honeywell, I just know she has. What if she's pregnant and gone to get an abortion? What if he's given her VD? Or AIDS?"

She started crying in earnest then, and I knew I was out of my depth. I put my arms around her and let her cry into my shoulder, and mouthed a message at Richard. He went out to the kitchen to call for reinforcements.

I know it couldn't have been more than ten minutes, but it seemed like an eternity until Aunt Nora arrived. Without speaking to me or Richard, she bundled Aunt Ruby Lee up and took her upstairs to her bedroom. A few minutes later Aunt Nellie showed up, and she was followed closely by Aunt Edna and Aunt Daphine.

"Did you call all four of them?" I asked Richard when they all went into the bedroom.

He said, "You bet I did."

We waited there together, feeling awkward and useless.

"Do you think Aunt Ruby Lee has called Roger?" Richard asked.

I shrugged. "She didn't mention it."

"Do you think we should?"

"Not yet. Let's see if her sisters can calm her down first."

"Do you think that Ilene is with Honeywell?"

I nodded. If she had been lying to her mother about him, it seemed pretty likely.

Finally, Aunt Nellie came back into the room. "Laurie Anne," she said, "Ruby Lee wants to see you for a minute."

I followed her back to the bedroom. Aunt Ruby Lee was propped up on the bed, with Aunt Nora on one side of her, Aunt Daphine on the other, and Aunt Edna perched at her feet. I had never really minded being an only child, but seeing them together like that made me a little wistful for what I was missing.

Aunt Ruby Lee's eyes were still red, of course, but she

looked a lot more composed. She said, "Laurie Anne, do you think you can find Ilene for me?"

"I don't know, Aunt Ruby Lee, but I'll do my best."

"What do you want us to do first?" Aunt Nellie asked, and Aunt Nora added, "Just tell us what you need."

"I think the first thing we should do is call Junior." Junior Norton was Byerly's Chief of Police and an old friend of mine.

My aunts nodded, and Aunt Edna dialed the number and handed me the phone.

"Byerly Police."

"Junior? This is Laura Fleming."

"Hey, Laurie Anne. Are you already in town for your aunt's wedding, or did you come in early for the Jamboree?"

Junior usually knew everything that was going on in Byerly, not that finding out about the wedding would have been hard with Vasti running the show. "I'm here for the wedding," I said, "but that's not why I called. You know my cousin Ilene, don't you? Ilene Bailey."

"Of course."

"Well, she's run away."

"Is that a fact? How long has she been gone?"

"Since last night. She never came home."

"How do you know she didn't just stay out with friends or something?"

"Aunt Ruby Lee says she always calls." I hated adding the next part, even to Junior, but it had to be said. "And she had a fight with her father yesterday at the Jamboree." I comforted myself with the reminder that Junior probably would have heard about it soon enough.

"Have you called any of her friends?"

"I called Cheryl Lender, Ilene's best friend, but Cheryl didn't know anything."

"Boyfriend?"

"That's where we think she's gone. She's been dating Tom Honeywell and we're afraid that she's gone off with him."

"I heard about them two. Isn't he a bit older than her?"

"Yes," I said, but that's all I said. I couldn't very well give Junior my opinion about that in front of Aunt Ruby Lee.

"I think he's still got that trailer at Evergreen Acres. I'll ride over there and see if there's any sign of her there. Are you over at Ilene's house now?"

"Yes. Aunt Ruby Lee is here, too, and my other aunts."

"Already called in the cavalry have you? I'll be over there after I go by Honeywell's place. In the meantime, I'd like you to check on a few things for me. See how much money Ilene is likely to have—that's a good way of knowing how far she can get."

"I'll ask."

"And see if she's taken any of her clothes and stuff with her."

"I don't think that will help much," I said. "She was at the Jamboree when we saw her last, so she probably didn't plan to run off."

"Are you sure?" Junior asked.

I really wasn't, not after the fight Ilene and Roger had had the night of Aunt Ruby Lee's bridal shower. Maybe she had never intended to come home after the Jamboree. "I guess I don't know for sure. I'll check on that, too."

"Good. I'll be there shortly."

"Thanks, Junior."

"No problem. You tell your aunt not to worry. We'll find Ilene for her."

I hung up, and relayed what Junior had said to my aunts. Then I said, "How much money do you think she's got?"

"Not much," Aunt Ruby Lee said. "She hasn't done any baby-sitting since she took up with Tom. Most of what she had went toward her outfit for the Jamboree, and what was left went toward the entry fee."

"I hate to say this, Ruby Lee," Aunt Nellie said, "but have you checked your pocketbook?"

"You don't think she'd take money from me, do you?" Aunt Ruby Lee said, but when none of us answered, she sighed and said, "I guess I don't know what she'd do anymore. Nora, would you go get my pocketbook from the kitchen?"

Aunt Nora did so, and Aunt Ruby Lee looked into her wallet. "I think it's all here," she said, sounding relieved.

I said, "What about her clothes? Did you check her room?"

Aunt Ruby Lee hesitated. "No, I didn't. I can't."

"Did she lock the door?" I asked.

"No, it's not that. You see, she and I had a discussion about privacy a long time ago. I had gone into her room to clean, and she got all bent out of shape because I saw something she was making for me as a surprise. So I promised her that I'd never go into her room without permission."

"Ruby Lee," Aunt Daphine said, "don't you think that this is a special circumstance?"

"I know it is, Daphine, but what good is a promise if you break it every time a special circumstance comes up?"

Aunt Edna said, "I don't think I'd be worried about a promise like that at a time like this. Not after what she's been up to. Ruby Lee, didn't I tell you that you were letting her get away with too much?"

"Yes, you did, Edna, but I can't help that now."

"I think you should march right into that room and see what you can find out. And if you won't, I will."

"No, Edna. I'm not going to do it, and neither are you. Laurie Anne will."

"Me?" I said. I had been staying as far out of that argument as I could. "Why me?"

"You're closer to her age," Aunt Ruby Lee said, "and I don't think she'd mind it as much. Is that all right?"

"I suppose so." I didn't love the idea, and considering the way Ilene and I had been getting along, I didn't think she would either. Still, Junior had said that it had to be done, and if it would make Aunt Ruby Lee feel better for me to be the one to do it, I would. "I'll be back."

I went down the hall to Ilene's room. I opened it, half-expecting a creak like something out of a horror movie. It was a silly thought, of course. Ilene had only been gone for a day.

The bed was neatly made, covered with a boldly striped bedspread. In fact, the whole room was pretty neat. I would have thought it would be a mess from hurried packing for the Jamboree, the way Richard and I usually leave our bedroom when getting ready for a trip. Did Ilene always leave it that nice, or was this was a kind of good-bye? I had read that suicides often straightened up beforehand. Then I shook that thought right out of my head. Ilene might be mad, but she wasn't suicidal.

I went to the closet door and slid it open, envious of the amount of storage space compared to what I had in Boston. It was filled with clothes of all descriptions, mostly bright colors that would look wonderful on my fair-skinned cousin. There were also a fair number of black blouses and shirts, which I suspected were more recent additions.

There were three or four empty hangers right in front. Now, if Ilene was like me, she never had enough hangers, which could mean that she had taken at least a couple of outfits with her. One would have been her costume for the Jamboree, of course.

The big bags I had carried upstairs for her the other night were crumpled down on the floor of the closet, but now they were empty. I picked them up to check out Ilene's shoes. She had a fair number of pairs, enough to go with all her outfits, no doubt. I didn't see the black ankle boots she had been wearing at the shower.

The dresser was my next target. There was a clear plastic makeup caddy on the top, but it was mostly empty. Wherever Ilene had gone, clearly she wanted to look her best. There had been lots of makeup in her dressing room, but would she have taken all of her makeup just for the Jamboree? I peered into the small, wooden jewelry box, but couldn't tell if anything was missing.

The top drawer was about one quarter filled with panties and bras and the drawer of blue jeans looked like it could hold several more pairs. Most women, no matter what age, keep their drawers well filled, so she could have taken clothes for a few days.

What else? There was a bookshelf, filled mostly with music books. Ilene had stacks of sheet music, too, and some biographies of musicians from Hank Williams to Buddy Holly to Pearl Bailey to Naomi Judd. The sheet music was of an even greater variety. Most of my cousins were country-

and-western fans, with a dab of top 40 music. Ilene had much wider tastes.

There were several notebooks pushed in among the rest, and I flipped through them. As far as I could tell, they were original songs. I knew that Clifford had tried his hand at songwriting, but nobody had ever mentioned that Ilene wrote songs, too. I couldn't read the notes, but the lyrics were decent. The notebooks seemed to be in chronological order, with space for another notebook, which might mean that Ilene had taken her latest compositions with her.

Next was the stereo. Ilene's collection of albums showed the same far-ranging taste as the sheet music. Country, big band, rock and roll, bluegrass, rhythm and blues, heavy metal, rap, and even some classical. My young cousin knew a lot more about music than I did.

There was a stack of cassette tapes, including some tapes labeled only COLLECTION 1, COLLECTION 2, and so on. I looked around for the Walkman Ilene had been using before, but apparently she had taken that with her. So I took a few minutes to figure out how to run her stereo and put on the latest of the collections.

The recording technique was primitive and of course I was biased because I recognized Ilene's voice, but I thought it was pretty good. Definitely better than amateur, and well on the way toward professional. Much better than what she had sung at the Jamboree, or so I thought.

Had Ilene played these for Roger? Did he have any idea of how good she really was, or did he close his ears as thoroughly as he did his mind?

Maybe I wasn't being fair to Roger, but hearing Ilene's work after the way he had been putting her down really made me mad. I had heard him encourage Clifford and Earl for far lesser efforts than these. Not that they weren't good, too, but that Ilene had done so much on her own really impressed me.

I shut down the stereo feeling pretty sure that I knew why Ilene had felt like she had to run away. When I was growing up, my parents had encouraged me in just about everything I tried. When they died and Paw took me in, he had done the same. Richard still did. I couldn't imagine how I could have achieved *anything* without them behind me, and Ilene had done all of this on her own.

Then I realized that that idea wasn't fair to Aunt Ruby Lee and Ilene's brothers, or even Tom Honeywell. Maybe I had misjudged Tom. I had thought that he was about as low as a man could get without sinking into the ground, but if he was helping Ilene along, maybe he wasn't so bad after all.

I looked around the room for the guitar that Ilene had been using on the tapes, but it wasn't around. She hadn't used it in her act, and I couldn't remember if I had seen it in the dressing room or not.

I had been hoping for something definite, but I really couldn't tell if Ilene had planned to run away or not. As I was closing the bedroom door behind me, I heard the doorbell, and by the time I got to the living room, Aunt Edna had let Junior Norton in.

"Hey, Miz Randolph," Junior said. "Good to see you Laurie Anne, Richard."

"Hi, Junior."

"Ruby Lee will be down in a minute," Aunt Edna said. "Won't you have a seat? Can I get you something to drink?"

Junior accepted her offer of a cup of coffee, and Aunt Edna went to fetch it.

I never could figure out how Junior gave off that air of

competence. She was just barely five foot tall, and had a friendly face and a quick smile. Her uniform was neat, but not pressed to a sharp crease, and though she carried a gun, she was so natural with it that I usually didn't notice it. Still, when Byerly's Chief of Police spoke, most folks listened.

Maybe it was in her blood. Her father, and his father, and I think his father before him, had all been police chiefs in Byerly. Junior's daddy, Andy Norton, had had his heart set on a son to carry on that line of law enforcement. Only his first four children were daughters. When Mrs. Norton got pregnant a fifth time, Andy was sure that he was going to get his son, and refused even to consider a name for a girl. When Mrs. Norton presented him with another daughter, he decided she was going to be his Junior, and that's all there was to it. If Junior ever considered a job other than being police chief, I never heard tell of it.

As it turned out, the Nortons had another child a few years later, and this one was a boy. Andy didn't see anything wrong with naming him Andrew Norton III, Trey for short. He was still in college, but worked as Junior's deputy during the summer.

By the time Aunt Edna served the coffee, Aunt Ruby Lee had come down with Aunt Nora and Aunt Nellie. She had gotten dressed in a pair of slacks and a striped blouse, and fixed her hair and makeup.

"I appreciate your coming over, Junior," Aunt Ruby Lee said. "How's your family doing?"

"They're just fine, ma'am." With the bare minimum of pleasantries taken care of, we could get down to business. "I hear you've lost track of Ilene."

"I'm afraid so, Junior," she said sadly.

"Well, I went over to Tom Honeywell's trailer, but he

wasn't there and there wasn't any sign of Ilene, either. I woke up one of his neighbors, and she doesn't remember seeing him since yesterday morning. Honeywell is a door slammer, and he woke her up. Anyway, she doesn't think that he's been back."

"Did you look inside his place?" Aunt Nellie wanted to know.

"I couldn't do that, ma'am, not without a search warrant," Junior said formally. Then she grinned and said, "Now, since Honeywell had left his curtains gaping wide open, it was perfectly legal for me to look through the window. Which is what I did, once I found a milk crate to stand on. I don't know what his usual housekeeping is like, but it looked to me like he had left in a hurry."

"Does he not have a job?" Aunt Nora asked. "Didn't his boss know anything?"

"He had been working at a gas station in Hickory, but when I called over there, the manager said he fired him over a week ago. Never on time, the cash register always short, rude to customers—all in all, not an ideal employee."

"Then you'll have to put an APB out on him," Aunt Edna said. To the rest of us, she explained, "That's an all points bulletin."

"I can't do that, ma'am," Junior said. "We don't know for sure that Honeywell has done anything illegal."

"What about contributing to the delinquency of a minor?" Aunt Edna said. "That's still a crime, isn't it?"

"Yes, ma'am, but we don't know for sure that he has Ilene with him."

"That's silly," Aunt Nora said. "Where else would she be?"

"I was hoping that y'all might have found something in her room that would answer that," Junior said.

"I let Laurie Anne look around in there," Aunt Ruby said. They all turned toward me. "Did you find anything?"

"I can't tell if she took anything other than her Jamboree stuff, or not," I said. "She might have."

Junior nodded. "Well, I didn't really expect her to leave a map. Now, the last time she was seen was at the Jamboree?"

"That's right," Aunt Ruby Lee said.

"Then maybe I should talk to the folks over there. Is it all right if I use your phone?"

"Of course."

"Forrest Jefferson is in charge," Aunt Nora offered.

Junior nodded and, after consulting Aunt Ruby Lee's phone book, dialed a number. "Hello? This is Chief Junior Norton from Byerly. I need to talk to Forrest Jefferson. . . . Yes, I know the Jamboree is going on but this is official police business. . . . No, I'll hold while you run and find her." There was a long pause. "Miss Jefferson? This is Chief Norton over in Byerly. I was wondering if I could ask you a couple of questions." Another pause, and Junior grimaced. "Yes, ma'am, I know you're awfully busy right now, what with the Jamboree going on. This shouldn't take but a few minutes. I'm trying to find a young woman named Ilene Bailey. . . . Yes, that's the one. . . . No, I'm sure she's not planning to disrupt anything. The problem is that she didn't come home last night, and her mama is awfully worried, as I'm sure you can imagine. . . . No, of course I don't expect you to keep up with every participant. . . . Is that a fact? I didn't have any idea that there were so many people out there. You must have your hands full, and I really appreciate your taking the time to talk to me. Now, I understand she had her things in a dressing room. Can you tell me if she left them there or not? . . . Of course you're not responsible if anything is missing. I'm just trying to find out if she left on her own hook or if somebody took her. You wouldn't want word getting around about young women disappearing from there, would you?"

The last was a not very veiled threat, which showed how annoyed Junior was getting. I wasn't the only one Forrest Jefferson rubbed the wrong way. It was also a thought that hadn't occurred to me—I had been assuming that Ilene had run away, not been taken away.

Junior went on, "I sure would appreciate it if you could send somebody to check. . . . That would be fine. Just have your assistant call me at this number." She read out Aunt Ruby Lee's phone number, thanked Miss Jefferson again, and hung up.

She said, "I suppose you could tell that Miss Jefferson doesn't have any idea of where Ilene might be."

"Then I don't know what to tell you," Aunt Ruby Lee said in a tight voice. "I don't know where she's gone."

"Don't you worry, ma'am. They're going to check to see if her things are there, and chances are that she'll be back on her own anytime now."

"You are going to look for her, aren't you?" Aunt Ruby Lee asked, sounding alarmed

"I'll do everything I can," Junior said firmly. "If you've got one, I'd like a recent picture of Ilene. Something that shows her face."

While the aunts went to find Aunt Ruby Lee's pictures, and then decide which one to use, I asked Junior in a low voice, "Do you think you can find her?"

"Well, Laurie Anne, if she has run off and really wants to

stay gone, she'll stay gone. Especially if she's left the imme-
diate area. I'll keep my eyes open, make some phone calls,
drive around and look, but it wouldn't hurt none if you were
to get some of your cousins out there looking for her."

"I'll do that."

My aunts finally picked a picture and handed it to Junior.
"That'll do fine," she said. "I'm going to hit the road and see
what I can find out. That woman is supposed to call back
from the Jamboree in a few minutes, and if she doesn't, you
call back and give them what-for. I'll be in touch, but you be
sure to call if you hear from Ilene."

"Thank you, Junior," Aunt Ruby Lee said.

"That's all right, ma'am. I'm glad to help out." She nodded at the rest of us and left.

Chapter 10

"I suppose all we can do now is wait," Aunt Ruby Lee said morosely once Junior was gone.

"The heck it is," I said. "Junior told me that we should get out there and look for Ilene ourselves, and that's what we're going to do. With as many people as we've got in this family, we should be able to cover the whole town and most of the county besides."

"Laurie Anne's right," Aunt Edna said. "There's no reason to sit on our hands. Let's get out there looking!"

I think they'd have all stormed out the door if the phone hadn't rung then. It was Miss Jefferson's assistant from the Jamboree. It turned out the person assigned to Ilene's dressing room for the day had found a lot of her things still there. I promised the woman I'd send somebody to pick them all up, and thanked her for her help. "It looks like she went off on the spur of the moment," I said to the others, and that cheered us up somehow. Ilene getting angry and running off didn't seem so bad as Ilene carefully planning an escape.

Of course, the paranoia I've picked up from living in Boston reminded me that Junior's idea of a kidnapper was another possibility. For now, I decided to keep that thought to myself. There was no reason to get Aunt Ruby Lee any more upset than she already was.

The first thing I did was call Aunt Nora's house to get Uncle Buddy and Thaddeous on the job. Willis, Aunt Nora's youngest, was still asleep because he works the night shift at the mill, so I wasn't sure if we should wake him up or not. Aunt Nora decided that he had had enough sleep and told Thaddeous to drag him out of bed.

Aunt Nellie called her husband Ruben, and then went to pick him up to start looking. They also had the job of going to the Jamboree to pick up Ilene's things and to track down Carlelle, Idelle, and Odelle. We decided to keep Ilene's brothers out of it for a little while longer, until they performed. Clifford and Earl had been practicing for months, and it wasn't going to make that much difference if they didn't join in on the search for a couple of hours.

Aunt Edna called her boyfriend Caleb in Greensboro, and he said he'd be there as soon as his assistant manager got in to take over the store. Then she called her son Linwood, and told him to start looking around that part of town in case Ilene was trying to get to the Lender house. Sue wanted to help, too, so Aunt Edna asked her to keep an eye on the Lender house and to make phone calls. Next Aunt Edna called the Ladies Auxiliary of the Byerly Baptist Church, and got them looking. Then she hit the road herself.

Aunt Nora, knowing that hungry people were going to start reporting in, headed for her house and the grocery store to round up provisions.

Aunt Daphine, who had already canceled her appointments at the beauty parlor she ran, called her employees to get them to ask around. If anybody in town had seen Ilene in the past twenty-four hours, one of the women there to get her hair done was likely to know. She also put Gladys, the manicurist and most knowledgeable gossip, on the job. Then Aunt Daphine went out to start looking herself.

Next I called Vasti. She said she couldn't go out herself because of wedding arrangements, but got her husband Arthur to send out all the salesmen from his Cadillac and Toyota dealerships. She also wanted to know what was going to happen to the wedding if Ilene didn't show up, but I cut her off as fast as I could. That was a question I didn't want to think about yet. I tried to track down Aunt Maggie at the flea market, but had no luck.

Still, within an hour and a half, we had most of the Burnette family out on the road looking for Ilene. I wanted to go out, too, but I finally decided that it would be better if I stayed at Aunt Ruby Lee's to answer the phone and hold her hand. Richard said that he'd stay, too, to be available for whatever errands needed running and, though he didn't say it, to hold my hand.

"I think that's all we can do right now," I said to Aunt Ruby Lee. "I hate to say this, but don't you think you should call Roger?"

She looked sick at the thought, but she nodded. "He's over at the Jamboree." I found the number for the Rocky Shoals High School, and dialed it. The person answering the phone this time was as reluctant to go get Roger as the other one had been to find Forrest Jefferson, but when I insisted and implied that I was a police officer, he agreed. When Roger came to the phone, I handed the receiver to Aunt Ruby Lee.

"Roger?" she said tentatively, then paused. "I'm fine. Well no, I'm not. Roger, Ilene is gone. . . . I mean she's gone. She never came home last night. She's run away. . . . I think you know why. You saw how mad she was yesterday, and I know you heard about what happened last night. . . . Junior already checked over at his place. They're not there. . . . I know I should have called you sooner, but I was hoping she'd show up. . . . No, we haven't told the boys yet. I didn't want to mess up their performance. You'll have to make up some excuse for my not being there. . . . Of course we're looking for her. Laurie Anne and my sisters have everybody out looking who can get away. . . . No, I think you should stay there until after the boys play. Then tell them. . . . I'm all right over here. You find my baby, that's all I want. . . . All right, you look around out there. I'll be here if you find out anything. . . . I love you, too. Bye."

She hung up the phone. "He's mad I didn't call him sooner."

"Well, you didn't and there's nothing you can do about it now," I said firmly. "He ought to know that you're not thinking straight at a time like this. Hurting people's feelings should be the last thing on your mind."

Aunt Nora made it back with enough sandwich fixings and Cokes to feed an army, arriving just before the first batch of people started coming by. I had just been expecting our family, but Aunt Nora knew better. Once word got out, all kinds of neighbors and friends showed up. Most wanted to help, but some just wanted to find out what was going on. I put the helpful ones to work and shooed off the others so Aunt Ruby Lee wouldn't be bothered any more than absolutely necessary.

I swear we must have covered every inch of Byerly and the nearby towns of Granite Falls, Rocky Shoals, and most of Hickory besides. I had people calling every hospital, police department, hotel, motel, and bed-and-breakfast in the

county and several surrounding ones as well. When Junior
checked in, she said she couldn't have done a better job if she
had brought in the National Guard.

We might have sat and watched the grass grow for all
the good our searching did. Nobody found hide nor hair of
Ilene or of Tom Honeywell. Oh, there were flurries of excite-
ment all throughout the day. A young couple had checked
into the Bide-a-Wee Motel in Hickory that morning, but
they turned out to be honeymooners from New York stop-
ping on their way to Florida. And somebody thought sure
that she had seen Ilene at Kmart, but when Thaddeous
raced over there to check it out, it turned out to be somebody else. There was even a frightening hour when the hos
pital in Hickory had a dead Jane Doe from a car accident
who was about Ilene's age. Only somebody else identified
her before Aunt Ruby Lee and I could get to the hospital.

By three o'clock, I couldn't decide if I was more tired or
frustrated. Most of the friends had given up, and the family
was out of ideas, too. We had had people look everywhere
we could think of and had called everybody we could think
of. If there was a stone left unturned, it wasn't for lack of
trying. I had been reduced to sitting around, hoping for the
phone to ring.

When it did ring, I jumped like a scalded cat and grabbed
it. "Hello?"

"Laurie Anne? This is Junior."

"Have you heard anything?"

"Yes and no." There was a pause. "Laurie Anne, I don't
want you to get all upset, but there's been a development
over at the Jamboree."

"Did they find Ilene? Is she all right?" By now, Aunt

Ruby Lee, Aunt Nora, and Richard were right there with me.

"No, they haven't found Ilene."

I shook my head for the benefit of my family, and they relaxed just a touch.

Junior continued. "They found Tom Honeywell."

"Does *he* know where she is?"

"We can't ask him. He's dead, Laurie Anne."

It didn't really sink in, but I automatically asked, "What happened?"

"He was found shot in the Ramblers' bus. From the looks of it, he's been there since late last night."

"Is there any sign of Ilene? Was she with him?"

"We don't have any way of knowing right now. There weren't any obvious signs of her around."

"You don't think—You don't think she's been . . ." I just couldn't finish the sentence.

"I don't know any more than what I've told you, Laurie Anne. He's dead, and there's no sign of Ilene. We're just going to have to keep looking."

"Junior, what if she's with . . . with whoever it was who did this?" Every lovers' lane killing I had ever seen in the headlines ran through my head. Had the killer kidnapped Ilene? Had he killed Tom to get at her?

"Laurie Anne," Junior said softly, somehow bringing me back to earth. "I know this is frightening, but you can't fall apart now. Your family needs you, no matter what's happened."

I took a deep breath. "I'm all right."

"We're going to keep right on looking for Ilene, both me and the Rocky Shoals police. And y'all keep on looking, too. You hear me?"

"I hear you."

"Good. Have you seen Roger?"

"Not lately. He's out looking."

"When he comes in, tell him that I've got two of the Ramblers checking out the bus because I didn't think he'd want to mess with it now. Al and Cotton are over here, and they say it looks like things have been moved around, but it doesn't look like anything's missing."

"I'll tell him."

"Good. I've got to go now. I'll be in touch."

"Thanks for calling, Junior."

I put down the phone, and as luck would have it, Roger, Clifford, and Earl showed up about then. I started to tell them what Junior had said, trying to emphasize that it didn't necessarily mean that Ilene was in trouble, but they all caught the implications just like I had.

Aunt Ruby Lee had been strong most of the day, but when I finished, she just broke down crying again. Roger took her in his arms and led her upstairs.

Clifford and Earl watched after them helplessly until Aunt Nora pulled them into the kitchen and started feeding them sandwiches.

I started pacing. "I just can't stand this," I kept muttering.

"Laura," Richard said, holding out his hand. "Come here."

I went, and let him hug me.

"Richard, I'm going nuts. Ilene's out there and she could be in terrible trouble." I didn't want to think about how terrible. "I've got to *do* something."

"You *are* doing something," he said. "You're doing a lot."

"I know, but I can't just sit here anymore."

"Okay. Wait here." He went into the kitchen, and returned a minute later. "Aunt Nora will listen for the phone and the door, and the boys will stay with her."

I don't know if my eagerness to get out of that house was unseemly or not, but I nearly flew out the door, car keys in hand.

"Where to?" Richard asked once I had the car started.

I was unwilling to admit that I didn't know where else to look, so I said, "She was last seen in Rocky Shoals, so we might as well go there."

Richard tactfully refrained from reminding me that a lot of people had already looked in Rocky Shoals.

Hoping that I'd see Ilene along the road, I drove slowly enough to make even normally polite North Carolina drivers lose their tempers and honk their horns.

For a minute when we got there, I couldn't figure out why there were so many people in Rocky Shoals, but then I remembered the Jamboree was still going on. It seemed like it had been forever since Ilene went missing, instead of less than a day.

I was tempted to go to the Jamboree, too, to see if they had found out anything more about Tom Honeywell, but decided against it. The place was bound to be a zoo. Besides, I didn't think the police would tell me a whole lot. Chief Monroe wasn't like Junior.

Not knowing what else to do, I drove around and around Rocky Shoals, getting angrier and angrier at the traffic, and driving more and more as if I were back in Boston. Richard, bless his heart, didn't say a word as I cussed at every other driver in town. He knew I was just letting off steam, even if I didn't realize it myself just then.

Eventually Richard said, "I don't know about you, but I could use something to drink. Can we stop somewhere?"

"Sure," I said. "We're not doing any good anyway." The Hardee's that marked the back road to the high school was closest, and at first I thought I'd go through the drive-through. Then Richard pointed out that it might be about time to call Aunt Ruby Lee's house and see if there was any news. I parked, and he went to the phone while I headed inside the restaurant to order drinks.

It was crowded in there with folks heading to and from the Jamboree, and most of them were talking about the discovery of Tom Honeywell's body, though they didn't use his name. All the commotion must have been the reason I didn't see her right off. Sitting in a booth by herself was Ilene.

I just stared for a few seconds, afraid that I was seeing things. She was facing to one side, looking out the window, but it was her all right. I abandoned my place in line and went over there.

"Ilene?" I said, still afraid she'd turn out be somebody else. "Are you all right?"

She turned and looked at me with the expression I usually reserve for finding something unpleasant in the refrigerator. "Of course I'm all right."

Ilene did look healthy enough, if a little bit worse for the wear. There was a scratch on her right cheek, and some smaller red marks on her hands. She didn't have on a bit of makeup, which was unusual for her, and her hair could have used some shampoo. The jeans she was wearing were muddy in places, and there were a couple of small holes in her shiny black cowboy shirt.

I slid into the other side of the booth. "Where have you been?"

"Nowhere," she said, and turned back to the window.

Now that I could see with my own eyes that she was all right, I was suddenly angry. "Jesus Christ, Ilene! You had us all scared to death. Why didn't you call your mama?"

She didn't even bother to look at me.

"Ilene—" I started, then Richard came up beside me.

"Ilene?" he said.

"Hello, Richard," she said without turning.

"Are you all right?"

Her only response was an exasperated sigh.

"Where's she been?" he asked me.

"Hell if I know," I snapped. "She obviously doesn't care that the police and our family and everybody else in Byerly has been out looking for her since the crack of dawn."

"I should have known that Mama would overreact," she said.

"Don't you dare talk about her like that!" I said.

"She's my mama and I'll talk about her any way I damned well please!" Now she was looking at me, all right, her face as angry as mine must have been. "Laurie Anne, I am sick and tired of you trying to run my life."

"Well, excuse me for caring about you, and for trying to help you."

"Help me? Is that what you call it? Why don't you tell me how getting Daddy out there to embarrass me to death at the Jamboree was helping me."

Of course, I knew doggoned well that I shouldn't have interfered at the Jamboree, but I was too mad to admit that now. "I told you that I only got Roger out there because I thought he'd like your singing."

"Sure you did."

"I did," I insisted. "How was I to know you were going to

come out there dressed like that? Why didn't you sing one of the songs from your tape?"

Ilene's face went red, and I knew I had made yet another mistake. "You *bitch!* What the hell were you doing snooping around in my room?"

"Aunt Ruby Lee asked me to," I said. "Junior said we had to look and see if there was any clue of where you had gone."

"You can't make me believe that you thought you'd find out where I was from listening to my tapes."

I flinched at that. She was right—I had listened to those tapes only out of curiosity, or rather, nosiness. What I needed to do was apologize, but I wasn't about to do that.

"Ilene," Richard said, "do you know about Tom?"

"I know as much as I need to know," she snapped. "I don't need you telling me I-told-you-so."

We looked at one another, realizing that she didn't know what had happened to him.

She caught the look between us, and said, "What?"

I said, "Tom's dead. They found him this afternoon. Somebody shot him."

"Are you serious?" She looked at our faces, and realized that we were. "Jesus! I heard a couple of folks talking about them finding somebody dead at the Jamboree, but I didn't know it was Tom."

"I'm sorry, Ilene," I said awkwardly. "I know you two were close."

"I *thought* we were close, anyway." She looked away from us again, but this time I saw tears in her eyes. "What happened?" she asked.

"We don't know," I said.

"I don't think we need to discuss this here," Richard said. "Ilene, are you going home?"

She said, "I might as well. I haven't got anyplace else to go."

"Laura, I think you should call Aunt Ruby Lee. And call Junior, too."

I nodded, and slid out of the booth so Richard could take my place while I went out to the pay phone in the parking lot. Clifford answered the phone at Aunt Ruby Lee's house, and was so excited that Ilene had been found alive and well that he didn't ask for any explanation. That was just as well, since Ilene hadn't given us one. Junior's brother Trey answered the phone at the police station and promised to radio Junior right away.

I went back inside to the table where Ilene and Richard were sitting, and asked "Are y'all ready to go?"

Ilene didn't say anything, just got out of the booth and pulled out her guitar case from where it had been beside her. She didn't say anything during the drive, either, or when we got to her house.

After we pulled up, I started to say, "Do you want us to go inside—"

She was already out of the car, and slammed the door behind her.

Richard said, "Maybe it's best to let her and her parents work it out for themselves."

"Probably so," I agreed, and we drove on to Aunt Maggie's house. As we went inside the door, I sighed and said, "Now we have to call everybody and tell them she's been found."

"Not everybody," Richard said. "Just Aunt Nora. She can call everybody else."

As it turned out, I didn't have to call anybody because the word had already spread. Aunt Maggie was on the phone when we came in the door, talking to Sue about Ilene, which meant that Aunt Ruby Lee must have already told at least one sister.

Aunt Maggie, who is nothing if not pragmatic, decided that since everything had come out all right, she might as well go out to an auction, and after making sure that we didn't want to come with her, she left.

"Only it didn't come out all right," I muttered to Richard. "Ilene is furious at Roger and Aunt Ruby Lee. And at me."

"She's a teenager," Richard said. "She's supposed to get furious now and again."

"Not like that. You saw her."

"Yes, I did. And I see that you're blaming yourself when you don't need to. You were only trying to help."

"You mean I had good intentions? Isn't the road to hell paved with those?"

"Laura," Richard said in exasperation. "The problems between Ilene and her parents started a long time before we got here."

"I helped make them worse."

"You got caught in the middle of them, that's all."

"Really?" I said, wanting to believe him.

"Really. You did what you could. So what if it didn't work? At least you tried. 'If to do were as easy as to know what were good to do, chapels had been churches, and poor men's cottages princes' palaces.' *The Merchant of Venice*, Act I, Scene 2. And that's not in the contest so don't try to come up with a colorful retort."

I nodded, because goodness knows I was in no mood to be colorful.

"Do you want to get something to eat?" he asked.

"I'm too tired to be hungry." The day's emotional ups and downs had worn me slap out.

"Then let's go to bed."

"I'm too riled up to be sleepy."

"I bet I can change your mind."

He was right, too. Once we got upstairs, he made me lie down and proceeded to rub every single tense muscle out of my back. I tried to brood, I really did, but under the circumstances, I just couldn't. All I could do was fall asleep.

Chapter 11

When the ringing woke me the next morning, I just knew I was having a bad dream. It was around the same time of day as before, and Richard was still asleep. So of course, I wasn't all that surprised when I answered the phone and it was Aunt Ruby Lee.

"Laurie Anne! Thank goodness you're there."

"What's the matter?"

"It's Ilene. She's in jail."

So much for the dream. Now I was wide awake. "What for?"

"Laurie Anne, they think she killed Tom Honeywell. They came and talked to her about him last night, and this morning they came back and arrested her."

"Junior arrested her?"

"No, not Junior. It was the chief of police in Rocky Shoals. That's where I am now. Laurie Anne, I don't know what to do. I know my baby didn't kill anybody."

"Is there anybody there with you?"

"No. Roger and the boys had already left for the Jamboree before this happened. I called over there, but the woman said she didn't know where to find them."

"You call over there again and *make* her find them. Richard and I will be there just as fast as we can. Do you want me to call anybody else?"

"Maybe Nora?"

"I'll take care of it." Aunt Nora would have been my choice, too, because her shoulder was the best to cry on. "I'm going to call Junior, too."

It only took a couple of minutes for me to call Aunt Nora and leave a message for Junior. In no time at all, Richard and I were back on the road to Rocky Shoals. I was inwardly fussing at myself the whole way there. I should have realized that Ilene would be a suspect in Tom's death. The way they had argued in public and then she disappeared—if she hadn't been my cousin, I'd have suspected her myself.

The Rocky Shoals police station was a little bit bigger than Byerly's, and everything looked a bit shinier. In the mood I was in, I didn't attribute that to it being any better, but to the fact that they didn't have enough to do. Judging from the familiar cars filling the tiny parking lot, so many Burnettes had already shown up that they were going to have plenty to do.

The young officer at the desk looked as if he was under siege, which he was. Roger was glaring at him, Aunt Nora was looking at him reproachfully while Aunt Ruby Lee sobbed on her shoulder, and Uncle Buddy, Thaddeous, Clifford, and Earl were watching him with that deadpan look that makes me more nervous than any ugly expression.

He looked up at me and Richard hopefully, but he wasn't going to get any relief from us. "What's going on?" I asked nobody in particular.

"Chief Monroe has Ilene in the back," Thaddeous said. "This fellow," he added while nodding at the desk officer, "said we can't see her without Monroe's say-so."

"Is that right?" I asked him.

"Yes, ma'am."

"Then get Chief Monroe out here," I said.

"Did you want to see me?" said the man I recognized from the Jamboree as he came out from the back of the station.

"Actually, I want to see my cousin Ilene."

"And you are?"

"Laura Fleming."

"Well, Mrs. Fleming, I told your family that they'd be able to visit her as soon as she was processed, and I just now finished."

Roger boomed, "You can damned well *un*process her! My little girl hasn't done anything!" He stepped closer to Monroe, but then somehow Richard was there between the two men.

All he said was "Roger?" in an even voice.

Roger didn't move back, but he didn't move forward either.

Monroe said, "Mr. Bailey, I'm sorry, but your daughter has been arrested for the murder of Tom Honeywell. I explained all of this to your wife." Nobody bothered to correct him on the ex-wife, future-wife issue. He looked around the room. "I'm afraid I can only allow one of you in to see her right now. Department policy."

Roger said, "You go ahead, Ruby Lee," but Aunt Ruby Lee shook her head, still crying. Roger nodded, and said, "I'd probably just upset her. Laurie Anne, you go."

"If it's all right with Aunt Ruby Lee," I said. When she nodded, I turned to Monroe and said, "Let's go."

He said, "You'll need to leave your pocketbook here."

I handed it to Richard.

Monroe led me through a door to the rear of the station and into a small room. "If you'll wait here, I'll bring in the prisoner."

I sat down and counted to ten, then did it in binary. His calling Ilene "the prisoner" as if she weren't a person anymore just made me mad, and I needed to get over that mad before I could do her any good. I think my breathing was under control by the time Monroe came back in with Ilene.

She looked both better and worse than she had when I'd found her at Hardee's. Her jeans and hair were cleaner, and her makeup was in place, but the expression on her face was sullen, even more so than it had been lately. I couldn't really blame her for that, not after what she had gone through in the past few days.

I moved as if to hug her, but Monroe said, "I'm afraid you're not allowed bodily contact." He pulled out a chair for Ilene, and she sat down.

"Can I be alone with her?" I asked.

"I'm afraid not," he said. "Department policy."

Aunt Maggie has a look of disdain that she uses to freeze people at fifty paces. She tells me that it's a Southern woman thing. I'm not as good at it as she is, but at point-blank range, I do all right. I gave Monroe the look. He stiffened, but didn't say anything.

To Ilene I said, "Are you all right?"

"Just dandy. I've always wanted to spend time in jail."

"What happened? Aunt Ruby Lee said they questioned you last night."

She nodded. "They wanted to know where I had been, and when was the last time I had seen Tom. I told them, but I could tell that they didn't believe me. They already knew about our fight at the Jamboree."

"Then what?"

"Then they left. But they came back this morning and arrested me. The sons of bitches put handcuffs on me."

"Department policy, no doubt," I said icily, not looking at Monroe.

"Then when we got here, they had a woman come and search me."

"Did she hurt you?" I said, ready to explode if she had.

But Ilene shook her head. "No, it just . . . no she didn't hurt me."

"Have they questioned you?"

"A little. They wanted to know where I got the gun, and what I did with it afterward. They kept saying that they didn't blame me for shooting Tom, but they wouldn't believe that I didn't do it."

"It sounds like we've got grounds for a suit for false arrest," I said, which was talking through my hat but I was angry.

"No, what we've got here," Chief Monroe said, "is a young lady who caught her boyfriend cheating on her. And this fellow had already been mistreating her. So in the heat of the moment, she gave him just what he deserved. I think we can get that down to something reasonable like manslaughter."

"But I didn't kill him!" Ilene nearly screamed.

Chief Monroe shook his head slowly. "I'd like to believe you, I surely would, but I just don't. Once you calm down and have yourself a good cry, I bet that you're going to realize that the best thing for you is to plead guilty and take what's coming to you. Your being so young will work in your favor."

"Is that your legal advice, Chief Monroe?" I asked coldly.

"I beg your pardon?"

"Well, apparently you've appointed yourself my cousin's lawyer or you wouldn't be trying to advise her. For the record, you did read my cousin her rights, didn't you?"

"Yes, ma'am, I did."

I looked at Ilene, and she nodded. I said, "Then I think we'll just take advantage of her right to remain silent until she speaks to a lawyer."

"You can do that, but I'm not trying to do that little girl any harm. I was just trying to—"

"You were trying to convince Ilene to commit a crime."

"I beg your pardon?"

"You were trying to talk her into confessing to a murder, weren't you? Since she *didn't* kill Tom Honeywell, any confession would be perjury, and I seem to recall that perjury is a crime."

He pushed back his hat and scratched his forehead. "I don't believe I've ever heard it put that way before." He shrugged. "If she doesn't want to talk anymore, that's fine. I'm afraid I'm going to have to take her back to her cell now."

"Ilene," I said urgently, "don't worry about a thing. Your mama and daddy are here, and we're going to get you out of here. It's going to be all right."

I don't know if I convinced her or not, because she didn't answer, just let Monroe take her away. A minute later the officer who had been at the desk came in to lead me back out front.

Chapter 12

By the time I got back to the front office, Junior had arrived and was listening to everybody trying to explain at once. She saw me and looked relieved.

"Laurie Anne, I'm all kinds of confused. Can you give me a rundown of what's going on around here?"

Everybody else quieted down, and I gave as brief an explanation as I could without leaving anything important out. I ended it with, "The next step is to get Ilene a good lawyer."

"You don't think she'll need one, do you?" Aunt Ruby Lee said.

"Yes," I said firmly. "That police chief is already trying to railroad her into confessing. We need somebody to look after her interests."

"Do you have somebody in mind?" Richard said.

"Not really. Aunt Ruby Lee, who did you use for your divorces?"

She looked a little embarrassed at the question, but I didn't have time to be delicate. "Shaw Stevens."

I knew Mr. Stevens myself, but before I could suggest calling him, Junior said, "He's gone to Memphis for his an-

nual trip to Graceland. And I don't think this is his usual
kind of thing anyway."

"Who else is good, Junior?" I asked.

She thought for a minute. "Florence Easterly usually
does all right with criminal cases. I don't know that she's
handled a murder before, but I expect she can handle it."

"Aunt Ruby Lee? What do you think?"

"If Junior says she's good, then that's all right with me.
Junior, do you have her number?"

Junior asked the officer at the desk if she could borrow
the phone, dialed the number, and handed the phone to Aunt
Ruby Lee.

The rest of us kept quiet while Aunt Ruby Lee made arrangements with Miss Easterly. "She'll be here as soon as
she can," she said when she hung up the phone.

"What about getting Ilene out on bail?" Roger wanted to
know.

"That will have to be decided by a judge," Junior said,
"but I don't think there's much chance of it. It's a murder
case, for one, and for another, she's a runaway." Roger and
Clifford tried to argue with her, but all she did was shrug.

Chief Monroe came in then, and seemed a bit taken aback
by Junior being there. "Chief Norton," he said, "what can I
do for you?"

"Hey there, Lloyd," Junior said. "I just came by to check
on Ilene Bailey. You know how it is when one of yours is arrested in somebody else's town. Have you got a minute to
talk?"

"You bet. I'm just waiting for somebody from the prosecutor's office to call."

"We've got a lawyer coming," I said, wanting him to
know that he was in for a fight.

"I expected you would," he said, "but I think it'd be a lot easier if you'd just let your cousin confess and get it over with." Before I could respond, he looked at Richard and said, "You're that Shakespeare fellow, aren't you?"

I had almost forgotten that Richard had kept Monroe distracted so I could sneak past him at the Jamboree, and I wondered just what I had missed.

Richard nodded.

"Didn't Shakespeare have something to say about lawyers?"

" 'The first thing we do, let's kill all the lawyers,' " Richard said. "*King Henry VI, Part Two*, Act IV, Scene 2."

"That's what I thought."

"Of course the character who said that was Dick the Butcher," I said as sweetly as I could, "and he was a complete ass."

Richard nodded solemnly.

Monroe blinked a few times, then said, "Come on into the back, Chief Norton." Clearly, he wasn't going to talk in front of all of us.

As soon as they were gone, Thaddeous congratulated me and Richard for insulting Monroe so politely, but I did feel bad about it. Getting Monroe angry wasn't going to do Ilene any good and might do her harm.

After that, there wasn't a whole lot for us to do but wait for Miss Easterly. Uncle Buddy went outside to smoke a cigarette, and Thaddeous went to keep him company. Aunt Nora collected quarters and went to find a pay phone to start calling the rest of the Burnettes. Clifford and Earl went to the diner across the street to get everybody something to drink. Roger kept his arm around Aunt Ruby Lee, who would cry a bit, pull herself back together, and then start crying again. As soon as he was sure that it wouldn't offend anybody, Richard pulled out a paperback copy of *Much Ado About Nothing* to read. I just sat. It was one of the longest hours I had ever spent.

It was just before ten when a petite blonde about fifty years old, dressed in pink and aqua, stepped inside the police station. She looked around, and asked, "Ms. Burnette?"

"I'm Ruby Lee Burnette," Aunt Ruby Lee said.

"You poor thing," the woman said. "I know you're just having the worst day of your life. But don't you worry. I'm going to take care of you and that little girl of yours." Then she realized that Aunt Ruby Lee was confused. "I'm sorry, I'm just forgetting every bit of my manners. I'm Florence Easterly."

She wasn't exactly what I had expected from a criminal lawyer, but if Junior recommended her, I was willing to give her a shot.

Miss Easterly went on, "Now do you think you can tell me what's happened?"

"I better let Laurie Anne tell it," Aunt Ruby Lee said, wiping her eyes.

Miss Easterly nodded sympathetically. "Of course." She looked around again. "And which of you is Laurie Anne?"

"I am," I said, and went back over the story. It didn't improve any on the second recitation, but though it sounded damning for Ilene, Miss Easterly just nodded.

"Well, young girls do make their mistakes. I know I've made my share." She shook her head as if remembering. From the looks of her, I couldn't imagine her making any mistake more serious than forgetting to acknowledge an invitation to tea. She then turned to Roger. "You must be Ilene's father."

Roger said, "Yes, ma'am. I'm Roger Bailey."

"I know this is difficult for you, Mr. Bailey, but you have to be patient. The wheels of justice turn slowly, but they do turn, and I'm here to speed them up a bit."

Roger nodded, and turned his attentions back to comforting Aunt Ruby Lee.

Miss Easterly spoke to the officer at the desk. "Hello, Wade. I'd like to speak to Ilene Bailey."

"Yes, ma'am. I'll just call Chief Monroe to let him know you're here."

"That would be just wonderful." She turned back toward us, and smiled as if to say that everything would be just wonderful.

Wade used the intercom to call Chief Monroe, and then started to escort Miss Easterly into the back.

"Y'all just wait here," she said before following him. "I want to have a talk with Ilene, and then I'll speak with Chief Monroe."

She was gone about forty-five minutes, and came back looking grave. Junior was right behind her.

"What's going to happen now?" Aunt Ruby Lee asked.

Miss Easterly said, "Chief Monroe has called the judge to set up an arraignment for this afternoon. That's when Ilene will be formally indicted."

"And that's when they set bail, isn't it?" Roger asked. "I don't care how high they set it—I'll get the money."

But Miss Easterly was shaking her head. "I don't think that we're going to be able to get Ilene out on bail at this time. With a capital offense, it is granted only rarely, and I'm afraid it will never be granted to a runaway. I'll ask the judge at the arraignment, of course, but I want you to be prepared for his refusal."

Roger looked thunderous. "What kind of country is that when a little girl like Ilene can be locked up with criminals?"

Miss Easterly patted him on the arm. "I do understand your feelings, Mr. Bailey. I could tell right away that Ilene is a fine young lady. But don't you worry—Chief Norton has come up with a solution I think you'll approve of. Chief?"

Junior was standing a little awkwardly, and I think she was ill at ease in the face of Miss Easterly's amazing, old-style femininity. "Well, folks, this is the best I can do. With Ilene being under age, by rights there should be a woman looking after her. The only thing is, there's just the one female police officer in Rocky Shoals and she's going on vacation after her shift ends today. Lloyd doesn't have any other woman who can keep an eye on Ilene, so he's willing to let me keep her in the Byerly jail. She'll be that much closer to home, and I'll make sure that she doesn't come to any harm."

"Isn't that wonderful?" Miss Easterly said brightly. "Not as comforting as having her back home, but much better than being here with strangers." She glanced at her delicate gold wristwatch. "Now it's nearly eleven o'clock, and the arraignment is scheduled for one. Ms. Burnette, I'd like you to get something else for Ilene to wear. Her outfit isn't quite what we want for making a first impression on the judge."

"I'll call my sister Daphine to bring something, if you'll tell me what you think she should get."

"Perfect. Would that be Daphine Marston, of La Dauphin Beauty Parlor?"

"Yes, ma'am."

"Even better. Ask her to bring her brushes and things, too. Ilene's hair is lovely, but I think that a slightly different style would make a big difference." She turned to the rest of us. "I know y'all think I'm being silly, worrying about these things, but Judge Daley is a conservative man when it comes to a young woman's appearance."

"I'll say," Junior said, half under her breath.

"Whatever you say is fine with me," Aunt Ruby Lee assured her. They conferred for a minute before Aunt Ruby Lee called Aunt Daphine.

When the clothing arrangements had been made, Miss Easterly said, "That's all we can do until the arraignment. Now I think we should all get ourselves a late breakfast. Or perhaps an early lunch."

"I couldn't eat a thing," Aunt Ruby Lee said, and I had to admit that food was the last thing on my mind.

"Nonsense," Miss Easterly said. "You've got to keep your strength up, and you know these fellows are growing boys." She smiled at Clifford and Earl. "I bet you two didn't get any breakfast this morning, did you?"

"No, ma'am," Earl admitted. Though he was a small fellow, he normally put away an awful lot of food.

"Then that's settled." Miss Easterly asked the desk officer, "Wade, does Andrews Brothers still have that scrumptious chef's salad?"

"I've never had the salad, ma'am, but it's still on the menu. The cheeseburgers are awful good."

"Then I shall have to try one." She turned to Junior. "Chief Norton, will you be joining the Burnettes and myself?"

"Not this time, Miss Easterly, though I appreciate the invitation. I've got some business to take care of, but I'll see you at the courthouse later."

"I'll be looking for you." Then, to the rest of us, she said,

"Shall we? It's only a block or so away, and I know a short walk will do wonders for me."

We all followed her. If Florence Easterly was as good at leading a judge around as she was at leading us, Ilene was in good hands.

Once we got to Andrews Brothers, Miss Easterly charmed the hostess into putting us into the back room, even though it wasn't usually opened except for dinner parties, and made sure that everybody ordered something substantial and ate it. I hadn't thought that I would want anything, but I put away one of those cheeseburgers the desk sergeant had recommended, a mound of French fries, and several glasses of iced tea.

Besides feeling full, I felt a lot more normal afterward. That time spent sitting in the police station had that same unreality as waiting in a hospital. The everyday business of deciding who would sit where, ordering food, and sharing a meal made the day real.

I don't know if Miss Easterly ate anything or not. She was busy speaking to every one of us, "trying to get to know Ilene's family," as she put it. I could tell from her questions that she already knew quite a bit about the Burnettes, which wasn't surprising for somebody from Byerly. I wasn't sure what Richard's published papers or my career plans had to do with Ilene's defense, but I was willing to talk about them if it would help.

Miss Easterly was congratulating Clifford and Earl on winning third place in the intermediate class at the Jamboree, and telling Roger how wonderful it was that they were taking after him, when Aunt Ruby Lee waved for me to come over to her.

She said, "Laurie Anne, in all the confusion, I haven't had

a chance to thank you for finding Ilene for me, but I do appreciate it."

"Considering where she is now, maybe she'd have been better off staying gone."

"No, Miss Easterly says that's the worst thing that could have happened. It would have looked like she was an escaping felon, not a runaway."

That made sense, but I still felt as if I had gotten my cousin out of the frying pan only to toss her into the fire.

"Now I need to ask you to do something else for me," Aunt Ruby Lee said. "Miss Easterly said Chief Monroe is pretty certain that Ilene killed Tom Honeywell. She doesn't think that he'll believe she's innocent without finding the real murderer."

I knew where this was heading, of course.

"Laurie Anne, what I'm asking is for you to see if you can find out who really did it."

I hesitated for just a minute, but this still wasn't the time to abandon my role as troubleshooter. "All right, Aunt Ruby Lee, I'll do what I can. You know I can't guarantee anything, but I'll try."

"Thank you, Laurie Anne. Ilene will be real happy to hear that you're on the job."

I wasn't so sure of that, but I didn't argue with her, just went back to Richard.

"Did she just ask what I think she just asked?" he said.

"Yes, she did."

"And did you just answer the way I think you did?"

"I said I would, if that's what you mean." I put my hand in his. "Is that all right? After what we've been discussing about family responsibilities?"

"You know, Romeo worried about his role in the Montague family all the time, but when Mercutio was killed, he did what he had to."

"Which means what?"

"It means that an emergency is no time for a soliloquy, and your cousin being in jail for murder is an emergency. I will remind you that you don't have to do this alone. There are resources you can call upon, including me and the rest of the family, and perhaps Junior."

"Noted," I said, and gave him a kiss. "Thank you, love."

Just then Miss Easterly announced that it was time for us to get back to the police station. Aunt Daphine was already there, and she, Miss Easterly, and Aunt Ruby Lee went to see Ilene and get her ready.

After that, Miss Easterly briefed the rest of us on what we should and shouldn't do at the arraignment. Basically, we were to stand and sit when told to, look concerned but not angry, and not say a word. She looked at Roger directly when she got to the part about not speaking, and I think he got the message.

The courthouse was a short drive away. It was a white building with columns, probably because nothing looks quite so official as a white building with columns. The courtroom itself was smaller than I had expected, with a dozen rows of benches that would have been at home in any church if they had added racks for hymnals.

The procedure was very quick. At one o'clock, Judge Daley came in, everybody rose until he got to his seat, and then we all sat down again. In about twenty minutes, he disposed of three cases. One traffic violation was dismissed, and a drunk-and-disorderly and a petty theft were assigned bail. Then the clerk called out Ilene's case, and she came into the courtroom.

To tell the truth, she looked less like someone I knew than she had in her getup for the Jamboree. That demure, blue dotted swiss dress with the lace collar must have been borrowed, and I had never seen her with her hair coiled at the neck like that. She looked as if butter wouldn't melt in her mouth, an illusion that would never have held if she had been expected to speak. Still the judge looked approving, so I guess Miss Easterly knew how to play to her audience.

They went over the bare bones of the case, and then Miss Easterly pleaded not guilty on Ilene's behalf. As predicted, the judge refused bail after the prosecutor told about Ilene's running away. That's when Junior, who had arrived at the courthouse a few minutes after we had, asked to approach the bench as a friend of the court.

Junior, Miss Easterly, the prosecutor, and Chief Monroe spoke to the judge for a few minutes, then they all returned to their seats and the judge announced that Ilene would be temporarily housed in the jail in Byerly in order to provide "accommodations suitable to her tender years." That was it, and after Ilene was led away, Miss Easterly gestured for the rest of us to follow her out.

"That went well, don't you think?" she asked brightly.

While she took care of a few matters, I pulled Junior aside. "Junior, is this really going to trial?"

Junior shrugged. "Lloyd thinks he's got a pretty good case. Ilene was seen fighting with Honeywell just hours before his death, and she hasn't got a scrap of an alibi for the time he was shot. She said she was out in the woods all night."

"In the woods?" It sounded pretty thin, even to me. "You don't think she did it, do you?"

"If Ilene says she didn't do it, I believe her," Junior said.

"The problem is going to be proving it, and I'm guessing that the only way to do that is to find out who did kill Tom Honeywell."

"Then that's just what I'll do," I said.

She nodded. "I'd have been surprised if you had said anything else. Now you do realize that I'm not going to be able to help you, not directly anyway. Rocky Shoals is Chief Monroe's town. It's his case, and I can't interfere."

"Not directly?" I said.

"Oh, I might be able to advise you on some points."

"Thanks, Junior. I appreciate that." Junior's full-fledged assistance would have been valuable, but I understood why she couldn't butt in.

Miss Easterly called us over and said, "Chief Monroe is ready to release Ilene into Chief Norton's custody."

"Fine," Junior said. To Aunt Ruby Lee she added, "You can follow me back to Byerly if you want to, or you might want to run by your house and get anything she might be needing for the next couple of days."

Aunt Ruby Lee nodded. "I'll do that, Junior. You tell her I'll be there as fast as I can. And thank you."

"That's all right, ma'am. I'm glad to be able to help."

Monroe came out with Ilene, and either department policy allowed it or he wasn't about to argue the point, because he let Aunt Ruby Lee hug her. He did watch pretty carefully, probably to make sure that no weapons changed hands. Junior signed some papers, and Monroe said, "Chief Norton, I release the prisoner Ilene Bailey into your custody."

"Then I'll be taking her off of your hands, Lloyd," Junior replied.

Aunt Ruby Lee said, "Junior, you're not going to have to put handcuffs on her, are you?"

"It is standard procedure with a murder suspect," Monroe said stiffly.

"Now Lloyd," Junior said, "if you insist on it, I will, but I think that I can handle a slip of a girl without handcuffs."

"Well . . ."

"And I don't seem to have mine with me," she added. "I wouldn't dream of taking yours, because then you'd be violating standard procedure by not having a pair with you."

"I might could dig up an extra set," Monroe began, but when he saw Junior's expression, he said, "but I guess it will be all right." He touched his hat, and left.

I didn't have any idea that Junior had "forgotten" her handcuffs, and I appreciated her sparing Ilene that indignity.

Aunt Ruby Lee asked, "Laurie Anne, are you coming back to Byerly with us?"

I shook my head. "I think I'm going to head for the Jamboree and see what I can find out there. I know Monroe won't tell me a thing."

Junior said, "You might be interested in knowing that Chief Monroe is planning to hold a press conference at two-thirty."

"Where?"

"Back at the police station."

I checked my watch. It was already two o'clock. "In that case, I'll go to that first."

"Should I head on to the Jamboree?" Richard asked.

"Good idea," I said, "except that we're a car short."

"I'll take him over," Thaddeous said.

"Great," I said. "You two see what y'all can find out, and I'll catch up with y'all later."

Junior escorted Ilene out to her cruiser, and the rest of us headed for our cars. Richard gave me a quick kiss before getting into Thaddeous's pickup truck, and I drove back to the Rocky Shoals police station.

Chapter 13

The press conference wasn't much of a much, just a few people standing around in the front of the police station. Hank Parker from the *Byerly Gazette* was there, as usual wearing his straw hat with a press pass stuck in the band. A middle-aged woman who looked like she was more used to covering church socials than murders represented the Rocky Shoals weekly paper, and a yawning man who didn't bother to use the camera slung over his shoulder was there from Hickory.

Still, Chief Monroe looked nervous. He rattled his piece of paper twice and cleared his throat three times before beginning.

"I've got a statement about the incident," he said. "After I read it, I'll answer questions." Then he read from his paper. "At approximately three-thirty yesterday afternoon, Homer Caldwell, the janitor at Rocky Shoals High School, discovered the body of Tom Honeywell, of Byerly, in a bus in the parking lot of the Rocky Shoals High School. Honeywell had been shot twice, once in the chest and once in the head, and seems to have died instantly. The coroner estimates time of death as sometime after midnight Friday night. The bus is owned by Roger's Ramblers, a country music band from Byerly, who had left the bus there while participating in the Rocky Shoals Memorial Jamboree. This morning, the Rocky Shoals police department arrested Ilene Lee Bailey, Honeywell's girlfriend. The two were seen arguing Saturday night, and Miss Bailey was missing for nearly twenty-four hours after that."

He looked relieved to have finished. "Are there any questions?"

"Chief Monroe," I said, "was a murder weapon found?"

"I'm sorry, Mrs. Fleming," Monroe said, not sounding very sorry. "This conference is only for members of the press."

Hank Parker piped up, "Chief Monroe, was a murder weapon found?"

Monroe looked put out, but answered. "Not at this time. However, Miss Bailey was not apprehended until over twenty-four hours after the shooting."

I moved closer to Hank Parker. "Ask him what kind of gun it was."

Hank complied.

Monroe said, "Tests are not complete, but we believe that it was a .22 handgun. A gun of that caliber was reported missing from backstage at the Jamboree, an area to which Miss Bailey had access."

How kind of him to keep dumping on Ilene. "Ask who owns the missing gun," I said to Hank, and he did.

"The gun belongs to Maureen Shula, one of the finalists in the Jamboree."

"Anything else?" Hank asked me.

I started to shake my head, but then said, "What was Honeywell doing on the Ramblers' bus?"

Monroe had heard the question, and this time didn't bother waiting for Hank to repeat it. "Since the bus belongs to Miss Bailey's father, our guess is that Miss Bailey had made an appointment to meet with Honeywell, and when they argued, she became angry and shot him."

That didn't make much sense to me. Ilene's supposed motive was their fight earlier, and Monroe was saying that they were going out there to neck after that. Even if they had arranged this assignation beforehand, would either of them have shown up after fighting? "And why would they meet on the bus?" I asked, more to myself than to Monroe, but he answered anyway.

"Several items on the bus had been disturbed, including some pieces of equipment that I've been told are quite valuable. A guitar was found next to Honeywell's body, where it had apparently been dropped when he was shot. It appears that they were attempting to steal it. Honeywell's car was parked next to the bus, presumably so the stolen property could be loaded into it."

Now as bad as Ilene had been acting, I did not believe that she would have stolen from her father. If she had wanted money, it would have been a whole lot easier for her to take it from Aunt Ruby Lee, and she hadn't. I started to suggest that Ilene had been trying to stop Tom from robbing her father, but that didn't hold water either. It didn't explain why she had a gun, why she had run off, or why she didn't admit to having shot Tom.

"Were there any signs of a struggle?" I asked. "Was Honeywell armed?"

Monroe shook his head. "There's no sign of it being self-defense, if that's what you're asking."

That was exactly what I had been asking.

"Now, if there are no further questions . . ." Monroe said. Hank looked at me, and I shook my head. I still had plenty of questions, but none that Chief Monroe could answer.

Monroe nodded, and walked away hurriedly.

"Thanks, Mr. Parker," I said. "I owe you one."

Hank tipped his hat. "My pleasure, Mrs. Fleming. You seem to know a lot more about this case than Chief Monroe is saying."

"Not really," I had to admit. "All I know right now is that my cousin didn't shoot Tom Honeywell, no matter how it looks."

"Perhaps you'll let me know as soon as you find out something more definite."

"You know I will." I glanced over at the reporter from the Rocky Shoals paper, who looked a bit dazed by it all. "Are you trying to scoop the competition in her own town?"

Hank sniffed loudly. "There is no competition in this town." He tipped his hat again. "If you'll excuse me, I think I'll mosey on out to the high school and see how the Jamboree is progressing."

"I'm heading that way, too," I said. "I am surprised that they didn't cancel it. A man was murdered there, after all."

"Heaven forbid! I don't think that anything short of an atom bomb would convince Forrest Jefferson to cancel her beloved Jamboree. When I called her yesterday, she insisted that the show must go on, because surely poor Mr. Honeywell would want it that way."

That didn't sound much like the Tom Honeywell I had met, but it probably wouldn't hurt anything for the Jamboree to continue. I had to wonder if Forrest hadn't pushed Monroe to make an arrest so quickly to keep from disrupting the event.

"Will you be conducting your own investigation, Mrs. Fleming?" Hank asked.

"Is this off the record?"

He nodded.

"You're darned right I will be!"

Hank grinned, and handed me a business card. "Like I said, call me when you find out something."

We walked outside together, and both of us headed for the Jamboree.

Chapter 14

If I hadn't known about Tom Honeywell's murder, I sure wouldn't have been able to tell from looking at the crowd at the Jamboree. The music was just as loud as it had been two days before, the people were just as rambunctious, and the lines to the bathroom were just as long.

One thing that was different was the yellow tape strung up around the Ramblers' bus and the Rocky Shoals police officer standing guard next to it. A number of people were milling around nearby, sharing rumors and speculation. They seemed a bit like vultures to me, but since I was there for the same reason, I couldn't very well look down on them.

I slowly walked around the bus, being careful not to touch the tape. It sure didn't look like the place I'd pick to kill somebody. The bus was slap dab in the middle of the parking lot, right next to a light pole, which meant that nobody could have snuck up on Honeywell. Did the killer walk right up to him and shoot?

Like Chief Monroe had said, Honeywell's silver Camaro was parked next to the bus, and it was roped off, too. That looked odd to me. If Ilene had killed Tom in anger the way Monroe thought she had, why hadn't she driven away? If she had been cold-blooded enough to take the gun, surely she'd have been cold-blooded enough to get the keys out of Tom's pocket so she could take the Camaro. Instead she had gone off on foot. It didn't fit, but I didn't think it would convince Monroe of anything.

There was a broken window on the driver's side of the bus, at just about the place to reach over to open the door. Didn't that make it more unlikely that Ilene would be involved? Couldn't she have gotten the keys somehow? Of course, I was sure Monroe would argue that she could just as easily have broken the window to make it look like it was somebody else.

I walked around another time, trying to picture what it must have looked like the night of the shooting. I didn't know what the exact time of death was, but it was late enough that Tom wouldn't have expected there to be anybody else around. Maybe somebody saw him and came to investigate. Like Roger, or one of the other Ramblers. If he had realized what Tom was doing, there could have been angry words, followed by a gunshot.

That still didn't make sense. I didn't know about the other Ramblers, but as far as I knew, Roger didn't carry a gun. That meant that he'd have to have seen Honeywell, found the gun, and then gone back to shoot him.

Of course, I could be wrong about Roger carrying a gun. What if he came to check the bus, saw Tom, and got carried away and shot him? Certainly Roger would have had a good motive for wanting Tom dead, what with the way he had been treating Ilene.

I shook my head. No, if Roger had shot Tom, he'd be shouting it from the rooftops. Certainly he'd never let his daughter go to jail for his crime. That was true for Clifford and Earl, too, and for all of the Burnettes. Anybody who thought enough of Ilene to kill for her wasn't likely to let her stay in jail.

That still left the other Ramblers, who could have seen Tom messing with the bus. The only thing was, if one of them had shot Tom while defending the bus, he could have claimed self-defense. Tom had no good reason to be on the bus, and surely his fingerprints would have been on the items that had been disturbed.

What if one of the Ramblers had been in on the robbery, and he and Tom had quarreled? That scenario didn't work well either. Items had been disturbed, but nothing was missing. Would a thief have killed somebody, and then left everything?

Why had Tom been shot anyway? I hadn't known him well, but he didn't strike me as the kind of person to resist if somebody aimed a gun at him. Besides, Monroe had said that there were no signs of a struggle, and that Tom hadn't been armed. It didn't sound as if he had been killed in anger at all, but deliberately. I wasn't about to mention that conclusion to Monroe. It would have made things look even worse for Ilene.

I walked around the bus one more time, but nothing else came to mind. All I knew for sure was that I just couldn't picture Ilene shooting Tom in the middle of the parking lot, right under a light that must have made it nearly as bright as day. I was heading back to the school building when I saw Chief Monroe, who did not look happy to see me.

"Mrs. Fleming," he said, and tried to keep on going.

"Just the man I was looking for," I said cheerfully.

He sighed heavily, but he did stop.

I said, "Chief Monroe, I was just out by the bus and I noticed that it's parked right under a light pole. Don't you think my cousin would have had more sense than to shoot somebody in bright light?"

"It's been my experience that people about to commit murder aren't known for their common sense."

"But—"

"Excuse me, but I need to talk to my officer." He walked briskly away.

Chapter 15

After I counted to ten three times, I decided that continuing to talk to Chief Monroe right then would only get me in trouble. Instead, I went looking for Richard and Thaddeous. I found the two of them sitting at a picnic table and drinking Cokes with a dark-haired, dark-eyed woman who was pretty enough to have made me a tad jealous if I hadn't trusted Richard completely. Of course, trusting him didn't stop me from putting my arm around him possessively as soon as I sat down next to him.

"Hi," I said. "What's up?"

Thaddeous said, "Laurie Anne, this is Maureen Shula. She won the novice competition Friday afternoon."

"Congratulations," I said, wondering why her name sounded familiar.

"Maureen is also the one who reported a missing gun," Richard added.

That's why the name sounded familiar. Chief Monroe had mentioned her at the press conference.

"I always carry a gun with me," Maureen said. "Show business can be awfully rough for a woman alone."

"I don't imagine you're alone all that often," Thaddeous said gallantly.

I sighed inwardly. My cousin was smitten again. "I take it that Richard and Thaddeous told you why we're interested."

Maureen nodded. "Sorry to hear about your cousin. I saw the first part of her act. She could have given me a run for my money if she hadn't been interrupted like that."

"I don't know about that," Thaddeous said. "I bet you're awfully good."

I nudged Thaddeous under the table to remind him of why we were there, but I don't think he noticed. "Do you have any idea of when your gun was taken?" I asked.

She shook her head. "I was so busy that day that I didn't hardly know if I was coming or going. I know I saw it that morning, when I set up my dressing room, but that's the last time I remember noticing it. I wanted to lock the room, but they wouldn't give me a key. Forrest Jefferson said that only performers were allowed back there, so everything should be safe." She tossed her curly mane back over her shoulder. "If she'd been around musicians as much as I have, she'd know better than that. I've seen some pretty scuzzy characters at these competitions. That's why I got the gun in the first place."

"Did anybody else know you had it?" Richard asked.

"Of course," she said. "What good is it if nobody knows you've got it? That first morning a fellow 'accidentally' came into the room while I was changing, and the only way I got him out of there was to pull the gun. He hightailed it out of there pretty quick, let me tell you. If he hadn't, he'd have been singing soprano."

Richard flinched, but Thaddeous just looked even more admiring. "That's the way to handle that kind. Men like that don't know what to do with a *real* woman."

"Anyway," Maureen went on, "he started squawking and everybody came running to see what was going on. Miss Jefferson wanted Chief Monroe to take the gun away from me, but I told her that I have a license and I have a right to protect myself, and that if she had let me lock my dressing room door, it wouldn't have been a problem. She fussed about it, but she backed down eventually."

"You didn't leave it loaded, did you?" I asked.

"Of course I did. What use is it if it isn't loaded?"

The NRA would approve, I supposed. "When did you notice that it was gone?"

"After the dance Friday night. Funny thing is, I went looking for it *because* of that fellow who got killed."

"You mean Tom Honeywell?" I asked.

She nodded. "He had been hitting on me at the dance, said he admired my style and could really help me with my career." She rolled her eyes. "Help himself to my prize money is more like it. Still, I didn't mind letting him buy me a beer or two. Then your cousin came in and let him have it with both barrels. I didn't need trouble like that, so I let him know right quick that I wasn't interested in his company anymore. He didn't like that, not one bit. So before I went outside to my car, I thought I'd get my gun out of the dressing room, just in case. Only it wasn't there."

"Did you report it?" I asked.

"Not then. There wasn't anybody around then to report it to."

"Honeywell didn't try anything, did he?" Thaddeous asked indignantly.

"He didn't have a chance," Maureen said. "I found a crowd who were heading to their cars at the same time, and went with them."

"That was smart," Thaddeous said.

Richard asked, "Was anything else taken from your dressing room?"

"Just the ammunition."

Of course, I thought. What good was it to have a gun without ammunition? "What did Miss Jefferson do about finding the gun?"

"Not a doggoned thing, as far as I can tell," Maureen said. "When I first told her, she didn't even want me to tell the cops. She just kept saying that I should have hid it better, and that she didn't want any trouble because of it. By the time I finally got past her and to the cops, they had just found the body, they didn't have any time for my problem. Then they decided it was my gun that killed him, and all of a sudden they had plenty of time. Chief Monroe even tried to get me to say I had gone out to that bus with Honeywell myself, but I told him right quick that he was barking up the wrong tree."

I was glad to hear that Monroe had at least considered other possibilities before settling on the wrong suspect.

Maureen continued, "Lots of people saw me drive away that night, and Lee was awake when I got back to the hotel and could swear to what time it was."

"Lee?" Thaddeous asked. "Is that your roommate?"

"He's my boyfriend," she said. "He'd have been at the dance with me, but he had some folks in town he was visiting."

Thaddeous didn't say anything after that. Another fledgling romance shot down, this time before it even got started. One of these days, I told myself, we were going to have to find that cousin of mine a woman.

"Thanks for your time," I said to Maureen.

"No problem," she said. "I just hope it works out for your cousin. We musicians have to stick together, you know. If she comes back to the Jamboree next year, I bet she'll walk away with the novice prize."

"I'll tell her you said that," I said. It would do Ilene good to hear it.

She left, with Thaddeous looking after her regretfully.

"It looks like we can pretty much limit ourselves to the people who could get backstage," I said to distract him.

Richard said, "That's a lot of people."

I nodded, remembering how many I had seen on the way to Ilene's dressing room. "Still, Forrest Jefferson must have a list." As annoyed as I had been when they wouldn't let us back there, it must might work in our favor this time. "Did y'all see her around?"

"She's here, trying to emulate Puck and 'put a girdle round about the earth in forty minutes.' " He raised one eyebrow. "That's *A Midsummer Night's Dream*, Act I, Scene 1."

I had nearly forgotten about our contest. "You mean that she's running around like a chicken with her head cut off?"

"You win that round, I think."

I didn't disagree, and he pulled out the notebook and added a mark to my score. Thaddeous looked a little confused, but just shrugged. He had been around us too much to worry about such things. I noticed him looking at his watch.

"Did you need to be somewhere?" I asked.

"Nothing major," he said, "but I did tell Vasti that I'd help get Aunt Ruby Lee's lawn in shape for the wedding. Clifford and Earl have been busy rehearsing, so they haven't been keeping it up."

"But the wedding and the reception are going to be at the church," I said.

"I know," Thaddeous said, "but Vasti says she wants them to take pictures over at the house before the wedding, and the photographer might want to take some outside."

For Vasti, that made sense. "I think we can handle it from here," I said.

"Thanks for the ride," Richard added.

"No trouble," Thaddeous said. "You just call if you need anything else."

He headed for the parking lot, and Richard and I went looking for Forrest Jefferson. While we were looking, I filled him in on what I had learned at the press conference and what I had guessed by looking at the bus. He didn't find any holes in my reasoning, or come up with any other ideas.

He and Thaddeous had spent most of their time trying to ferret out rumors about the shooting, but hadn't learned much that I hadn't heard elsewhere.

It didn't take us long to find Forrest. All we had to do was look for a crowd of upset people, and there she was in the middle of it, dispensing orders just as fast as she could. We waited around the edges until there was a lull, then moved in closer.

"Miss Jefferson, can I talk to you a minute?" I asked.

"What is it?" she said, flipping through the stack of pages she was still carrying.

I started with, "I'm Laura Fleming, and this is my husband Richard," because I didn't know if she'd remember us. "We're investigating the shooting of Tom Honeywell, and we need a list of the people who were backstage and had access to Maureen Shula's gun."

"I thought Chief Monroe wouldn't need that list now that

he's made an arrest." She looked up at us. "You're not with the police."

"No, ma'am, we're not. Ilene Bailey is my cousin."

"Trying to get her off, are you? I don't think you'll have much luck. The way I hear it, it's an open-and-shut case."

"I disagree," I said as evenly as I could. With no official standing, I didn't want to make her mad. "We really would appreciate that list."

"I don't know that I should give it to you," she said. "You don't have any business with important Jamboree information."

A familiar voice behind me said, "Is there some reason you don't want the names on that list known, Miss Jefferson?" I turned and saw Hank Parker, peering at Forrest with his best suspicious look. "Were there people back there who shouldn't have been?"

"Of course not, Mr. Parker," Forrest said. "You know that Chief Monroe has been supervising security personally."

"Then why are you withholding the list?"

"I'm not, it's just that . . ." She saw him jotting down her every word and said, "It's just that I don't have it with me right now, and I'm very busy during these last few hours of the Jamboree. As you know, it has been extraordinarily successful, despite the unfortunate incident with Mr. Honeywell." That last sounded like something she wanted Hank to quote. She smiled at me and said, "I'll be glad to give you a list of participants if you can come back tomorrow, when I have had time to put that information together."

"And their addresses?" I asked.

Her smile looked a little strained, but she said, "Of course. Shall we say around noon?"

Chapter 16

Despite having spent most of the day asking questions, there were really only two things I was sure of. The first was the fact I had started with: Ilene didn't kill Tom Honcywell. The second was something that seemed more reasonable the more I thought about it. The way Tom was killed, where he was killed, and when he was killed kept telling me that the murder didn't have anything to do with Ilene at all. The problem was, I didn't know enough about Tom to figure out who else would have wanted him dead.

We were driving back to Byerly when I announced, "I think we should get some gas."

Richard peered over at the gauge. "But we've got half a tank."

"I know that, but I really think we should get gas, and it just so happens that Sid Honeywell's is on the way."

"I take it that Sid Honeywell is related to the late Tom Honeywell."

"His father."

"Will Mr. Honeywell be there? I mean, his son was just found dead yesterday."

"I didn't think about that," I admitted. "Well, if he's not

"That would be wonderful."

"Fine. My office is here at the school. Just knock on the front door, and I'll tell Mr. Caldwell to expect you."

"Thank you."

She nodded, the smile still glued on, and said, "Well, if you will excuse me. I still have some details to attend to." She beat a hasty retreat.

"Mr. Parker, that's two I owe you," I said. "He helped me out at the press conference, too," I explained to Richard.

Hank grinned. "Happy to put the power of the press at your service. Any luck so far?"

I shook my head. "Nothing definite. We talked to the lady whose gun was stolen, but she couldn't tell us anything except that any of the participants could have taken it because most of them knew she had it. How about you?"

"Nothing so far. I've been looking for Homer Caldwell, the janitor that found the body. Initial reactions can add tremendous flavor to a story." He tipped his hat, said, "I expect I'll be seeing you around," and left.

"What now?" Richard said.

"I'm not sure. Wander around, I guess. See if we can eavesdrop on anything interesting."

It wasn't much of a plan, but it was the best I could come up with. We walked through the Jamboree two or three times, listening in to all kinds of conversations, but didn't hear anything we could use. Most of the people who said anything about the murder knew that Ilene had been arrested, and were satisfied that she was guilty. If Richard hadn't been there, I don't know if I would have been able to resist arguing with them.

The Jamboree started winding down after awhile. The dealers and food vendors packed up, and about the only people left were going to see the awards ceremony. Under the circumstances, Clifford and Earl had decided not to attend to accept their award, so there wasn't much reason for us to hang around.

We were on our way back to the car when we saw Hank Parker backed up against a wall by a serious-looking man in a coverall talking a mile a minute. Hank glanced our way with a look of near desperation, so Richard and I went over there.

The man in the coverall was saying, "You know, I don't know how long I had been up on that ladder, not realizing what was lying there below me, before I looked down. And even then, I didn't see him at first. But there he was, as dead as can be. Poor fellow, him so young and all." He went on for several minutes about the shame of a man dying so young, and how his nephew had been even younger when he died.

When he finally took a breath, Hank said, "Hey there! Mr. Caldwell, this is Laura Fleming and her husband Richard."

Mr. Caldwell nodded. "Nice to meet you. I was just telling Mr. Parker here how finding that body plumb knocked me for a loop." He proceeded to tell us just how shocked he had been, and that he was glad he didn't have a weak heart like his brother-in-law, and that he was convinced that physical labor was the best thing in the world for keeping a body healthy.

No wonder Hank looked so desperate. I waited for Homer to take another breath and said, "Excuse me, but aren't you the janitor here?" Knowing that he was, I didn't wait for his answer, because it could have taken half an hour. "Miss Jefferson was looking for you a few minutes ago, something about a spill on the stage."

"Is that right? Well, I better go find her right no Jefferson is mighty particular about this Jamboree that's a fact. I just wish you had told me right away. walked quickly away.

Hank took off his hat and wiped his forehead. "I sure a preciate that, Mrs. Fleming. I didn't think I was ever going to get away from that man."

"You haven't been here since we saw you before, have you?" Richard asked.

"Near about. I've never known a man to talk so much and say so little."

"He 'speaks an infinite deal of nothing,' " Richard said. *The Merchant of Venice*, Act I, Scene 1."

"He could talk the hind leg off of a mule," I said.

Richard thought about it, then pointed at himself. I n ded, and he pulled out the notebook.

"That's one less favor you owe me," Hank said, obliv to our exchange.

"My pleasure," I said.

"I suggest that we leave before Homer finds ou you've fooled him."

"I expect Forrest will have found something for do by the time he gets there," I said, but we all he the parking lot anyway, just in case.

there, whoever is there will be able to tell me where to find him."

As it turned out, Sid Honeywell was in the cashier booth at the station. Perhaps I shouldn't have been surprised. As far as I knew, he and Tom had never reconciled after Tom ran out on him, taking every bit of money he could put his hands on. Still, it just didn't seem right, even if it did make things easier.

A lot of the self-service gas stations I've seen have fortresses for cashier booths, with only the tiniest openings for you to hand them money. Sid Honeywell's place wasn't that way at all. The door to the booth was always open, and Mr. Honeywell was always ready to chat with you when you paid for your gas.

I pulled up next to the pump, left Richard to deal with the gas, and went on up to the booth. Mr. Honeywell was a chubby man, with a full beard. His father had played Santa Claus at the elementary school Christmas party for years, and it wouldn't take much longer for Honeywell's hair to go solid white so he could follow in his father's footsteps. Normally, he looked jolly enough for the part, but today he only half smiled when I came in.

"Hey, Mr. Honeywell," I said, handing him a twenty-dollar bill. "My husband's filling up that blue Escort over there."

He nodded and said, "How are you doing?" in that toneless way that really doesn't call for an answer.

Another customer came in to pay for his gas, so I waited for him to go before saying, "I wanted to tell you how sorry I was to hear about Tom."

He nodded again and took a breath that was almost a sigh. "Well, I can't be surprised that he ended up that way. I don't know where his mother and I went wrong with him, but we sure went wrong somewhere."

There wasn't much I could say to that. I had heard that Mrs. Honeywell drank and that she was drunk when she had her fatal car accident, but I didn't know whether or not that was true or, if it was true, whether or not it had anything to do with Tom turning out the way he did. Some people from good families go bad, just like some people from bad families go good.

"Still," Mr. Honeywell said after a long pause, "I loved him. Even after what he did to me."

"I know you did," I said awkwardly.

He saw that Richard had finished filling the tank of our car, and checked the meter. "That'll be $7.50." He handed me change and a receipt. "I appreciate your stopping by. I know you've got your own troubles about now, with Ilene in jail. I don't know what she ever saw in Tom, and that's a fact."

Now I really felt awkward. When I came by, I wasn't thinking that the cousin of a suspected murderer wouldn't necessarily be welcome in the business of the bereaved. "Ilene didn't shoot him, Mr. Honeywell."

"I heard that's what she said, so maybe she didn't. There were lots of others who had reason to. Tom stayed in trouble of one kind or another, ever since he was a boy. Gambling, drinking, stealing, always something." He shook his head sadly. "I don't know if it's a good thing or not that we never had another child. Lord knows I don't think I could have taken another one like Tom, but a good son or daughter sure would be a comfort to me now."

"I am sorry," I said, mainly because it's all I could think of. "You take care now."

He just nodded, and I went back out to the car. "That is one sad man," I said to Richard. "First to have Tom turn out the way he did, and then to have him die so young."

Richard took my hand. "Are you all right?"

I nodded. "He's just *so* alone. Here I had been thinking that it was tacky of him to be at the station at a time like this, when the fact is that he probably hasn't got anybody to help him. His father's in the nursing home, his mother and wife are dead, and Tom was their only child. I just wish there was something we could do."

"Maybe there is," Richard said. "Not us personally, but the Burnettes could. Why don't we call Aunt Nora and see if she can come up with something?"

"That's a great idea." I checked my watch. "We could go over there and tell her about it now, if you like."

"Isn't it about dinnertime?" Richard asked.

"Is it?" I asked innocently.

It was, of course, and when we got to Aunt Nora's house, she promptly added two places to the table and wouldn't take no for an answer. Not that our refusal was all that firm, especially when I saw that she had baked a ham. I've never been able to decide what goes best with Aunt Nora's biscuits: ham, roast beef, country-style steak, or pork chops. That means I have to try out each dish every chance I get.

I told Aunt Nora about Sid Honeywell's predicament, and, as Richard had predicted, it didn't take her long to come up with a solution. Earl had been talking about getting a summer job, now that the Jamboree was over, and helping out Mr. Honeywell would be perfect. Earl needed something to keep him busy so he wouldn't be fretting about Ilene. It only took two phone calls for Aunt Nora to get it all set up.

Then Aunt Nora caught us up on what had been going on

in Byerly while we were gone. Ilene was at the jail, but Junior didn't have any objections to visitors, and she certainly didn't mind if they brought food, as long as there was enough for her, too. She'd be spending the night there at the jail with Ilene.

"How is Ilene doing?" I asked.

Aunt Nora said, "About as well as you'd expect. Edna keeps saying that she brought it on herself, but I just can't believe that."

"Aunt Edna doesn't think Ilene did it, does she?" I asked.

"Of course not! It's just that she thinks that Ilene should have known better than to run around with somebody like Tom in the first place. I had to remind Edna of some of the scrapes she got into when she was younger."

"Like what?" I asked.

Aunt Nora just grinned. "I promised her I wouldn't tell."

"But now you've got me curious."

"That's too bad. Besides which, with Ilene's problems, you've got enough to keep you occupied. You are going to be working on that, aren't you?"

"Of course," I said, and told her what we had been up to so far. That got me to thinking again. It had been a horrendous couple of days, and I think Richard would have been happy to just sit and relax for the evening, but I was getting antsy. He saw me fidgeting and manfully said, "We hate to eat and run, but I'm afraid we've got places to go."

"That's fine," Aunt Nora said. "You do what you have to."

Chapter 17

It wasn't until we got back into the car that Richard said, "I assume that we do have places to go."

"Just one," I said. I had thought of something when Aunt Nora was talking about Earl. "Have you ever met Alton Brown? Earl's father?"

"I don't think so."

"Well, Sid Honeywell mentioned that Tom was a gambler, and so is Alton Brown. Maybe he knew Tom."

"It's worth a shot."

I stopped at the first pay phone I came to, got Alton's number from information, and called to ask if we could stop by. Alton said that he'd be glad for us to, and gave me his address.

Alton opened the door promptly when we rang the bell. "Laurie Anne, how nice to see you again. This must be the husband I've heard so much about. Won't you come in?"

He had us inside the door and on the couch with glasses of iced tea almost before I could confirm our identities. I was pleased that he was so glad to see me. I didn't know Alton well, because he and Aunt Ruby Lee hadn't been married all that long. Earl was the result of their marriage, and he was just a toddler when they divorced. I saw Alton every now and again because Byerly just isn't that big, and of course he visited Earl pretty often and Clifford, too, even though he was only Clifford's former stepfather.

Alton was always neatly dressed, with creases in his pants and his button-down shirts carefully tucked in. No hair was ever out of place, and he frequently pulled off his wire-rimmed eyeglasses to hold them up to the light and make sure they were perfectly clean. Even now, when he was sitting around the house on a Sunday evening, he looked as neat as a pin. To look at him, he's the last person on Earth you'd expect to be a compulsive gambler.

"To what do I owe this delightful surprise?" he said.

If anybody else talked like that, I'd think they were teasing me, but that's just the way Alton talks.

"Actually, we've come to ask a favor."

"I'm honored."

"I suppose you've heard about Tom Honeywell getting shot."

"And little Ilene has been arrested. Yes, news spreads rapidly in Byerly." He shook his head. "Poor Ilene, to go through such a thing. I've always been fond of her, though we have no formal relationship. How can I help?"

"Obviously, I don't think Ilene killed Tom."

"Obviously."

"I'm trying to find out why somebody else might have wanted him dead. I've heard that he was a bit of a gambler."

"So you've come to a thief to catch a thief, as it were," he said, but he didn't sound offended. He pressed his hands together as if in prayer, and rested his chin on them.

"Something like that," I said with a grin. "Did you know him?"

"Only by sight, and by reputation. We did not frequent the same circles."

I did find the idea of Tom gambling and throwing back beers with fastidious Alton ridiculous. "Do you suppose you could find out more about him? Whether he was winning or losing? If he owed money or not? Maybe he had been caught welshing, or cheating?"

"I would be happy to assist you. In fact, I'll venture out tonight to see what I can learn. I don't normally indulge in contests on a work night, but for Ilene's sake, I can bend a rule."

"Will there be gambling on Sunday night?"

"My dear Laurie Anne, a dedicated searcher can find gambling every night of the week, even in Byerly. I shall call you tomorrow. Where can I reach you?"

"We're staying at Aunt Maggie's house."

I started to give him the number, but he said, "I still remember it, as a matter of fact. Card counting is remarkable training for memorizing numbers."

"Thank you, Alton. I really appreciate it."

"Think nothing of it. I'm happy to do it for Ilene, and for Ruby Lee. I was so pleased to hear about her impending nuptials. I think Roger is an excellent choice for her." He flashed a smile. "Much better than I was."

Alton was showing us out when he said, "Richard, I understand you are a scholar of Shakespeare. Tell me, what did the Bard have to say about gambling?"

Richard hesitated only for a second. " 'If Hercules and Lichas play at dice, which is the better man? The greater throw may turn by fortune from the weaker hand.' *The Merchant of Venice*, Act II, Scene 1."

I was afraid that Alton would be offended, but he only

nodded and said, "Quite true. Though I am an aficionado of cards rather than dice, it works just as well for me."

Once we were back in the car, I said, "Couldn't you come up with something a little more tactful?"

Richard shrugged. "I don't think Shakespeare liked gamblers. The only other quote I could come up with was worse. 'False as dicers' oaths.' "

"Ouch. I see what you mean." I noticed him looking at me pointedly, but for the life of me, I could not come up with a Southernism about gambling. "Take the point," I said, and he cheerfully did so.

I could tell Richard was bone tired by that point, and so was I, so I didn't even ask. I just drove us back to Aunt Maggie's place, and we went on up to bed.

Chapter 18

Ilene had been in trouble one day, missing the next, and in jail the day after that. I thought that surely nothing else could go wrong, and we could be sure of getting a good night's sleep. I was wrong. The phone woke me the next morning.

" 'Once more unto the breach, dear friends,' " I muttered to myself on the way down to the kitchen to answer the phone, not certain where the quote came from but fairly sure that it was Shakespearean. "Aunt Ruby Lee?"

"No, it's me. Vasti."

Of course it was. "What's the matter?"

"That's what I was going to ask you. What took you so long to answer the phone?"

"I was asleep, Vasti."

"It must be nice. *Some* of us have too much to do to lie around in bed all day."

I checked the clock on top of the stove. It was all of eight o'clock. We were burning daylight for sure. "What's up, Vasti?"

"It's a disaster, Laurie Anne, a pure out-and-out disaster!"

"What?" I honestly couldn't think of anything else that could have gone wrong.

"Aunt Ruby Lee is talking about canceling the wedding! She says she won't get married with Ilene in jail."

"I guess it would be awkward," I said. "Especially since Ilene is supposed to be the maid of honor." To tell the truth, I hadn't even thought about the wedding in days.

"Awkward? I tell you what's awkward. Awkward is having to cancel the caterer, and the hall, and the flowers, and the photographer, and the videographer. You know that nobody is going to return the deposits. And somebody is going to have to call every single one of the guests to tell them not to come. Laurie Anne, what am I going to do?"

"Vasti, don't you think you're overreacting?"

"Overreacting?" I could tell she was either rolling her eyes in exasperation, throwing up her hands, or shaking her head in disbelief. Maybe all three. "I have spent months putting this wedding together. Months!"

"Everybody knows how hard you've been working, Vasti, but things happen. Ilene didn't exactly plan on getting arrested."

"I'm not so sure."

"Vasti . . ."

"Anyway, I need to know something and I need to know right now. Are you going to be able to get Ilene out of jail by Saturday?"

"I don't know. I'm doing the best I can."

"Well, how can I plan around that?"

There wasn't any answer I could give, so I didn't even try.

Vasti sighed. "And if I do cancel everything, I just know you'll find the murderer and it will be too late to put things back together and they'll end up eloping or getting married at a justice of the peace. How would that look?"

I thought it would look fine, and I seemed to remember that something like that had been the original plan.

"Well," Vasti said as if she had come to an important decision, "I'm not going to cancel anything for now. I'm just going to have to trust you."

"I appreciate your confidence," I said dryly.

"That's all right. Just remember that I'm counting on you. I better hang up now so you can get to work. It's Monday already! That gives you five days, and you're just lucky that Aunt Ruby Lee wouldn't let me set up a rehearsal dinner or you'd only have four."

I hung up the phone, and then stuck my tongue out at it. Okay, it wasn't mature, but I wasn't feeling very mature. What I was feeling was tired and grumpy. I went back upstairs, intending to treat both symptoms by crawling into bed and going back to sleep.

Richard was still sound asleep, of course, so I snuggled back up to him and got comfortable. And lay there, wide awake. All I could think of was Ilene in jail, and Aunt Ruby Lee being upset, and Vasti and her darned wedding plans. After twenty minutes or so, I gave up and headed for the shower.

I was planning to wake up Richard once I was dressed, but he looked so peaceful lying there that I didn't have the heart to. This was his vacation, after all, and he had had a particularly tough spring semester. There was no reason I couldn't make my first stop by myself, so I left him a note and took off.

While trying to get back to sleep, I had decided to go to the police station and take Junior up on her offer of indirect help. If anybody in Byerly had a reason to kill Tom Honeywell, Junior was likely to know about it.

I went through the drive-through at Hardee's and picked up a bunch of biscuits, thinking that Junior and Ilene would be hungry. I needn't have bothered. I could smell breakfast as soon as I walked into the station, and sure enough, Junior was sitting at her desk with a plate of eggs, grits, and bacon, with a glass of orange juice on the side.

"Hey, Laurie Anne," she said, taking a bite.

"Good morning, Junior." I held up the bag. "I thought you might want something to eat, but I guess not."

"Your Aunt Nora beat you to the punch," she said. "There's plenty more if you want some."

"That's all right. I can get eggs and bacon anywhere, but I can't get a Hardee's sausage biscuit in Boston." I pulled up a chair and joined her.

"You can go see Ilene if you want," she said. "Your Aunt Nora is back there, too."

"Actually, it's you I came to see. I wanted to pick your brains about the late Tom Honeywell."

She took a bite of eggs, and thought about it for a minute. "I suppose that wouldn't count as interfering," she said. "I'm not going to be telling you a thing that I didn't already tell Lloyd Monroe."

I turned over a paper napkin and pulled out a pen, ready to take notes, and Junior pulled out a file folder from the wooden IN basket on her desk.

"Were you expecting me?" I asked.

"Let's just say that I'm not surprised." She opened the folder. "I guess you know that Honeywell was in trouble pretty much from day one."

I nodded.

"Most of it was pretty minor at first. Truancy, vandalism, picked a couple of fights before he realized that he wasn't as tough as he thought he was." She turned a page. "He eventually graduated to petty theft. Nothing too awful, and his daddy always bailed him out."

"Sid might have done better to let his son take his punishment," I said righteously.

"Easy to say when it's not your own," Junior said, and while I tried to decide if she was trying to make a point, she turned to the next page. "Later on, there was a string of more serious thefts, but we could only pin one of them on Honeywell, and he got off with probation. He got into gambling about then, too."

"I've already asked Alton Br—," I said.

Junior held up one hand to stop me. "Laurie Anne, gambling *is* illegal and I *am* Chief of Police, so please don't tell me if anybody you like is involved."

"Sorry," I said. "What were you saying?"

"I was saying that Honeywell got involved in gambling, and got pretty heavily in debt as a result. I think that's why he decided to take his daddy's money the way he did. He paid off what he owed, and took off with the rest. I'd have loved to catch him and pay for that, but Mr. Honeywell just would not press charges. I couldn't really blame him, but I wish I could have changed his mind."

"I'm surprised Tom ever came back to town," I said.

"I'm not. Around a little bitty place like Byerly, somebody like Tom Honeywell can play like he's a big shot. Put him in a town of any size, and it's just too plain that he's not much of a much. Plus he ran out of money, and I imagine he thought his daddy would take him back. He showed up at the front door one day like the prodigal son, wanting Sid to forgive him."

"Sid didn't, did he?"

Junior shook her head. "Wouldn't even let him in the door. He called me to chase Tom away from the gas station once or twice after that. It hurt him worse than anything, but he knew he couldn't trust his son anymore."

"Junior, I just thought of something awful. Do you suppose Mr. Honeywell could have shot Tom? I went by his station yesterday, and he seemed to be grieving, but people can fake that."

"Since Sid closes up around ten, and Tom wasn't shot until the wee hours of the morning, it's possible. Just not likely. How would Sid have known where to find Tom, since they weren't speaking? Where did he get the gun, because the only gun I know of him having is a shotgun at the station? If the gun is the one stolen from backstage at the Jamboree like Lloyd thinks, how did Sid get it?" She shook her head. "It seems to me that if Sid Honeywell was going to kill his son, he'd have done it a long time ago. Like I said, possible, but not very likely."

"Good," I said, agreeing with her reasoning. I wanted to get Ilene out of jail, but I didn't want to have to put Sid Honeywell in her place. "Did Tom get into trouble once he came back to town?"

"You know he did. Gambling again, and a drunk-and-disorderly in Hickory. There's been a couple of small thefts recently, but if it was him, he covered his tracks pretty well." She closed the folder. "Is that any help?"

"Not much," I said. "Petty theft and vandalism doesn't usually provide a motive for murder. No drugs?"

"Just alcohol, maybe a little pot. I don't imagine that he could afford anything stronger."

"Women? Other than Ilene, I mean?"

"Not that I know of. He played kissy-face at bars now and again, maybe even a one-night stand here and there, but I never heard of anybody regular other than Ilene. Like I said, I don't think he could afford it."

I looked at the pitiful collection of notes I had taken, and frowned. Maybe Alton would have something more for me. "Thanks, Junior," I said.

"For what?" she said with a look of wide-eyed innocence. "We're just a couple of women gossiping over breakfast."

Aunt Nora came out from the back right then. "Laurie Anne! I didn't know you were here. Have you solved the case yet?"

Had she been talking to Vasti? "I'm afraid not," I said. "How's Ilene?"

She shrugged. "All right, I guess. She won't talk much."

"I should go speak to her," I said, but I wasn't enthusiastic about it. "Is that all right, Junior?"

She nodded. "I don't need to warn you about helping her escape or anything like that, do I?"

"Don't be silly."

"Just checking."

Aunt Nora said, "I've got to run. Ruby Lee said she'd be up here after a bit to keep Ilene company."

"See you later," I said to her, and went on in the back. I had never visited anybody in jail in Boston, but I was fairly sure that the procedures involved were more complicated than just walking in. Junior hadn't even bothered to close Ilene's cell door, let alone lock it. If Chief Monroe had been there, he'd have had a conniption.

Aunt Ruby Lee must have brought some of the comforts of home. Ilene's Walkman was sitting on a TV tray next to a stack of cassette tapes, and there was a pile of magazines next to that. Plus there was a small cooler against one wall. Still, it was a jail cell, and it bothered me to see my cousin there.

Ilene was sitting on one of the two single beds with her guitar on her lap, picking out notes. She looked up when I walked in and sat down on the other bed, but then looked back at her guitar.

"Hi!" I said.

"Hi."

"How are you doing?"

"Why is it that *everybody* who comes in here has to ask that?"

That was a question I'd be better off not answering. "Richard and I have been trying to find out what really happened to Tom." I gave her the high points of what we had found out, unhappy at how little there was to tell. "Of course," I added, "we're just getting started." I paused, thinking that she'd thank me or something. She just kept picking at the guitar.

After a bit, I said, "I better get your story, too. What happened that night?"

"Ask anybody. Everybody on this planet must have heard about it by now."

"I've heard about what happened at the dance," I said, "but I don't know what happened afterward."

She sighed deeply. "Fine, if it will make you happy. After the mess with Tom, I ran. Just ran, as fast as I could. I got to the woods behind the high school before I stopped."

"Why didn't you call your mama, or somebody to come get you?"

"I didn't want anybody to come get me! I was sick and tired of everybody messing up my life! I just wanted to be alone for a while. Is that so terrible?" She glared at me, daring me to argue with her.

"I guess I'd have felt the same way," I said.

She glared a minute longer, as if she didn't quite believe me, then went on. "I didn't actually decide to stay out there all night, I just never decided to leave."

"Did you get lost?"

She looked at me like I was crazy. "No, I didn't get lost. I was a Girl Scout for eleven years, Laurie Anne. I had a flashlight and my Swiss Army knife in my pocketbook, and I knew exactly where I was."

Spending the night out in the woods would never have occurred to me, but I hadn't lasted a year in the Girl Scouts. "Did you sleep out in the open?"

"I would have, but I found a sugar shack to use."

"A what?"

"A sugar shack. Somebody had built himself a little lean-to between three trees so he could go out there with his girl-friend. Or maybe girlfriends, judging from all the old rubbers in there. Didn't you ever hear of a sugar shack?"

I shook my head.

"I don't suppose you ever did," she said with disgust. "God forbid you should ever go off into the woods with a boy."

"Ilene . . ." I started to say, meaning to defend myself, but I decided that it wasn't the time. It wasn't any of Ilene's business anyway. "So you were out there all night. What about the next day?"

"I slept pretty late, and after that, I found a spot to sit and play my guitar. I just wanted to think. When I got hungry, I walked to the Hardee's and got something to eat. That's where you found me."

It didn't sound like much of an explanation for so long an absence, and I could understand why Chief Monroe hadn't been convinced. "Didn't you see or talk to anybody who can prove where you were?"

"Why? Don't you believe me?"

"Of course I believe you, but Chief Monroe doesn't."

"No, I didn't see anybody."

"Can you think of anybody who might have wanted to kill Tom?"

"Just me."

"Ilene!"

"No, I don't know of anybody."

I took a deep breath and silently counted to ten, but I was still mad. "Do you not want me to get you out of here?"

"What difference does it make what *I* want? Since when does that make a difference?"

"Of course what you want makes a difference," I said, forgetting that I was mad. There was something going on inside Ilene, and I didn't know what. "Why would you ask a question like that? Who's been going against what you want?"

"Nobody important, just my mother and father. Why in the hell did they decide to get married again anyway?"

"Don't you want them to?" It had never occurred to me that Ilene would be against her parents getting back together.

"No, I don't! I'm supposed to be tickled to death about it,

but if anybody had bothered to ask me whether or not I'm happy, I'd have told them. I'm not!"

"Really?" I asked without thinking.

Ilene rolled her eyes heavenward and sighed.

"I'm sorry, Ilene, it's just that I thought every child of divorced parents wants them to get back together again."

"Not me."

"Why not?"

"Do you *really* want to know?"

I nodded.

"Because I remember how it was when they were together. The two of them were always fussing about Daddy being out late and who he was out late with. They tried to hide it from me and the boys, but my bedroom was right next to theirs and I heard it all. Maybe I didn't know what it meant then, but I do now. I don't want to go through that again."

"I'm sorry, Ilene. I never realized how bad it was for you. But don't you think it will be different now? They've both changed a lot."

"Maybe it will be different," she allowed, "but only if Mama learns to stand up for herself and not go along with everything Daddy says."

"She does give in to him a lot," I had to admit, remembering how Aunt Ruby Lee had gone back on giving Ilene permission to be in the Jamboree.

"She's a doormat," Ilene said. "Even if they do get along this time, I'm not sure I want to live with Daddy anymore."

"Why not?"

"Because he won't let me alone! He doesn't like my clothes, and he fusses about me wearing makeup, and he thinks I ought to be home and in bed by nine o'clock every night. I can't live like that."

I saw what she meant. I hadn't worn makeup or stayed out late when I was seventeen, but that was because of personal preference, not because Paw wouldn't have allowed it. "Have you tried talking to him?"

"Of course I have, but he won't listen. Not *really* listen. He just pats me on the head and says, 'Daddy knows best.' " Then she seemed to change the subject. "When you were looking around in my room, did you go into the closet?"

I still felt guilty about that. "I looked in, but not all that closely."

"Did you look in the box on the top shelf?"

I shook my head.

"In that box is a china doll Daddy gave me for my birthday. She's got blond curls, a pink satin dress, and eyes that open and shut. He gave it to me last year."

It took me a minute to catch on to what she was saying. "Last year? But that's when you turned sixteen. Roger gave you a baby doll for your sixteenth birthday?"

She nodded. "I know Daddy loves me, but he doesn't know me. He still thinks I'm the same as I was when he and Mama first split up."

"How about your mama? Have you talked to her about it?"

"I've tried. When I just saw Daddy on holidays and weekends once in awhile, it wasn't so bad and Mama said I should just put up with it. But now he's over at the house all the time and I can't hardly breathe."

Come to think of it, the complaints about her behavior had begun about the time Roger and Aunt Ruby Lee started getting serious again. No wonder she had taken up with Tom Honeywell.

She went on. "I think I could have stood it if it were just the clothes and makeup. I mean, I could sneak around him on that if I had to. But not the music!" She stroked her guitar. "I'm as good as Clifford and Earl, and Daddy keeps telling them that he's going to put them to work in his band. When he hears me, all he says is that I ought to join the church choir!"

"Ilene, I am so sorry," I said. "I had no idea of what you've been putting up with. Once we find out who killed Tom and get you out of here, I'll see if there's something I can do."

The funny thing was, the mention of getting her out of jail didn't seem to console her. I could almost see her close up again. "Well, you go on and play detective, then. I'm not going anywhere."

I was starting to think that she wanted to stay in jail. She must have realized that her parents wouldn't get married until she was out, but would she be willing to stay there just to stop the wedding? That seemed awfully cruel, and more than a little reckless.

"If you think of anything that might help," I said, "you can get word to me, can't you?"

She snorted. "Are you kidding? I haven't been left alone for more than ten minutes at a time since I've been here. Either Mama or Aunt Nora or Aunt Daphine or somebody has been right here with me. Do they think I'm going to kill myself over Tom Honeywell?" She started plucking discords, and I knew she wasn't going to say anything else to me.

Chapter 19

Junior was typing when I went back to the office, but stopped when she saw me. "Did she tell you anything?"

I shook my head. "She was in the woods, and she doesn't know why anybody would kill Tom."

"Do you think she does know something else?"

"I don't know, Junior." I didn't think I should tell Junior any details about why Ilene was so troubled, but I did say, "Even when she gets out of here, she's got a lot to deal with." I felt so bad about her, and now I was getting angry at Roger and Aunt Ruby Lee for not realizing what had been happening. But it didn't seem fair to lash out at them right then either. So I picked what I thought was a safe target. "If Chief Monroe had the sense God gave a milk cow, Ilene wouldn't be here right now!"

"Now simmer down," Junior said.

"I don't want to simmer down." In fact, what I wanted to do was kick something, preferably Chief Monroe's shin. "I cannot understand why he's being so stupid!"

"Is that what you think he is?" Junior shook her head. "I've known Lloyd Monroe for many years, and he may be a lot of things, but he's not stupid."

"Well, he's sure acting stupid," I insisted.

"What makes you say that?"

I looked at her, not sure what she was getting at. "The way he's been acting. Arresting Ilene, and not considering somebody else. Don't *you* think he's going about this the wrong way?"

"I'll admit that I might take a different approach, but that's not saying that Lloyd is stupid. Laurie Anne, do you read the newspaper back up in Boston?"

"Of course I do."

"Do you read about murder cases?"

"Yes."

"Then you remember that case where a man said his pregnant wife was killed by a stranger, and it turned out he killed her himself."

"I remember."

"It usually does turn out to be the person closest to the victim. I know you've heard tell of people who get beat up and killed by their ex-boyfriends and ex-girlfriends, ex-husbands and ex-wives."

"Of course."

"Then you know that when somebody gets killed, especially if there's no sign of drugs or other criminal activity, the first person the police look at is the spouse, or the boyfriend or girlfriend. In more cases than not, that's where they find their killer."

"But Ilene didn't do it."

"Still, look at it from Lloyd's perspective. A man gets killed just hours after he dumps his girlfriend. The body is found in a bus belonging to the girl's father, with a gun that she had access to, and during a time when she doesn't have the first scrap of an alibi. You think about that."

I did, but opened my mouth to argue some more.

Junior stopped me with, "Are you *sure* she didn't do it?"

"Of course I am."

"Are you saying that you never for an instant thought that Ilene could have shot that man?"

That hit a nerve. "Just for a second," I said slowly. "When Aunt Ruby Lee first called me, I did wonder. But I'm sure now."

She nodded. "I wondered a bit myself."

"But you never would have arrested her."

"Yes, I would have. With circumstances like that, I'd have been stupid not to. Just like Lloyd Monroe would have been stupid not to. And like I said, he's not stupid."

"Maybe not," I had to admit, "but don't you think he's missing a bet by not looking elsewhere for the killer?"

"I think he is, but I'm a hunch player. Lloyd's right when he says there's no proof, because there's not. Just a hunch. Lloyd never accepts hunches. He plays it by the book, strictly by the book, and I can't fault him for that."

I remembered how he had politely but firmly kept me from going backstage at the Jamboree, and how he had insisted that only members of the press be allowed to ask questions at his press conference. It had been annoying, but he hadn't seemed like he was throwing his weight around just because he was in charge. And he had been right both times, in a way.

"I guess I can't fault him for it either," I said reluctantly.

"Do things by the book, and most times, the book will do right by you."

"I just never tangled with somebody who was so devoted to the book."

"Well, Lloyd's got his reasons."

"Oh?" That sounded like a story.

Junior hesitated for a minute, but only for a minute. "I don't suppose it's any big secret. You know the story of the Rocky Shoals bus wreck, don't you?"

"If I hadn't, that poem in the Jamboree program would have reminded me."

"Some poem," Junior said with a snort. "You know that the boy driving the bus that night wasn't the regular driver. The driver got sick, and they thought they'd have to cancel the trip. Then this fellow working at the county school bus garage said he could drive it, but he didn't have a license for driving a bus. He asked the police chief if it would be all right first. That was Lloyd Monroe, in his first year of being police chief. He wasn't so strict yet, and he said it would be all right."

"Oh my," was all I could say. If Monroe had played it by the book that night, those kids might not have died.

"It gets worse," Junior said. "Lloyd was going off to eat dinner that night, and he saw a light blue Volkswagen Beetle convertible speeding down the street. By rights, he should have hopped into his squad car and gone after it, but he was hungry and he figured that the driver was just heading for the concert. So he let him go."

"Was that *the* Volkswagen? The one that caused the accident?"

"There's no way of knowing, because they never found out who was driving it. The thing is, Lloyd is convinced that it was. When the accident happened that night, Daddy was one of those who responded to the call. Every cop and fireman from miles around responded, for all the good it did. Most of the kids were already dead.

"Still, they did what they could, and got the survivors

out of the bus. They ran out of ambulances, so they started using station wagons. Daddy and Lloyd drove the last two survivors to the hospital. One of them had been sitting near the front, and on the way, Lloyd asked her what had happened. She told him about the light blue Volkswagen passing the bus, just before the truck hit them. Daddy said he never saw a man look so stricken as Lloyd did that night. He didn't say anything, not one word, but Daddy could tell that, inside, he was crying like a baby."

Junior took a deep breath before continuing. "If Lloyd Monroe plays it by the book these days, I can't really blame him."

"I can't either." Then something else occurred to me. "Why didn't the girl who saw the Volkswagen see the driver? Or wasn't the top down?"

Junior said, "The top was down, all right, but she was a tad nearsighted, and she wasn't wearing her glasses that night because she wanted to look her best for her date. Neither the truck driver nor the bus driver had time to see the driver. It was a shame, too, because at least that way, Lloyd would have known for sure."

"But if he saw that Volkswagen in Rocky Shoals, doesn't that mean that the driver was from Rocky Shoals?"

"Not necessarily. Like I said, there's no way of knowing that it was the same car, and even if it was, it could have been passing through Rocky Shoals. Folks from all over this part of the state went to that concert."

"You're probably right."

"Laurie Anne," she said with a grin, "don't you think you ought to stick to one mystery at a time?"

I had to grin back. "Junior, I believe you're right." I checked my watch, and decided that Richard had had enough sleep by then, so I thanked Junior for her help and drove back to Aunt Maggie's house.

Chapter 20

Though I was halfway expecting that Richard would still be asleep, I found him fully dressed and talking on the telephone when I got back. I kissed him on the forehead and got myself a Coke while waiting for him to finish.

He said, "That's all I need, Aunt Ruby Lee. Thanks!" and hung up.

"What's up?" I said.

"Just trying to match your industrious example," he said. "I've been trying to trace Honeywell's movements at the dance the night of the murder."

"Any luck?"

"Not much. I found out from Aunt Nora that Aunt Edna went, so I called her. She and Caleb were there, but they didn't stay long because they ran into Roger and quickly realized that he wasn't in good shape for a dance."

"Still upset about Ilene?"

"Very much so. He was worried that it would cause problems between him and Aunt Ruby Lee. Plus he was threatening to 'teach Tom Honeywell a lesson' if he saw him, and Aunt Edna was afraid that there would be trouble. So she decided to get him out of there, and they took him out to dinner at Fork-in-the-Road. After that, they went to Aunt Daphine's house and the four of them played cards all night."

"Without Aunt Ruby Lee?"

"Aunt Edna says they called Aunt Ruby Lee, but she said she was tired and wanted to go to bed early."

"She told me that she sat up all night waiting for Ilene," I said.

"You're not suggesting that—"

"I'm not suggesting anything of the kind. I'm just thinking that it's a shame that she was sitting there all by herself when she could have gone over to Aunt Daphine's." Just for a second, I tried to imagine Aunt Ruby Lee killing Tom Honeywell. "Nope, she couldn't have done it. She doesn't have a gun, she couldn't have gotten backstage at the Jamboree to steal one, and she'd have confessed to get Ilene out of jail by now."

"Good," Richard said. "Anyway, neither Aunt Edna, Caleb, nor Roger saw Tom Honeywell that night.

"Next I called Clifford and Earl, or rather, I tried to. Clifford is at work, and Aunt Ruby Lee had just sent Earl to the jail to take some things to Ilene."

"I must have just missed him."

"She suggested we join them for dinner this evening and talk to Clifford and Earl then."

"That sounds good. Were there any other Burnettes at the dance?"

"The triplets, but they're all at work, too."

"Maybe we can catch them after dinner."

"How did your researches go?"

"Not terribly impressive," I said, and told him what I had found out from Junior and about my conversation with Ilene. "For a little while, she was really talking to me, but then she froze up again. She knows *something*, but I'll be darned if I know what."

"You'll thaw her eventually," he said. "Like Hamlet, your fate cries out and makes each petty artery in this body as hardy as the Nemean lion's nerve."

"I appreciate the confidence," I said, even if I didn't understand the quote, "but if I have to come up with a Southernism to match, it kind of takes the joy out of it."

"Then I won't count it," he said generously. "What next?"

"I suppose we might as well go see if Forrest has that list of Jamboree participants ready, unless you've got a more exciting idea."

Richard didn't, so we left for Rocky Shoals. Unlike the other times we had driven there, traffic was nearly nonexistent. There were lots of beer cans by the side of the road, and tired-looking welcome banners hanging on the buildings, but clearly the Jamboree crowds had departed. Rocky Shoals now looked the way it usually did, a sleepy town that was even smaller than Byerly.

As promised, Homer Caldwell was watching for us at the high school, and let us in the door.

"Hey there, Miz Fleming, Mr. Fleming," he said.

"Hi, Mr. Caldwell. How are you today?"

"Not too bad. My rheumatism is acting up a bit, which is unusual for the summer, but I suppose it was brought on by all the work I did for the Jamboree. It sure is a lot of effort putting this thing together. Now Miss Jefferson is real good about hiring help for during the Jamboree, and that's a fact, but there's an awful lot to do before they get here and after they leave. And I'm the only year-round worker here. Jim Emerson used to work year-round, but he retired and the other fellows already had summer jobs lined up and they didn't want to hire somebody new just for the summer. So it's been just me for the past five years. Of course, there's not much work to do once the Jamboree is over, just the parking lot and Miss Jefferson's office, because she does so much work for the Jamboree. She works all year round, just like me."

I knew he'd have to take a breath sometime, and as soon as he did, I said, "I think Miss Jefferson is expecting us."

"She sure is. Come on, and I'll show you to her office." He kept talking the whole time we were walking, but I have to admit that I tuned it out after that.

Despite Mr. Caldwell's monologue, I heard Forrest Jefferson's voice echoing through the hall long before we reached her office. She sounded like she was talking to somebody about a bill, and she didn't sound happy. She slammed down the receiver just before we got to her door, and glared up at us.

"Here's Mr. and Miz Fleming," Mr. Caldwell said, then quickly backed away.

I didn't much blame him. Forrest looked mean enough to bite. "You must be here for that list," she said.

"Yes, ma'am," I said automatically, although she wasn't that much older than I was. She just seemed like somebody to say ma'am to.

"I haven't had a chance to print it yet," she said. "You'll have to wait."

"That'll be fine," I said, knowing that if she changed her mind about giving it to us, there really wouldn't be anything we could do about it. I forced a smile and said, "I know you must be terribly busy."

"You have no idea," she said, somewhat mollified. "People think that once the Jamboree is over, I can relax until next year." She turned to the PC on her desk to access a file and entered a command. The laser printer on the stand next to the desk started whirring. "They have no idea of what it takes to put this all together. Do you know how far ahead I have to start working on the Jamboree?"

"I'd say at least a year."

"That's right. Today I start working on next year's Jamboree. Some items have to be negotiated even sooner." She gestured at the phone. "Those sanitary facilities people insisted that I sign a three-year contract, and even after their pitiful performance, they expect me to abide by that contract. I told them in no uncertain terms that the contract is null and void as far as I'm concerned, and it's their own fault. I have no time to deal with their sort."

I nodded sympathetically.

Richard diplomatically, if not truthfully, said, "I'm amazed at how smoothly it all went. I've seen professionally organized events in Boston that didn't run nearly so well."

She nodded, and even seemed disposed to think about smiling. "I have been told that before. I probably have more experience organizing events than most so-called professionals. I have worked on every Jamboree, and have been chairwoman of the committee for every year since the first."

I was surprised that she mentioned a committee. The way she had been talking, I thought she did it all by herself. "This year must have been particularly trying, what with the murder and all."

She bristled. "I think that everything went smoothly, despite that incident."

"That's what I mean," I said hurriedly. "When I was here

on Sunday, I would never have guessed something like that had happened if I hadn't already known it."

That soothed her again. "Thank you. It really was horrifying to have something like that happen. I shall have to see about screening our participants more carefully. A person like Tom Honeywell should never have been allowed access. Imagine, him attempting to steal equipment that way. It's no wonder he was shot, and he has no one to blame but himself. If that young woman hadn't shot him, I expect one of the people he stole from would have."

"That young lady is my cousin," I reminded her as politely as I could, "and she didn't shoot him."

"No? Well, you must admit that if she hadn't been associating with someone of his ilk, she wouldn't be in the position she's in now."

I wasn't about to admit any such thing, but I before I could admit what I wanted to admit, Richard spoke up.

"That's a fine laser printer," he said.

Forrest patted it. "Nothing but the best for the Jamboree. A donation, of course. Nearly every penny that we raise goes to the scholarship fund."

"I didn't realize there was a scholarship involved," Richard said.

"Oh, yes. The original purpose of the Jamboree was, of course, to keep Rocky Shoals's youth out of trouble, but I quickly realized that it could also be a fund-raising opportunity. What better memorial for those who died in the Rocky Shoals Bus Tragedy?"

I could hear the capital letters when she spoke, and I caught her looking up at a picture of three teenagers leaning against the hood of a car. "You must have known some of those who died," I said sympathetically.

She nodded. "I was supposed to be on that bus myself, but my parents forbade me from going. I had done poorly on a test, so they insisted that I spend extra time at the library. My boyfriend Archie and my best friend Mary both died that night."

"I'm sorry," I said. I hadn't realized that Forrest was the student who couldn't go to the concert. "I can't imagine how it must have been for you."

"Archie and I were to have been married. He would have made a fine husband."

No wonder she put so much effort into the Jamboree, and no wonder she had never married. I stepped closer to the photo. Forrest was in the center, looking a little younger and a little slimmer in the photo, but not much. The girl on the left was a little bitty thing, fair-haired and slender, who looked like she was smiling because somebody had told her to. The boy on the right wasn't much bigger than the girl, and had dark hair and pale skin. He had his arm around Forrest, but didn't look very comfortable in that position.

"He was very nice-looking," I said, which wasn't too far off from the truth.

"I had great plans for the two of us," she said, "but there's no sense in looking back. One must go on."

The printer finished with the list of participants just then. Forrest jogged the pages together neatly and handed them to me. "Here you go."

"Thank you," I said, but I was dismayed at how thick the list was. I hadn't realized how many participants there were.

"Good luck helping your cousin," she said. "If I were you, I'd tell Chief Monroe to check Honeywell's home for other stolen goods. I wouldn't be at all surprised to find that he had stolen from someone else, and perhaps that person was the one to kill him."

"Thank you," I said again, both for the good wishes and the suggestion.

Richard and I didn't quite run back to the car, but we did walk as fast as we could to make sure we didn't get cornered by Homer Caldwell again.

"Can you believe this list?" I said once we were safely on the way back to Byerly. "It could take us years to talk to all of those people."

Richard flipped through it. "Not to mention the travel involved. Here's one who came from Los Angeles, and one from Wyoming."

"Maybe we can rule out folks from out of the state," I said. "Surely Tom didn't have time to get somebody from Wyoming mad at him."

"Unless he went to Wyoming when he embezzled his father's money."

"Oh Lord, I hadn't thought of that. He was gone for months, so there's no telling where he got to."

"And then there's Forrest's suggestion."

"Don't remind me," I said. "It's starting to look like it would be harder to find somebody who *didn't* want Tom Honeywell dead."

Chapter 21

Aunt Maggie was actually at the house when we got there, but she told us she only had time to eat a sandwich before heading for a mini-warehouse auction. "Y'all got a phone call from Alton Brown," she said. "That's one of Ruby Lee's ex-husbands, isn't it?"

"Earl's father," I said.

"I can't keep that girl's men straight. Then again, she couldn't either. Anyway, he wanted y'all to come see him at the bank 'at your earliest convenience.'" She snorted. "Who does he think he's fooling, talking so fancy. He was born and raised here in Byerly, same as the rest of us."

"That's just Alton," I said with a shrug.

She left, and then Richard and I fixed a couple of sandwiches ourselves before getting back in the car.

"Why the bank?" Richard asked on the way.

"That's where Alton works," I said.

"A compulsive gambler works in a bank? Isn't that a bit risky?"

"Just because he's a gambler doesn't mean that he's dishonest," I retorted. "You know that Big Bill Walters wouldn't let him work there if he wasn't trustworthy." Big

Bill, the man who owned the bank and much of Byerly, was too sharp to let anybody else get away with anything.

Alton's office was just as neat as his house. No dust, no papers out of place, and even the leaves on his Wandering Jew wandered in a straight line. He showed us to chairs, and then leaned on the edge of his desk.

"Any luck?" I asked.

"Quite a bit, as a matter of fact. It was one of my more successful forays for several months. That is to say, I was hot."

I said, "Congratulations."

He nodded in acknowledgment. "More importantly, of course, I learned much about the late Tom Honeywell. He was quite a gambler, as you already had learned. Mostly cards, occasionally dice. Fervent interest in sports activities was mentioned." He sighed. "I only rarely bet on a contest which relies on another man's skill—only one's own skill is to be trusted."

Considering how often Alton had lost his paycheck playing poker when he and Aunt Ruby Lee were married, I didn't think he should rely on his own skill either, but it wouldn't have been polite to say so.

"What about a horse's skill?" Richard asked.

"With a horse, the real skill is that of the jockey. The hounds bypass the jockey, but are still dependent on a trainer."

"True," Richard said thoughtfully.

To bring the conversation away from the philosophy of gambling, I said, "Had Tom been winning these days?"

"Sadly, he had not been."

"Had he lost a lot of money?"

"More than he had in hand, apparently."

"A beer budget, and a champagne appetite," I said. "Richard?"

" 'Whose large style agrees not with the leanness of his purse.' *Henry VI, Part Two*, Act I, Scene 1."

Alton raised an eyebrow.

"It's a contest we're having," I explained. "Which expressions are more colorful: the Bard's or the South's."

"I see. Which of you is winning?"

"Neck and neck," I said, "but this round goes to Richard."

Richard pulled out his notebook and added a hash mark to his score.

"Now back to Tom Honeywell," I said. I felt a little silly for letting a game interrupt us, but then, Alton knew the appeal of games better than I did.

Alton said, "As I was saying, Honeywell's accounts were far in arrears. His debtors were quite concerned."

"Could somebody have been concerned enough to shoot him?"

"Quite the opposite. You see, the money he owed will now have to be written off as a loss. He left no estate, and even if he had, illegal gambling debts can hardly be legally recouped. Despite his personality, he was worth more alive than dead."

"I take it that he didn't make many friends," Richard said.

"He did not. A few said they had initially been charmed by him, but after borrowed money was not returned, the friendships soured. Also, it seems that he had been suspected of changing the odds, but what he won by such methods, he quickly lost on contests he could not directly affect."

I said, "What about the people he cheated? Wouldn't revenge come into it?"

"You have been watching Westerns where the crooked card player dies amidst a hail of bullets and the cheers of the townspeople. This is not accurate. The accepted ways of dealing with such a fellow around here are either to avoid him completely, or cheat more skillfully than he does. The players I know are split fairly evenly between the two options."

"Rats! I was hoping this would lead somewhere." Then I had a new thought. "Did you ask what he talked about during games? Maybe he mentioned something significant."

But Alton was shaking his head. "I'm afraid that serious players tend to discourage casual conversation. The reason behind any gathering is, after all, the contest itself. I was told that this was a point of etiquette that took some time to impress upon young Honeywell, but as of late, he had realized that his boasts of masculine prowess were not appreciated. His only conversation in recent times was to crow upon winning, and to curse when losing. Neither is considered good form."

So much for Byerly's gambling mafia. I looked at Richard, hoping he had a question, but he shook his head.

"I'm afraid that I've been of no help to you after all," Alton said.

"Well, even negative data is data," I said, trying to be philosophical. "I do appreciate your helping out."

"Not at all. If there is anything further I can do, don't hesitate to call."

"I won't."

He escorted us to the door.

"Thanks again, Alton," I said, and gave him a small hug,

suitable for a former uncle. Richard followed suit with a handshake.

"It was a pleasure seeing you again," Alton said. "No doubt we will see each other at Ruby Lee and Roger's wedding. The wedding is still expected to take place, isn't it?"

I shrugged my shoulders. "To tell you the truth, I don't know. Aunt Ruby Lee won't even consider it while Ilene's in trouble, so we're doing our best to try to get things straightened out before then."

Alton did look pained at this, which I thought was awfully nice, considering that it was his ex-wife who was getting married. "What a shame! I hope all goes well."

I nodded, and started out the door. Then Richard said, "So, what are the odds for their getting married?"

Alton smiled widely. "At this point, most of the local players consider the wedding a long shot. Of course, knowing that you two are investigating the case, I've placed my money on the other side." He closed the door behind us.

"He's betting on the wedding?" I said to Richard. "I'm appalled."

"Why? He's betting on us, isn't he?"

"Great. If we don't find out who killed Tom in time, we're going to have Alton mad at us, too."

Richard just patted my back comfortingly.

Chapter 22

Richard and I spent the rest of the afternoon around Aunt Maggie's kitchen table going through the list of Jamboree participants. We might as well not have bothered. As Richard had said, most of the people weren't from the area at all, and I didn't know all of the locals, and of the locals I did know, I didn't know of any reason they'd want to kill Tom Honeywell. We called Aunt Nora to see which of them she knew, but that was no help. She knew more than we did, but didn't know that any of them knew Tom.

We gave it up as a lost cause in time to go to Aunt Ruby Lee's for dinner.

Aunt Ruby Lee is nowhere near as good a cook as Aunt Nora, but there are meals she cooks very well. We didn't have any of those meals that night. It wasn't actively bad, but clearly her mind was not on her cooking. After she told us what her day had been like, I understood why.

Part of the time she had been with Ilene, but Ilene hadn't exactly welcomed the company. Part of the time she had been with Roger, and without her saying so outright, I could tell that she and Roger had had words. And the rest of the time, Vasti had been after her to do things for the wedding. I wanted to think that Vasti was only trying to take Aunt

Ruby Lee's mind off her troubles, but I wasn't convinced. Clifford and Earl were clearly worried about their mother, and so was I.

After dinner, Richard and I volunteered to help the boys with the dishes, and sent Aunt Ruby Lee off to bed. She needed the rest.

It didn't take long to get the dishes squared away, and then we all sat down in the living room. With the two brothers there together, it was easy to tell that they had different fathers. Earl was dark and dapper like his father Alton, and moved with that same smoothness. Clifford was much bigger, more so than the difference in ages called for, with that build Aunt Maggie always called big-boned, and he had his mother's blond hair.

"I don't have to tell y'all how much trouble Ilene is in," I started. "It looks bad for her right now, and the more we know about what happened the night Tom was shot, the better chance we've got of getting her out of there."

"Just tell us what you need to know," Clifford said, and Earl nodded.

"I need everything y'all can remember. I was there at the Jamboree on Friday, but I wasn't at the dance that night, so I want you to tell me exactly what happened."

Clifford said, "Well, Earl and I got there at around seven. We wanted to talk to Roger, but never could find him. We went and talked to Cotton, Al, and Slim instead."

"The other Ramblers," I explained to Richard. "Did you see Ilene?"

"No, but I did see Tom Honeywell."

"Who was he talking to?"

"He was talking to everybody who would listen, trying to make out that he was some kind of big shot and how he could get them equipment at a discount." He snorted. "A five-fingered discount is what it was. Mostly he was talking to Maureen Shula. She's the one who won the novice competition. I guess I should have been glad that he was with somebody other than Ilene, but I was mostly mad at him for two-timing her."

"I don't believe he was two-timing her," Earl put in. "He wanted to awful bad, but Maureen saw right through him and all his talk."

Clifford said, "Still, he had his arm around her when Ilene showed up." He shook his head. "Ilene looked fit to be tied when she saw them. At first she looked like she couldn't make up her mind whether to cry or to get mad, but she finally decided to get mad. She stomped right over there and pulled his arm off of her, and started laying into Maureen like it was her fault."

Earl said, "But it wasn't Maureen's fault at all. She told Ilene that she wasn't interested in Honeywell, and that if Ilene wanted him, she was welcome to him. You have to get up pretty early to fool somebody like Maureen."

And you'd have to be as dumb as a dishrag not to see that Earl had a crush on Maureen, just like Thaddeous had, and I told myself that I'd have to casually mention her boyfriend at some point. Still, Clifford wasn't contradicting Earl, so he must not have been blinded completely by infatuation.

"Anyway," Clifford said, "Maureen putting Honeywell down got him mad, and don't you know that he was going to take it out on Ilene. He grabbed her and pulled her off into the corner. I don't know what he was saying, but I didn't like the way he looked, so me and Earl went over there. If Ilene wants to make a fool of herself over Honeywell, that's one thing, but if he thinks he's going to get away with hitting her, that's something else."

Earl nodded vigorously. I was glad that even though they hadn't been getting along with their baby sister lately, they had still been willing to come to her defense.

"By the time we got there, Ilene was giving as good as she got," Clifford said.

"I didn't know she could talk like that," Earl said admiringly.

"The thing was," said Clifford, "I was afraid it was going to get out of hand. I went up behind Ilene, and said that maybe they should break it up. Well, Ilene turned around and lit into me something fierce. Said she was tired of people trying to live her life and all kinds of stuff like that."

"She didn't mean it," Earl said. "She was just mad. Clifford put a hand on her shoulder, and she shook him off like it burned her. Then she pushed right past and ran off faster than greased lightning."

I knew where she had gone after that. "What did Honeywell do?"

"He started cussing about Ilene," Clifford said. "I told him that he ought not to talk like that."

From the satisfied expression on his face, I knew that he hadn't put it quite that politely.

Clifford went on. "He stomped off, and we went to look for Ilene."

"But she was long gone," Earl said. "She always could run fast, even when she was a little bitty thing. So we went back to the dance, thinking that she'd show up eventually, but she never did."

"Did you see any more of Honeywell?" I asked.

"He was around," Clifford said. "Talking to a bunch of different folks. I think I saw him with one of the triplets."

"Which one?"

He looked sheepish. "I'm not real sure. It was all the way across the room from me, and the light wasn't good. She was wearing blue jeans."

I was pretty sure that Carlelle had been the one in jeans that night, and made a mental note to ask her what they had talked about. "Did you see him spending a lot of time with anybody else? Or fighting with anybody?"

Both of the brothers shook their heads, and then Clifford said, "He was still there when we left, probably trying to talk somebody into buying him a drink. We waited around as long as we could, hoping that Ilene would come back, but then we had to go pick up Liz. Her shift was over at eleven, so we left at ten-thirty to go get her and then we all went out to the Mustang Club with her brother and his girlfriend."

I looked at Richard, and he shrugged. "I guess that's all I need," I said.

"Did we help you any?" Earl said.

"Some," I said. "At least you've established that Tom and Ilene didn't leave together, and I don't know how Chief Monroe can think they'd set up a meeting on the Ramblers' bus after a fight like that." Of course, Ilene still could have followed Honeywell there, but I didn't see any reason to tell them that.

"I just wish I had taken care of Honeywell myself," Earl said darkly. Then he said, "You know, maybe I could tell—"

"Don't you dare!" I said. "Aunt Ruby Lee doesn't need you in jail because of a phony confession."

"I suppose not."

"And besides, your confessing would make it look like you don't believe Ilene is innocent. You do, don't you?"

"Of course I do," Earl said. "I just want to help."

"I know you do, Earl. Ilene knows it, too." A few days ago I had envied Aunt Ruby Lee her sisters. Now I envied Ilene her big brothers.

Chapter 23

I suppose we could have made another stop that night, but it was late and we were tired, so we went back to Aunt Maggie's to plan the next day's stops and to get some sleep. This time, nobody called to wake me up, and I woke up feeling rested.

Richard called the triplets the first thing, wanting to find out what Tom Honeywell had been talking to Carlelle about at the dance, and whether any of them had seen anything useful. They were on their way to work, and he arranged to meet them for their morning break at the mill.

As for me, I let Richard drop me at the police station so I could show Ilene the list of Jamboree participants and see if she recognized any names.

There wasn't anybody out front when I came into the police station, but a second later, Trey, Junior's brother and deputy, came out from the back. Though Trey was taller than Junior, he didn't quite have her presence. I knew that he was studying law enforcement in college, but wasn't sure if he was planning to keep his job as Junior's deputy or try to get a job somewhere else after graduation.

"Hi, Trey."

"Hey there, Laurie Anne. Ilene's mama had some things

she had to do, so I've been back there keeping Ilene company." Then he anxiously added, "Is there any news about the murder?"

"Not yet," I had to say.

He shook his head sadly. "I just hate that Honeywell was killed in Rocky Shoals instead of in Byerly. If me and Junior were on the case, we'd have it licked by now." I stiffened, and I guess he realized how that had sounded. He quickly added, "I didn't mean it like that. I just meant that Junior and I would be helping you, instead of getting in your way like Lloyd Monroe. I swear, that man just won't listen to reason."

I was amused that what he was saying sounded pretty much like what I had said about Monroe to Junior the other day. "Well, Chief Monroe is just doing what he thinks is right," I said mildly.

Trey's only response was a snort. "Is there anything I can do for you?"

"Actually, I wanted to see Ilene, if that's all right."

"Of course it's all right. You go on back, and I'll stay up here out of your way."

Ilene was sitting on the bed with her guitar in her lap, and a pencil and a half-filled sheet of music paper next to her. The cell looked considerably different from when I had been there last. Blue gingham curtains had been pinned up to hide the bars, and the bed was covered with a matching bedspread. A comfortable-looking chair had been added, and there was a hanging bag of Ilene's clothes on the cell door. All in all, it was pretty cozy.

"Hey, Laurie Anne," Ilene said, putting down the guitar. "How's it going?"

"All right. Just trying to stay busy to keep my mind off of

things." She halfway smiled. "Lots of musicians have done their best work in jail."

"Well, don't get too comfortable in here," I said. "We're going to get you out pretty soon."

There was a pause, and then she said, "I guess I should apologize. I haven't been very nice to you lately, and here you are trying to get me out of jail."

It wasn't the most gracious apology I had ever heard, but I thought it was sincere. "That's all right. You've had a pretty tough time of it. Right now we've got other things to worry about." I pulled the list of names out of my pocketbook. "I got a list of all of the Jamboree participants and I want you to look at them. I'm pretty sure that the killer must be one of these people because they're the only ones who had access to the gun that was stolen. I want you to tell me if Tom mentioned having any kind of a fight with any of these people."

"Tom had fights with lots of people," she muttered, but she took the list from me and started looking through it.

She had gotten through the first page when Trey poked his head in. "Don't want to interrupt, but I thought y'all might want something to drink."

"How about a Coke?" Ilene said.

"That sounds good to me, too," I said.

"Two Cokes. I'll be right back." He ducked out again.

I had thought that he meant that he'd be back in the room in a minute, so I was startled when I heard the front door open and shut. "Did he just leave?" I asked.

"He said he was going to get us a drink," Ilene said, not looking up from the list.

"How does he know we won't walk out of here?"

Ilene just shrugged and kept reading.

That was pretty casual, even for Byerly. I was fairly sure that Junior would have taken a dim view of her brother's lack of caution. And I thought I knew why he was acting that way. I looked at Ilene. Even in jail with a murder trial hanging over her, she was as pretty as ever, and with Tom Honeywell out of the way, she was available. Had Ilene realized what was going on? I thought about telling her, but decided that now was not the best time for her to be concerned with a new suitor.

Ilene finished with the last name on the list.

"Well? What do you think?" I prompted.

She shook her head. "I don't think any of them would have killed Tom."

That's what she said, but there was something in her voice that made me think that she wasn't telling the whole truth. "Are you sure?"

"I just said I was," she snapped, which only confirmed it for me.

At first I thought that she didn't want to say anything unkind about her boyfriend. "Ilene," I said gently, "I appreciate your loyalty to Tom, but now is not the time to hold things back."

"This doesn't have anything to do with Tom!"

"Then why aren't you telling me everything you know?"

"I don't know anything else." She picked up her guitar again and started plucking at the strings, pointedly ignoring me.

I didn't think she'd lie outright to me, but she was certainly lying by omission. Maybe she didn't *know* anything, but she sure *thought* something. If she wasn't trying to protect Tom's memory, then who was she trying to protect? I picked up the list and looked through it. There were three names on it that could have caused Ilene's reaction.

"What about Clifford and Earl? How did they get along with Tom?"

"You leave them alone! They didn't have anything to do with this."

"They didn't like Tom, did they?"

She didn't say anything.

"You're thinking that one or both of them might have killed Tom to keep him away from you, aren't you? Or because of the way Tom treated you that night?"

Ilene didn't say anything for a minute, then she spoke in a voice as cold as the grave. "If you think I'd say anything against my own brothers, you've got another think coming."

"Ilene, Clifford and Earl have an alibi. They picked up Liz from work at eleven, long before Tom was shot. Then they all went to the Mustang Club. Even if they had wanted to kill Tom, they wouldn't have gotten Liz mixed up in it. Besides which, Liz's brother Hoyle and Hoyle's girlfriend were with them."

She let this sink in, but still didn't say anything.

"Then there's your father," I said. "Aunt Edna and Caleb Wilkins were with Roger all night. Aunt Daphine was with them part of the time, too. They went out to eat and then went over to Aunt Daphine's place. I bet we could verify that with the people at the restaurant and with Aunt Daphine's neighbors, if we had to, so he's in the clear, too."

Ilene kept messing with her guitar, which meant that she had realized that there was one other person who might have killed on her behalf.

I went on, "Then there's your mama. She didn't have access to the gun, but I guess she could have found one somewhere. Clifford and Earl were out late that night, so she could have gone out without them knowing it, but they got back at around the time Tom was killed and she was there then. She wouldn't have had time to kill Tom and get back to Byerly."

"Really?" she said.

"Really," I said firmly.

After a long time, Ilene put the guitar back down and took a deep breath. "That's good to know."

"Now I found all of this out on the way to finding out other things, but I didn't really need to. The way I figure it, anybody who would have killed Tom Honeywell on your behalf wouldn't be letting you take the blame."

"I suppose not," she said. "It's just that you know I haven't been getting along with Mama and Daddy lately, or my brothers either."

"I don't care how much you've been fighting, your family loves you. They wouldn't get you in trouble like this."

She didn't look convinced.

"Ilene, I've got reason to know that it takes a lot to alienate this family. Look at me. Because of me, one of our uncles is dead and your former stepfather is in jail. They still put up with me."

"That wasn't your fault."

"Maybe not. But what about moving to Massachusetts? Ilene, I married a Yankee! What could possibly be worse than that?"

She had to grin then. "I guess you're right. I just didn't know where everybody else was that night, and I was ashamed to ask."

"So you *were* afraid one of them might have killed Tom?"

She nodded. "I didn't want to think that, but I just

couldn't help it. Daddy was madder than I've ever seen him that day, and I know Clifford and Earl hated Tom."

"Because of the way he treated you?"

"That, and because of how he was with them. Tom made fun of their music."

I nodded, but said nothing. Mama had always said that if you can't say something nice, you shouldn't say anything at all, and that it wasn't polite to speak ill of the dead either.

Ilene said, "I suppose that Tom wasn't easy to get along with."

I nodded again.

She shook her head ruefully. "Who am I trying to fool? Tom Honeywell was probably the meanest son of a bitch I've ever met."

"I'm sure he had his good points," I said.

"No, he didn't," Ilene said. "He was hateful to everybody, and he didn't have any more feeling for me than the man in the moon. He was only using me!"

So much for not speaking ill of the dead. "He must have put up a pretty good front, then. When y'all first met, I mean."

Ilene shrugged. "I suppose. I didn't realize that he'd dump me like he did, but I knew he wasn't the kind of man Mama wanted me to bring home." She looked at me. "Didn't you ever like somebody even if you knew your family wouldn't?"

"You bet I did. There was that one guy I dated in college—"

"Other than Richard?"

I nodded. "His name was Philip. At the time, I thought he was dark and brooding and very deep. What he really was, was full of himself." I shook my head, remembering what a fool I had made of myself over him. "But he was *so* different from anybody in Byerly. I kept imagining Aunt Edna's eyes bugging out if she ever met him. Maybe that's the real reason I dated him. Not in spite of the fact that the family wouldn't like him, but *because* they wouldn't."

Ilene looked a little sheepish, but she nodded. "I guess that's partly how it was with me, too. I wanted to stir folks up a bit. And I really did think Tom could help me with my career. He knew how I should dress, and what I should sing, and how to get people's attention."

I had to admit that Ilene's performance at the Jamboree had gotten a lot of attention, but said, "You don't need anybody like Tom, Ilene. You've got talent, and you've got your own style without him."

"Do you really think so?"

"Yes I do! I know that I shouldn't have listened to your tape, but I'm glad I did. You're good!"

"You know, you're the first person in the family who's said that to me."

"Seriously? I knew Roger didn't approve, but what about your mama? And Clifford and Earl?"

"They don't have *time* to listen to me. Clifford and Earl are too busy with their own music, and Earl's getting ready to graduate next year, and Clifford has Liz." Then she sadly added, "And Mama's been spending most of her time with Daddy for the past year."

"Oh, baby, why didn't you tell me?" a voice said from behind me. Aunt Ruby was standing there, holding a couple of canned Cokes. We had been so deep in our conversation that we hadn't heard her come in.

"Mama?" Ilene said.

Aunt Ruby Lee sat down next to Ilene and took her hand. "Ilene, you know that I love your daddy."

"Yes, Mama. I won't make any more trouble for you two."

"I know you won't," Aunt Ruby Lee said a little sharply. Then she smiled and said, "I don't mean that the way it sounded. What I mean is that what's between me and Roger is just that—between us two. Nobody can make trouble for us unless we let them."

Ilene nodded.

"Now, as much as I love Roger, I love you just as much. And nothing—and I mean nothing—can ever change that or come between us. And that includes Roger."

Though she didn't say anything, just for a minute all of Ilene's teenage years fell away, and she was ten years old again. Her eyes got very big, and she held on to Aunt Ruby Lee's hand like she was afraid to let go.

Aunt Ruby Lee went on. "Now Ilene, there's something I want from you."

"Anything, Mama."

"Will you play something for me? Right now?"

"Oh, Mama," Ilene said.

I could tell that Ilene was about to burst out in tears, so I quickly handed her the guitar. The weight of it seemed to steady her, and she started strumming, lightly at first, and then more strongly.

I didn't recognize the song she sang, so it must have been one she wrote herself. Throughout the whole song, Aunt Ruby Lee kept smiling like she was the proudest mother in the world. Maybe she was.

As Ilene finished the last notes, I snuck out of there. It was high time that the two of them had some time alone.

Chapter 24

Trey was at the desk out front. "Were the drinks all right?" he asked. "Miz Burnette got back about the same time I did, so she said she'd take them to you."

"They were fine," I reassured him, though I didn't think Ilene had noticed them at all.

"I brought Cokes, but then I got to thinking that maybe Ilene would prefer Pepsi. Some people say Coke when they mean Pepsi."

"I think Ilene prefers Coke."

"Was regular Coke all right? She drinks diet Coke sometimes, but I don't see why. She sure doesn't need to."

"Regular Coke was just what she wanted."

He bobbed his head a few times. "By the way, your cousin called looking for you a few minutes ago. She said she was on her way over here."

"Which cousin?"

"Vasti. I mean, Miz Bumgarner."

That I didn't need. Maybe having Vasti lecture me wasn't cause for panic, but it wasn't my idea of a good time either. "Could you excuse me for a minute?" I said, and fled back to Ilene's cell. Ilene was showing Aunt Ruby Lee some sheet music.

"Aunt Ruby Lee, can I borrow your car?" I asked.

"Sure," she said, reaching into her pocketbook for the keys. "Is anything wrong?"

"No, I just got an idea I want to check out, and Richard's got our rental car. I won't be gone long."

She handed me the keys. "Keep it as long as you want. I think I'm going to be here for a while anyway." She smiled at Ilene, who smiled right back.

I left the two of them and stopped by Trey's desk long enough to say, "I'm afraid something's come up. Could you tell Vasti that I had to go? If my husband comes by, tell him I'll catch up with him later. Thanks." I was out the door before he could answer, and into Aunt Ruby Lee's light blue Taurus just as fast as I could get there.

The only problem was, I didn't really have anyplace to go. Since Ilene hadn't recognized anybody on that list of names, the next logical step should have been to start trying to get in touch with each and every one of them, but I just couldn't talk myself into calling that many people right then.

I'm not sure why I ended up on the road to Rocky Shoals, and then back at the high school. It was just that so much had happened there that it seemed like I ought to be able to figure out *something* there.

The buildings were locked, so I could only walk around the grounds. It was quiet now, a far cry from what it had been like during the Jamboree. Of course, schools always look lonely during the summer, but since I had only seen this place when it was crawling with people, it looked even more forlorn than usual.

The Ramblers' bus was gone, and so was the barrier of yellow tape, though there were still some scraps of it stuck onto the light pole the bus had been parked under. It just didn't look like the setting for a murder. If Tom Honeywell had left a ghost, he sure didn't have a good place to haunt. Not that I believe in ghosts, but I still jumped when I heard a voice saying, "Hey there, young lady."

I turned around and saw Homer Caldwell. "Hi."

"Miz Fleming, isn't it?"

I nodded, and resisted asking him how he was doing today for fear that he'd tell me.

He leaned over and picked up a couple of pieces of the yellow tape. "I thought I had gotten the last of this stuff. The police left it all over the ground when they took the bus away. Not that I hold it against them, mind you. They've got bigger fish to fry than litter." He tucked the scraps into his pocket. "Can I help you with something?"

"I'm just looking around," I said, and realized that that sounded ghoulish. "You know my cousin is the one that's been accused of killing Tom Honeywell."

Mr. Caldwell nodded, and looked at the place the bus had been. "A terrible thing, a man dying that young."

"It is," I agreed. I hadn't liked Tom Honeywell, but he hadn't deserved to die like that. "I'm trying to find out who really did it."

"You don't think that little girl did it?"

"I know she didn't."

He didn't look convinced, but he didn't argue with me either.

I said, "It must have been awful, finding the body and all."

"That isn't the half of it. When I looked down and saw that boy, I could tell right away he was dead. I don't know what it is, but you can just tell somehow." I guess he could tell that I was trying to think of a tactful way to ask why he was so experienced with dead bodies, because he added, "I used to be a volunteer fireman here in town before Rocky Shoals got the money to hire a real crew. They'd call us out for most anything: fires, of course, and lost kids and car wrecks, and one time, an old barn collapsed." He shook his head. "I've seen more dead folks than I want to remember, I'll be frank with you. I was even there at the bus crash."

I didn't have to ask which crash he was talking about, not in Rocky Shoals.

He shook his head sadly. "My sister's boy died in that crash. He was a nice boy, too, smart as a whip."

"I'm sorry."

"Thank you. It was many years ago, of course, but I still remember finding him and knowing that I was going to have to tell my sister. Come to think of it, the bus crash was the first thing than ran through my head when I saw that Tom Honeywell. Looking down on him reminded me of looking down at the wrecked bus. Of course, it was nighttime at the bus and daylight here, but the angle was about the same."

I may be slow, but I'm not stupid. This was the second time he had referred to looking *down* at Tom Honeywell's body. "Where were you when you saw him?" I asked. "I thought you saw him from the parking lot."

"I did," he said, "but not from down here. He would have been visible from the ground, of course, but not until you got right up to the bus. He was laying half on the driver's seat, half on the floor of the bus, so you probably wouldn't have noticed him even if you walked right by. Lots of people walked by without seeing him, all morning long. I never saw him myself until I climbed up there." He pointed to the light pole.

"What were you doing up there?"

"Changing the light bulb. It went out early in the evening on Friday, and Miss Jefferson told me first thing Saturday morning that she wanted me to replace it so people wouldn't have to walk back to their cars in the dark. It took me most of the day to get to it, but I wasn't about to forget it. Miss Jefferson is mighty particular is about things for the Jamboree."

I guess I heard all of that, but I really only paid attention to the first sentence. "Changing the light bulb?" I repeated.

"That's right," he said, looking at me like my bulb needed changing, too. "They last a good long time, especially these new ones we've been getting, but eventually they have to be changed. I generally let one of the younger maintenance workers change them. I've always been happy to be a janitor, but they want to be maintenance workers. Be that as it may, I generally let one of the younger ones take care of the lights, but I'm the only full-timer one who stays here for the summer. We get temporary workers to help clean up after the Jamboree, but I do the regular maintenance work myself."

I looked around the parking lot. There were only a few light poles. "This area must have been awfully dark Friday night," I said, more to myself than to Mr. Caldwell.

"Yes it was," he agreed. "Dark as pitch, I'd say. It was a new moon this weekend. That's why Miss Jefferson was so insistent about my changing that bulb."

"Then how did the killer know it was Tom?" I asked.

"I'm afraid I don't follow you."

"You said that it was dark as pitch that night, and it would have been darker still in the bus. So how did the killer know it was Tom he was shooting?"

"I never thought about that," Mr. Caldwell said.

"I can't see how anybody could have seen well enough to be sure of who it was, and since Tom Honeywell had no good reason to be on that bus, doesn't it make sense that the person *wasn't* sure of who he was shooting?"

"That's an interesting idea," Mr. Caldwell said doubtfully. "What do you suppose it means?"

"It means that my cousin didn't have a motive," I said triumphantly. "Have you told this to Chief Monroe? The part about seeing the body from above?"

"I'm not sure that I did. I was trying to tell him the whole story, same as I did you, but he was in an awful hurry. He kept telling me to stick to the point, stick to the point, so I might not have gotten around to that part. Do you think it's important?"

"I sure do. Can you tell him now? Is there a phone we can use?"

"You bet there is," he said. "You come with me."

He let us into the building, and into the room where the janitors, or maybe the maintenance workers, kept supplies. There was a phone in there.

I probably should have let Mr. Caldwell make the call, but I was feeling far too full of myself.

"Rocky Shoals Police. Chief Monroe speaking."

"Chief Monroe, this is Laura Fleming."

I heard a small sigh. "What can I do for you, Mrs. Fleming?"

"I was just talking to Homer Caldwell down at the high school, and he told me something I think you should know."

"I have spoken to Homer already, Mrs. Fleming."

"I know you have, but you might not have heard this. Here's Mr. Caldwell now." I handed him the phone.

Listening to Homer must have driven Monroe close to

the breaking point, because it almost did me. Even knowing exactly what it was that I wanted Chief Monroe to know, it took forever for him to get to the important part. Only when he finally did, I could tell that Chief Monroe hadn't reacted the way I had expected.

Mr. Caldwell's face fell a bit, and he said, "It's just that Miz Fleming here thought it was awful important for me to tell you. Like she said, how did that killer know who it was he was killing? . . . I guess that's another way of looking at it. . . . Yes, she's still here." He handed the phone back to me.

"Chief Monroe?" I said. "What do you think?"

"I think it's very interesting, Mrs. Fleming, and I have to commend you."

That was more like it.

"It's not every citizen who would bring a fact to my attention that makes it look worse for a member of her own family."

"Hold on a minute! How does this make it look worse for Ilene?"

"You've just shown that the killer couldn't have seen who it was she was killing, unless she already knew who it was. The only one who would have known that Tom Honeywell was on that bus was Ilene Bailey."

"Ilene didn't know he was going to try to steal that stuff."

"That's what she says, but I have to say that I don't believe her. Unless you're postulating that somebody shot Honeywell without having the faintest idea of who it was, and I don't think that even you could believe that."

"What I'm postulating is that the killer didn't know it was Tom he was shooting. He was expecting somebody else on the bus. Probably one of the Ramblers. It is their bus, after all."

"Uh-huh."

"Don't you think it's possible?" I asked desperately.

"It is *possible* that the killer thought that somebody other than Honeywell was on the bus that night, although nobody else was as far as I can find out, and it is *possible* that the killer mistook Honeywell for this unknown person he was expecting and shot him. I just don't see anything to lead me to draw that conclusion."

"What about the light being out? How did the killer know who he was shooting?"

"What about a flashlight?"

"Did you find a flashlight on the bus?"

"No, but we didn't find a gun either. That doesn't mean that the killer didn't have one."

"But you can't prove there was a flashlight."

"I don't need to. It doesn't matter whether or not there was a flashlight. I don't know about you, ma'am, but there are some people I know well enough that I would recognize them in the dark. My wife, for instance. And Ilene Bailey knew Tom Honeywell pretty well. I don't think I'd be out of line in saying that she'd been with him before in the dark."

"You're not going to look for another killer, are you?"

"I'd be lying to you if I said I thought I needed to. I talked to a lot of people about what they saw that night, even after I had your cousin in custody, and nobody, not one person, told me anything to make me think that somebody else might have killed Tom Honeywell. Now if you find anything else, you've got my word that I'll follow up on it. That's the best I can do."

"All right," I said, feeling awfully tired. "Thanks for listening." I hung up the phone.

Mr. Caldwell said, "Sorry to disappoint you."

"It's not your fault," I said. "I should have realized that a burnt-out light bulb wasn't going to be enough."

"I'm sure things will work out all right."

"Thank you." He let me out of the school, and went back to cleaning up the parking lot while I headed for the car.

I wanted to be angry during the drive back to Byerly, I really did. It would have been a lot easier if I could have screamed at Chief Monroe, called him an idiot, and stomped off in righteous anger. I just couldn't. He was right. Not right in thinking that Ilene had killed Honeywell, of course, but right in thinking that she *could* have killed him. She was the most reasonable suspect.

It was funny. When I'd been talking to Junior, I had accused Monroe of having a closed mind. The fact was that *I* was the one with a closed mind. Monroe had looked at all the possible suspects and picked the likeliest one. I had started with the assumption that the killer was anybody but Ilene, which meant that it had to be somebody unlikely. Nothing but concrete proof was going to convince Monroe that somebody unlikely had killed Tom Honeywell.

I was fresh out of concrete proof.

Richard and I had spent all our time trying to track down somebody who would want to kill Honeywell, and all I had found was a possibility that Tom was an innocent bystander. Though he had to be the worst excuse for an innocent bystander I had ever seen.

I started out trying to find the murderer, and now I had to find the real target, too. And it was only four days before Aunt Ruby Lee and Roger were supposed to get married.

Chapter 25

"Richard?" I called out as soon as I walked into the house.

"He's not here," Aunt Maggie said. I found her eating a pimento cheese sandwich in the kitchen. "I thought I'd get myself a bite before tonight's auction," she explained. "They sell hot dogs there, but those dogs don't always agree with me. You want one?"

"No, thanks," I said. "I'm not hungry." I poured myself a glass of iced tea and sat at the table across from her.

"You look like you've lost your last friend," Aunt Maggie said.

"I feel about that low," I said, and told her what I thought I had found out, and how Chief Monroe had reacted to it. "Now I'm in worse shape than I was to start with." I took a swallow of iced tea. "You know, Aunt Maggie, you were right all along. You remember when we drove home from Aunt Ruby Lee's shower and you said I shouldn't stick my nose in other people's business? If I had listened to you then, everybody would be a whole lot better off."

I had expected her to agree with me, but what she said was, "You hold it right there! I was talking about people having a family spat that night. I didn't say anything about people being arrested for murder. There's a world of difference between that night and right now."

"But—"

"Besides which, this doesn't have anything to do with minding other people's business. Ruby Lee asked you to see what you could do for Ilene, didn't she? And Ilene wants you to help, doesn't she?"

"Yes, but—"

"If they want you to do what you're doing, you're not sticking your nose in their business, are you?"

"Not exactly, but—"

"You're just mad because it hasn't been as easy as you thought it would be. Isn't that right?"

I considered it for a minute, and finally had to say, "I guess I am."

"That's what I thought. Now if you want to give up, you go ahead, but don't expect me to tell you that it's the right thing to do. In my book, if you tell somebody you're going to help them, you do it. Or at least you keep on trying until there's nothing else you can do. Are you to that point now?"

"Yes, I am," I said, trying to make it sound definite. "I've just hit a brick wall. I've been investigating Tom Honeywell all this time, and now it looks like he wasn't the one the murderer meant to shoot at all."

"So?"

"So everything Richard and I have done has been a complete waste of time."

"So?"

There really was only one answer, especially with her looking at me like that. "So I've got to start over again."

She nodded. "That's what it sounds like to me, too."

I thought for a minute. "I told Chief Monroe that the real

target was probably one of the Ramblers because it was their bus."

"Seems reasonable."

"Well, I found out everything I could about Tom Honeywell from Junior. Maybe I should go pick her brain about the Ramblers, too."

"That would be a good place to start."

I stood up and reached for my pocketbook. "If anybody wants me, I'll be at the police station. Thanks, Aunt Maggie."

She grinned. "What are you thanking me for? All I've done is fuss at you and talk you into doing something you don't want to do."

"Maybe, but it's something I ought to do." Certainly something I would regret *not* doing. I was halfway out the door when I stopped. "I thought you said you weren't one for giving advice when it wasn't asked for."

"Laurie Anne, you didn't believe me when I told you that, did you?"

"Well . . ."

"Good. I'd hate to think that your mama raised a fool. Now get going."

"Yes, ma'am."

Chapter 26

Junior was at the station when I got there, but she was on the telephone. I went into the back long enough to say hello to Aunt Ruby Lee and Ilene and return Aunt Ruby Lee's car keys. Then I went back up front where Junior was.

"How's it going?" Junior said as she hung up the phone.

"Good and bad." I explained what I had found out, and how Monroe had interpreted it. "What do you think, Junior? Am I just clutching at straws?"

She shook her head. "No, I think you're on to something. If it were my case, I'd certainly investigate the possibility."

"But it's not your case," I said.

"I'm afraid not."

"If it were your case, I'm guessing that the first thing you'd do is take a look at the Ramblers and see if there's any reason somebody might want one of them dead."

"I hate to break it to you, Laurie Anne, but motive isn't the first thing we look at. Or even the second. What I'd do is all the usual investigative things. First I'd check out the body and the scene to see if there was anything useful there."

"Like ballistics?" I said, remembering the word from a television movie.

"Ballistics only works if you've got a gun to compare bullets with. What I mean is stuff like figuring out the angle at which the bullet entered the body to see where the killer was standing when he fired. Or any kind of physical traces of the killer on the body. You know—police stuff."

I felt a little silly for my ignorance, but tried to tell myself that Junior didn't know anything about programming. Of course, she didn't interfere when I tried to write a program. I might have backed down if I hadn't been so fired up from Aunt Maggie's pep talk.

I asked, "So what did the police stuff tell you in this case?"

"The shooter was a few feet away from Honeywell, and shooting upwards."

"Does that mean that the killer was shorter than Honeywell?"

"Not in this case. It looks like Honeywell was walking down the steps on the bus. He was probably on the first or second of the three steps, so he'd be taller than just about anybody. The first shot was to the chest. He then fell backwards onto the driver's seat, and the killer stepped onto the bus and shot him in the head, to make sure."

"How could you tell that?"

"The head shot was at a different angle, from somebody standing over the body. We know it was the second shot because there was a bloody smudge on the handrail, like you'd make if you were holding on while climbing those steps. The blood was Honeywell's, which means that he had already lost some. There wasn't any blood on his hands, so he didn't make the smudge. Therefore the killer did."

"Weren't there fingerprints?"

Junior shook her head. "Whoever it was was wearing

gloves, which were no doubt disposed of along with the gun. They didn't find anything useful on Honeywell, so I'm guessing the killer didn't even touch him. Either he was scared to, or sure that Honeywell was dead. And he was quite dead. Either shot would have been fatal."

I thought about somebody standing over a body in the dark, gun in hand, so confident that his shots had been fatal that there was no need to check. "Sounds pretty methodical for what Chief Monroe claims is a crime of passion, doesn't it?"

"That's the feeling I get, too, but it's hard to say."

"So once you've got everything you need from the scene, then you'd go after motive?"

"Not yet. First I'd talk to everybody who had been around the scene of the crime and try to find somebody who had seen something. And go back to anybody whose story was inconsistent with somebody else's or the facts as we know them."

"Sounds tedious."

"It can be."

"What did Monroe find out from that step?"

"Not much. Nobody saw anybody over there that night, not Honeywell or the killer. There were a few people still at the school, even as late as it was, but they were all at the dance. I was hoping Lloyd would get lucky with somebody having gone out there to make out in the car, but nothing doing. A security guy was in the school building to keep an eye on the dressing rooms, but he didn't go out to that back parking lot. So that part was a bust."

"Then what?"

"Then I'd trace the movements of the deceased. I might found out a motive, but the important thing is to find out who he was, where he lived, anything about him there is to find out. Since most people are killed by somebody they know, this is where you usually find the killer, if none of the other things have helped."

"Did Chief Monroe do all this?"

"Oh, yes. Like I said, Lloyd isn't a stupid man."

It did sound like he had covered all the bases. Except for the fact that Tom Honeywell was not the intended victim. "If he did all of that, then all there is for me to work with is the backgrounds of the Ramblers. Which is what I asked for in the first place."

"I think you're right."

"So what was that lecture about police procedure for?"

Junior grinned. "I just wanted you to know a little bit of what's involved here, other than motive. Most of the time, police investigations work out without any help from you."

She had a point. "I know they do, Junior. I certainly didn't mean to imply that you don't know your job. Or that Chief Monroe doesn't know his."

"I'm glad to hear that."

"It's just that this time, I think he does need some help."

"As a matter of fact, I think Lloyd's missing a bet this time, too. So which Rambler are you interested in?"

"Any and all of them. Roger first. I know he used to be my uncle, but he hasn't been for several years now, and to tell you the truth, I don't know him all that well."

Junior reached into her file cabinet, pulled out a folder, and flipped through it. I was glad to see that it was thin. "Roger Bailey. A few speeding tickets. His car inspection sticker expired once, but I let him off with a warning. The Ramblers got involved in a couple of brawls, but I think that both of them were cases of being in the wrong place at the wrong time. Your future uncle has a strong right cross, by the way. That's all I've got."

I said, "Maybe that's all the official stuff, but what do you know about him personally? And don't bother playing innocent. You hear about everything that goes on in and around Byerly, sooner or later."

Junior closed the folder, propped her elbows on the top of her desk, and her head on top of both hands. "I've always liked Roger, and I know Daddy does, too."

That was more important than it might have sounded. Junior was known for her good judgment when it came to people, and she had inherited the trait from her father.

Junior went on. "Born and bred in Byerly. The Baileys are decent folks. Nothing fancy, but good plain people. I can't remember any of them being in trouble. Most of them work at the mill, but I think there was a cousin who went into the music business in a small way. He wasn't as successful as Roger, but he might have paved the way for him.

"I thought it was a shame when Roger and your aunt split up, but he was doing a lot of carousing in those days. It got even worse after the divorce. Drinking more than he should have and seeing a fair number of women, especially after Ruby Lee remarried. But Roger eventually settled down, and it seems to me that he's sincere about wanting to take up where he left off with Ruby Lee and the kids.

"He's got a temper, but it's the kind that flares and goes away again. He doesn't hold a grudge. I suppose somebody who got in his way might feel differently, but I've never heard of anybody being out to get him." Junior shook her head. "No, I can't think of a reason why anybody would go after Roger Bailey."

I was glad to hear it. Not just because he was almost

family again, but because I liked him. Now if I could just get him to realize what century it was when it came to women and careers.

"What about Cotton Lewis?" I asked.

Before Junior could answer, the door to the station opened and Trey came in, carrying a paper bag from Hardee's. He kind of nodded at the two of us, then went on in the back.

Junior sighed and reached for another folder. "Cotton was in the same brawls as Roger, but he fights a bit meaner. Broke a chair over one man's head. Another time he got into a serious fight over a woman, but nobody wanted to press charges after I broke it up. That's all I've got officially, and unofficially, I don't know much else. He's not from Byerly, so I don't know his people. He seems to be a good enough fellow, and he sure can play a fiddle. That fight he was in would be the only motive I can think of, but that was a couple of years ago. It seems like they'd have pressed charges right then and there if they'd been a mind to, not waited all this time and then driven to Rocky Shoals to try for him."

"It doesn't seem very likely," I agreed. "What about Al Cunningham? He's quite the ladies' man, isn't he? Though I don't quite see the attraction myself."

"I don't know," Junior said thoughtfully. "He's not pretty, but there's something about him."

"Don't tell me that you've gone out with him?"

"No, but he asked me once. I might have gone, but I'm just not the sharing type. If I like a man well enough to be with him, I want him all to myself."

"You and me both," I said.

"Other than being a ladies' man, I'd say Al is an all right

fellow. He does hold a grudge, but is more likely to play a practical joke than to do anything serious."

"Did he ever play a practical joke that might have really made somebody mad?"

"Not that I've ever heard. Well, there was that time with Cecil, who used to be with the Ramblers. Cecil got pretty upset when Al put the strings onto his guitar backwards right before a performance, but I heard that Al took him drinking and they were friends again afterward. And Cecil moved to Tennessee a couple of years ago."

Trey came back through on his way out the door, with a silly grin on his face. He didn't seem to notice me or Junior. Junior sighed again, sounding even more exasperated.

"Anything in Al's folder?" I asked.

Junior shook her head.

"Don't you need to check?"

"I told you he asked me out. I looked then."

"You check out the records of everybody who asks you out?"

"Wouldn't you?"

"I guess I would." I had to ask, "Did you ever find out anything juicy by checking?"

She grinned. "One time I had to serve a warrant on my date."

"So much for that evening."

"It wasn't too bad. I didn't serve the warrant until after dinner."

"Are you serious?"

She just grinned. "Who do we have left?"

"Slim Grady. Though I imagine Slim is a nickname."

She looked at a folder. "Those same two brawls as the other Ramblers. He mostly stayed out of them—not much of a fighter." Then she put all of the folders back into the file cabinet and said, "I don't know much about Slim. He's a quiet sort, keeps to himself other than his music. I know your cousins have their eyes on him, and they're not the first. I guess women believe the old saying about still waters running deep. Even so, I don't know that I've ever seen him out on a date. I hear he goes to the library, reads a lot. Listens to music, too. Not just country either. He orders all kinds of CDs: classical, jazz, rock and roll."

"And Drew Wiley must be his mailman," I said. Nothing unusual ever came in the mail without Drew taking notice and spreading the word. The men in Byerly who read *Playboy* always went to the newsstand in Hickory to buy it, just to keep Drew from knowing.

Junior grinned again. "Does any of this help you?"

I shook my head. "Not a bit. I suppose that I'll have to talk to the Ramblers themselves and see whether they know anything useful. Though I can't imagine that there's a whole lot you've missed."

"I'll take that as a compliment," Junior said.

Trey came back in, this time with a tiny portable television set, and started to carry it to the back.

"Trey?" Junior said.

"Yes, Junior."

"Aren't you supposed to be on patrol?"

"This is my lunch break."

She nodded. "Did you actually eat anything?"

"I'll grab a bite later."

"All right."

He started into the back, then stopped. "Junior, have we got an extension cord I can use for this?"

"There's one in the closet."

"Great!" he said, and went on by.

"Laurie Anne," Junior said, "I imagine your family has already put a fair amount of pressure on you about this thing, and I hate to add to it, but I sure would appreciate it if you'd get your cousin out of my jail so my brother would get back to work."

"I thought he might have a crush on her."

"You can call it a crush, but I call it a royal pain in the rump. He's brought her fresh sheets for the bed, and a fan because it gets stuffy in there, and a rug for that hard concrete floor, and a lamp because the fluorescent light is hard on her eyes. He's brought her so much food that she's not going to fit out the door if she's here much longer."

"He's got it bad, all right. What is it? The Joan of Arc thing? Poor innocent Ilene locked up?"

"That might be part of it, but I think he's had a thing for her for a while. Just too shy to say anything. I keep telling him that he's not going to be any kind of a law officer if he can't talk to half of the human race, but he says that talking in the line of duty is different. It's off-duty conversation that he can't handle. I just can't see how any brother of mine could be afraid to speak up."

Actually, with Junior's mother, her four sisters, and Junior herself, I could see how Trey might have had a hard time getting a word in edgewise while growing up. I didn't think it would be a good idea to say that, so I changed the subject. "Have you seen Richard? I thought he'd be here."

"He was here when Miss Easterly came by to speak with Ilene, and they headed back over to her office to discuss strategy."

"Then I guess I'll go over there. Thanks for the look at your files."

"Don't mention it. To anybody."

Before I could leave, I heard Trey call out, "Junior, do you think Mama and Daddy would mind if I borrowed their VCR for a few days?"

Junior looked at me, clearly begging me once again to get Ilene out of there, and she looked so pitiful that I waited until I was outside to laugh.

Chapter 27

Since Florence Easterly's office was just across the street from the police station, I walked. The three-story building housed City Hall and its accompanying bureaus, with plenty of space left over for Florence, a notary, and a couple of other folks.

A young girl who looked vaguely familiar smiled and called me by name when I opened the frosted-glass door labeled EASTERLY, which probably meant that she was the sister of somebody I had known in school. I smiled back, made some small talk that wouldn't betray the fact that I didn't know who she was, then asked if my husband was there.

"He's in with Miss Easterl⁻ ⁻ ⁻rie Anne. You go right on in."

I could hear voices behind the door, so I opened it quietly so as not to disturb their legal brainstorming. Only the conversation I didn't disturb wasn't legal. That is, it was legal, but it sure didn't concern the law.

Miss Easterly was standing in the middle of the office wringing her hands and staring at them in despair. " 'Out, damned spot! Out, I say!' "

"Macbeth?" I asked when she got to a dramatic pause.

"Act III, Scene 4," Richard confirmed.

I had thought Miss Easterly would at least look embarrassed when she realized I was there, but instead she gave a delicate curtsy.

"How was I?" she asked.

"Pretty good," I had to admit. "Practicing for Ilene's defense?"

"We have strayed from our original discussion. Your husband happened to quote from the Bard, and one thing led to another. At one point I considered going into the theater and I still perform in the occasional local production."

"Richard quoted from Shakespeare?" I said, in mock amazement. "Fancy that."

Richard grinned, and gave me a quick hug and a kiss.

"Miss Easterly has a flair for Shakespeare, don't you think?" he said. "And acting isn't all that different from presenting a case to the jury."

I was imagining the reaction to her using a soliloquy to defend Ilene when there was a tap on the door. The receptionist came in carrying an honest-to-God silver tea set on a tray.

"Thank you, Amanda," Miss Easterly said, and Amanda carefully placed the tray on a low table on the opposite end of the room from Florence's desk, and backed out again.

"Won't you sit down?" Miss Easterly said, and gestured us toward armchairs next to the table. We sat, and she poured tea into white china cups with gold leaf on the rims, and pulled a lacy napkin off a plate of tiny sandwiches cut into diamond shapes. "I realized that it was getting toward noon, and thought we could eat while we talked."

I was hungry, now that she mentioned it. "Thank you," I said, and reached for one. Richard did the same, and we bit into them at the same time. Fortunately Miss Easterly was pouring tea at that point, and didn't see our expressions. They were cucumber sandwiches. I had heard of cucumber sandwiches, but this was the first time I had ever had to eat one. I fully intended that it would be the last.

"How does Ilene's case look?" I asked, hoping that she wouldn't notice I wasn't eating any more of that sandwich.

"I'm optimistic that we can get an acquittal," Miss Easterly said. "We've been discussing the evidence, and it is circumstantial and not terribly strong. It would be better if we could find out who really killed Mr. Honeywell, of course."

"As it turns out, Tom may not even have been the intended victim," I said, and explained.

"That's good work," Richard said. Then, to Miss Easterly, he said, "This should help, shouldn't it?"

"It would help add that shadow of a doubt," she said. "Still, I'm more concerned that the trial itself would brand Ilene as a killer. Rarely do the police try more than one person for a crime, and even an acquittal could follow her for life."

"I hadn't thought of it that way," I admitted. I should have. I knew a man who had been through the same thing. After being found not guilty, he had left town to avoid the stares. "So what you're saying is that we should find out who the killer is before it goes to trial." That was no big surprise. Everybody else in Byerly had already been pushing us toward that.

She nodded. "If at all possible."

"I've got a couple of leads to follow up on," I said with more confidence than I felt, "so I suppose we better get back to it."

"Thank you for the sandwiches," Richard said. "We'll be in touch."

" 'Parting is such sweet sorrow,' " she said with a smile.

"Now you've got her doing it," I said to Richard as we left.

"Are you saying that quoting Shakespeare is a less than desirable habit?" he asked with a sniff.

"Of course not," I said quickly. "It's charming, and shows how wonderfully educated you are. It's just that she doesn't have your style."

"True," he said, and realizing that we were alone in the stairwell, stopped to give me a real kiss. "What do we do next?"

The kiss had given me a few ideas about what to do next, but what I said was, "I'm thinking that one of the Ramblers was the real target, so I think we need to go talk to Roger."

"Only on one condition."

"What's that?"

"Can we go get some real food first?"

Chapter 28

After a satisfying stop at Fork-in-the-Road for barbecue, we drove to Roger's apartment. He lived in a brick building that had so little personality that it could have been anywhere in the state, or in the country, for that matter. The first thing we saw when Roger let us in the door was stacks of boxes all over the living room.

"Let's go into the kitchen," Roger said. "I'm not exactly set up for company these days."

"We're not company, Roger," I said. "We're family. At least we will be in a few days."

"I sure hope so, Laurie Anne," Roger said as he took us into the kitchen and pulled out chairs from around the Formica-top kitchen table. "I've just got this awful feeling that there's not going to be any wedding."

Richard said, "Cheer up. The worst that could happen is that the wedding gets postponed until we get Ilene out of this mess. Admittedly that means having to placate Vasti, but I'm sure that you and Aunt Ruby Lee can weather that storm."

But Roger was shaking his head. "I don't know. With all the bad luck I've had with Ruby Lee, I'm afraid that if we don't get married right on schedule, it's just not going to happen. What if she changes her mind now that she's had a chance to think about it?"

"Roger, she's not going to change her mind. She loves you," I said.

"And I love her, too, more than anything on this world. Except the boys and Ilene, of course. And I guess Ilene's the reason you've come over here, not to listen to me mope. What can I do for you?"

For the fourth time that day, I explained why I didn't think Tom Honeywell was the intended victim.

"That's some fancy figuring," Roger said. "It seems right funny that as many people as didn't like Honeywell, he was killed by accident."

"Of course, that means that we need to find out who the intended target was. Which is why I'm here."

"I don't follow."

"Since Tom was killed in the Ramblers' bus, it seems pretty likely that whoever it was was trying to kill one of the Ramblers."

Roger leaned back in his chair. "I see what you mean, but I can't believe that anybody would want one of the boys dead, Laurie Anne. They're good fellows, every one of them."

I said, "Nice people get killed, too."

"I suppose."

"Just tell me about them. I've met them, but I don't know any of them well." I didn't see any reason to mention that I had already quizzed Junior about them, and him.

"All right, but let me get something to drink first. Do y'all want something?"

While Roger got himself and us Cokes, Richard pulled out a pad and a pen, ready to take notes.

Once Roger was back in his chair, he asked, "Which one do you want to hear about first?"

"Cotton?"

"He's one hell of a fiddler, Cotton is. Now he's got a temper, I won't try to tell you different, but he's always real sorry afterward. He got into a fight at a bar we were playing at once, and the man he was fighting with had to get a dozen stitches in his head. You know, Cotton paid every penny of that man's medical bills, that's how sorry he was."

"With a temper like that, don't you think he might have made a few enemies?"

"If he has, he's never mentioned it to me. He's getting much better about keeping himself under control."

What Roger said fit in with what Junior had told me, and his paying the bills afterward didn't do much for the idea of revenge. Still, maybe Cotton had been in a fight with somebody who didn't forgive him, money or not. And there could have been other fights that Roger didn't know about.

"What about Al?"

"You got to admire a man like Al," Roger said with a grin. "He's got girlfriends in every town we play in, and when we go somewhere new, he picks himself out another one by the time we're there half an hour."

"A woman scorned?" I asked.

"Not hardly," Roger says. "He's never said no to a woman in his entire life."

"Maybe he met one who didn't like sharing him."

"Not that I've ever heard of. I don't know that I approve of what he does, but he's up front about it, never sneaks around. Al tells them right off that he's not ready to settle down."

"What about a jealous husband or boyfriend?"

"Maybe a boyfriend, but not a husband. Al's got a sixth sense about married women. He says he can tell within five minutes whether or not she's got a wedding band hidden in her pocketbook. He was married once himself, and she messed around on him, and he just won't do that to another man."

An interesting kind of honor, I had to admit. Still, the jealousy angle might be worth pursuing. "Slim Grady?" I prompted.

"Now you're barking up the wrong tree. Slim is a real straight arrow. As reliable and honest as the day is long."

"I know that the triplets have been chasing him, but he hasn't actually asked any of them out, has he?"

Roger shook his head. "I've never known Slim to go out with any woman, as a matter of fact. He'll have a drink with women when we're at a club, but it never goes any further than that."

"What about men?" I asked, not sure how he'd react.

Roger took it in stride. "I've never seen him with another man either. Just a loner." Roger took a swallow of Coke. "What else?"

"Well," I said, wanting to lead up to the next part delicately, "what about you?"

"Me?" he said. "I hadn't thought of that."

"Do you have any enemies?" Then I added, "I promise that none of this is going to get to Aunt Ruby Lee."

"Shoot, Ruby Lee and I don't have any secrets, but I don't have any enemies. Not that I know of, anyway. I don't have Cotton's temper, and I don't have Al's way with the ladies. I won't say I've never been in a fight or gone out with a woman other than Ruby Lee, but nothing that would get me into trouble."

"What about your business dealings?"

"I've had my share of problems with bar owners not wanting to pay out our contract, and with other bands trying to muscle in on our clubs. I had to take one of our former band members to court for trying to run off with two of my best speakers, but that didn't come to much. And he left this part of the country years ago."

"You're sure?" I said, but I was just as glad he didn't have anybody mad at him. The last thing Aunt Ruby Lee needed was more trouble.

Roger did think about it for another minute, but then he said, "I'm as sure as I can be. I always keep my side of a bargain, and I try to be careful about who I do business with."

He leaned back in his chair, shaking his head as if he was remembering something. "I've been lucky, but the music business can get pretty ugly. If you had seen some of the places I've had to play and some of the pure out-and-out trash I've had to deal with, you wouldn't want Ilene in the music business any more than I do. One so-called nightclub wasn't nothing but a hangout for Hell's Angels, with a manager who had more tattoos on him than I'd ever seen in my life. We spent the whole night ducking thrown beer bottles. And at least that place paid us what they promised. That's what it's like for a musician starting out."

"I know it's not a nice business," I said, "but don't you think Ilene should decide that for herself?"

"Not if it means her making a mistake."

"Paw always said a person had to make her own mistakes."

"Did he let you play in traffic when you were a little girl?"

"Ilene isn't a little girl anymore."

"She is when it comes to this business."

"What about Clifford and Earl? They're not much older than Ilene, and you've been talking about letting them play with the Ramblers."

"That's different."

"Why? Because they're boys?"

"That's right," he said, and he didn't even have the good grace to look embarrassed about it. "I wouldn't have to worry about them getting hurt if a crowd gets rowdy because they'd be able to defend themselves. There's no telling what could happen to Ilene."

"I bet she could take care of herself," I said, thinking about Maureen Shula. "She's smarter than you think she is, and tougher. I'll admit that she'll have to be careful about where she plays at first, but lots of women musicians have made it to the big time. What about the Judds, and Loretta Lynn?"

"Naomi Judd ruined her health on the road, Wynonna had an illegitimate baby, and Loretta has had more nervous breakdowns than I can count. Is that what you want to happen to Ilene?"

"Of course not, but I don't want Clifford and Earl to turn into alcoholics and die in a car crash like Hank Williams either."

"They won't," Roger said firmly. "I'll be looking after them. Now can I answer any other questions for you?" That made it plain that he wasn't going to talk about Ilene anymore.

"I don't think so, but I would like the rest of the Ramblers' addresses. We'd like to talk to them, too."

"I'll give them to you if you want, but I've got a better

idea. We've got to drive to Statesville for a show tonight. Why don't y'all come along with us, and talk to them on the way? The bus is plenty big enough."

"The same bus?" I asked, meaning the same bus as the one Tom Honeywell was shot in.

He nodded. "It's the only bus we've got. Chief Monroe said they're done with it. That's not going to bother you, is it?"

"I suppose not," I said.

"We're meeting here at about five-thirty. It takes about an hour to get there, so you ought to have time to talk to everybody."

I looked at Richard, and he nodded, so I said, "Thanks, Roger. It sounds perfect. We'll see you then."

As we were climbing back into the car, Richard said, "It's only two-thirty now, so we've got time if you've got another idea."

"Oh, I've got lots of ideas," I said, and batted my eyes.

He raised one eyebrow. "Are you suggesting that we go back to the house?"

For my answer, I raced the motor and zoomed out of the parking lot.

Chapter 29

When we got back to Roger's place that afternoon to join the band on the bus, we found out that we weren't the only guests. Carlelle, Idelle, and Odelle were there, too, clustered around Slim as closely as they could be without touching one another. Once again, they were dressed differently, but they all looked very nice. Each one trying to outshine the others, I suppose.

Poor Slim looked more than a little uncomfortable at the attention, and I knew he had to be wondering how he was going to be polite to all of them. Which is to say, which one was he going to sit next to?

"Shall we rescue him?" I whispered to Richard.

"It would be the humane thing to do," he replied.

"Slim," I called out. "Just the man we've been looking for. Richard and I would like to talk with you on the way to Statesville, if that's all right."

He smiled and said, "That would be just fine. Roger told me y'all have some questions."

The triplets looked disappointed, but didn't object. I suppose they were laying their plans for the show itself.

I have to admit that I felt funny climbing onto the bus, and couldn't help glancing at the driver's seat, where Tom's body had been found. The seat was covered with a tattered afghan, probably to hide whatever stains they couldn't wash off. I must have been staring, because Richard gently nudged me forward.

Richard, Slim, and I sat in the very back of the bus, while the other band members and the triplets stayed closer to the front. Roger was driving.

"What kind of questions can I answer for you two?" Slim asked.

I answered by telling him what direction the investigation was taking. "It seems reasonable that one of you Ramblers was the intended target, and I don't want to be rude, but I was wondering if you have any enemies."

He shook his head. "I can't imagine that I do. I've lived in Byerly for less than a year, so I haven't had time to make anybody that mad at me."

"What about the other musicians at the Jamboree?" Richard asked. "Do you have any professional enemies?"

Slim hesitated, but then shook his head. "I can't think of a soul."

I said, "There were a lot of folks who wanted to be in the Ramblers, weren't there?" Aunt Nora had told me about the auditions and all the demo tapes Roger had received when it got around that they needed a new guitar player. "Did anybody get particularly upset when you got the job?"

"There were a whole lot of fellows who were disappointed, but I can't imagine anybody wanting to kill me out of spite."

"What about to take your place in the band?"

He grinned. "Laurie Anne, this is a good band to be with, but it isn't *that* good."

"I guess you're right," I said sheepishly. "Roger has been

talking so much about how nasty the business can get that I got carried away."

"It can get nasty," Slim admitted. "I've been cheated a few times myself, but nothing has ever happened that would be worth killing for."

Richard said, "What about the other Ramblers? Have you ever known them to have any enemies?"

"I can't think of any," he said.

I looked at Richard to see if he had any other questions, and when he shook his head, I said, "Thank you, Slim. If you do think of anything, be sure and let us know."

"I sure will."

The triplets must have been watching us like hawks, because as soon as Slim got up, they nigh about broke their necks trying to get to the seat he was heading for. Carlelle won the race, and she triumphantly slid in beside him. Idelle jumped in the seat behind them and leaned forward, while Odelle took the seat in front and turned around.

Once that battle was over, Richard went to bring Cotton back to talk with us.

Cotton's hair was sandy-blond these days, but he must have been tow-headed as a boy to earn his nickname. Though Al was the ladies' man, I thought that, with his blue eyes and muscular body, Cotton was much better looking.

"Roger told me that you think one of us was meant to get shot," Cotton said.

I nodded. "Do you have any ideas of who the killer might have been after?"

"I've been thinking about that. Did you ever think that it didn't matter who it was? Maybe it was somebody making a statement about country music, like people claiming rock music played backwards says evil things. Or like them chasing after that Rushdie guy, trying to kill him."

I hadn't thought of that, and I could tell Richard hadn't either.

"Have you received any threats?" Richard asked.

"No," Cotton said, "but there's an awful lot of nut cases out there."

It sounded unlikely, even to me, but as Junior had pointed out, I was no expert. Richard wrote something down and I said, "We'll check into that."

"I was also thinking that it might have been one of those crazy fans that chase after famous people. Like the man who shot John Lennon, or the guy who slashed up that actress out in California. The fatal attraction thing."

That also hadn't occurred to me. "Have you noticed anybody stalking the band?" I asked.

Cotton shook his head. "We've got our share of groupies, I guess, but nobody sticks out. Except . . ." He looked over at the triplets for a minute, but evidently decided against saying what he was thinking. "I guess not."

Again, Richard took notes, just in case. I said, "That's something else we can look into. Is there anyone else? Maybe somebody you know personally?"

"I don't think so."

"I've heard that you've got a temper," I said as diffidently as I could.

Cotton stood up and roared, "Who told you that?"

I jumped back and Richard suddenly had his shoulder between me and Cotton. Then Cotton sat down and laughed.

"Just kidding," he said with what Paw used to call a shit-eating grin. He had to turn away and wave at everybody else in the bus to show them that everything was okay. "I

know I've got a reputation, but I've been working on that."
He lowered his voice a bit. "Roger was starting to get tired
of my getting into fights. It's not good publicity for the band,
not to mention the damage to our equipment. So I've been
seeing somebody to learn strategies for dealing with my
temper. I know now to mellow out, take a deep breath
before I start anything. The trick is not to repress it, because I've got a right to feel angry. I just can't let it get the
better of me. I like to picture the anger as a liquid, and I let it
drain right out of me, where it won't do anybody any harm.
And I think I've made peace with anybody I've had any
problems with."

"That's great," I said, though I was disappointed. I had
thought sure that he'd have at least one skeleton rattling
around in his closet. Neither Richard nor I had any other
questions, so Cotton went to tell Al it was his turn.

I've heard it said that drummers tend to be either
chubby or skinny, and Al was one of the chubby kind. His
brown hair was long and a little stringy, and his eyes were
nothing special. After all I had heard about his way with
women, I was expecting a little flirting, but he was down-
right businesslike. Polite and all, but no more than that.

I explained what it was we were after, and then said, "Do
you have any idea of who might have it in for a member of
the band?"

"I sure don't," Al said. "I've never had any kind of trouble that would lead to shooting."

I felt a little uncomfortable asking about his love life, so I
nudged Richard so he'd take over.

"We understand that you are acquainted with a lot of
women," Richard said in his stuffiest, college professor tone.
I guess he felt uncomfortable asking, too.

Al grinned slowly. "You might say that."

"Could one of these women have become angry with you over some slight, real or imagined?"

"I don't think so," he answered firmly. "I know how to treat women right."

"No jealousy among your companions, or former companions wanting to renew relations, or women who wished to be companions when you weren't interested?"

"No," he repeated. "Like I said, I treat women right. I respect them, and they respect me."

He sounded very sure of himself, though I couldn't quite reconcile the idea of respecting women with respecting so many at one time.

Richard said, "I understand you were once married."

Al said, "That's been over for years, and it's me that was slighted against, not her. Besides which, she moved out West not long after the divorce was final."

Richard looked at me, and I shrugged. Maybe somebody did have reason to dislike Al, but if so, he didn't know about it.

"Thank you," Richard said, and Al moved back up to the front of the bus.

"I just don't get it," I said when Richard and I were by ourselves.

"Me, neither. How can somebody have somebody else ready to kill him and not suspect it?"

"I don't mean that. I mean I don't get how Al gets all those women. He's nice enough and all, but nothing to write home about."

"Of course, he wasn't turning on the charm for you."

"Are you saying that I'm not his type?" I said, a little miffed.

"I don't think Al restricts himself to a type, usually, but you're a married woman, and he avoids married women."

"True," I said, and snuggled closer to him.

"Besides, he knew he couldn't possibly compete with *my* charm."

"Is that so?"

With a look of disdain, Richard quoted, " 'These fellows of infinite tongue, that can rhyme themselves into ladies' favors, they do always reason themselves out again.' *Henry V*, Act V, Scene 2."

I thought rapidly. "All marriages are happy; it's the living together afterward that causes all the trouble."

Richard raised an eyebrow.

"I bet Al would give me the point," I said, looking out the window in order to maintain a straight face.

"All right, but only because I'm going to win anyway."

That sounded like a challenge to me, so we kept up the contest. He was ahead of me by two by the time we hit Statesville.

Chapter 30

The rest of the evening was pleasant, but not very helpful. We got to Statesville, and I found out just how much work it is to set up for a show. Then came the show itself, which was lots of fun, even for people like Richard and me who aren't big country music fans. We all danced and had a great time. After the show, we helped load up the bus and drove back to Byerly.

Oh, we spoke to the Ramblers between sets and got to know them better, but we never could come up with a motive for murder. As Roger had said, they were all nice fellows.

Roger drove the bus back to the parking lot of his apartment, and the rest of us retrieved our cars. Except the triplets. They announced that they had gotten a ride to Roger's place because their car wasn't "acting right," and asked Slim if he would drive them home.

Slim looked like he was worn slap out, but he politely agreed, then watched helplessly as the three sisters nearly wrestled for the front seat of his Corolla.

"Poor Slim," Richard said as we pulled out behind his car.

"What's so poor about him?" I asked. "He's got three attractive women interested in him. You *do* think my cousins are attractive, don't you?"

"Of course I do," he said quickly. "It's just that if he accepts one, he gets the others mad at him. Besides which, I don't think he's interested in any of them."

"I thought men liked being chased by women. Heck, I thought they dreamed of such an opportunity."

"You're being sexist. If it was a woman being pursued by three men, you wouldn't be making jokes."

"You're right," I said. "I guess they are making Slim uncomfortable. Look at how fast he's going, trying to get them home as soon as possible." Slim's car was way ahead of me by then, and I was a few miles on the wrong side of the speed limit myself.

"He is driving fast," Richard said.

I sped up a little, trying to keep them in sight. "I think he's going *too* fast."

Slim's car reached a curve, and it looked to me that he just barely stayed on the road.

"Jesus!" I said. "What's the matter with him?"

"His brake lights went on," Richard said, "but I can't tell that he slowed down at all."

At that point, I had to slow down myself to make the curve. By the time we made it, Slim's car was even farther ahead of us.

"Richard, I think something's wrong. Do you suppose his brakes could have gone out?"

"They must have. He wouldn't be stupid enough to drive like that if they hadn't."

"Hold on, I'm going to try to stay with him," I said, and accelerated as much as I safely could. The road was straight at that point, but I knew there were more curves coming.

Slim must have realized that the road was going to get worse, because he started to veer off the road, swerving into areas of grass and dodging phone poles.

"He's trying to slow himself down," Richard said.

"Use the emergency brake!" I said, as if he could hear me.

Either he didn't think of it or he couldn't, because he kept veering from side to side. Thank goodness we were the only cars in sight. We weren't far from a really nasty curve when Slim's car left the road completely and tore across a field. The car slowed, but not enough to keep it from crashing into a tree with a horrible thud.

I followed them off the road, albeit more slowly, and stopped our car a few feet away. Richard was out of the car and running toward the wreckage before I could get the engine stopped. I left the headlights on, but didn't see anybody emerging from the car as I followed Richard.

All I could think of was those horrible scenes from the films they show in driver's education class. I'm not a praying person, but I prayed a lifetime's worth in the minutes it took me to reach the crumpled car.

As Richard grabbed on to the door handle on the driver's side, I heard a wailing from the car. I didn't know whether to be glad that at least one of them was still alive, or afraid that one of the others wasn't. I got to the door on the other side of the car, wrenched it open, and looked inside.

"Odelle? Idelle? Carlelle?" I didn't know who had won the battle to sit in the front seat. The windshield was shattered, and the dashboard bent into a V. One of the triplets was folded over, her hands over her head.

"Honey?" I said, touching her as gently as I could. I didn't see any blood, but there wasn't much light.

The head lifted, and a tearstained face looked into mine. It was Carlelle. "Laurie Anne?" she said. "How did you get here?"

"Are you hurt?" I asked. "Is anybody hurt?"

"Slim's out cold," Richard said.

I felt a hot streak of anger at that man for putting my cousins in danger, but it faded almost immediately. It wasn't the time or the place. "Carlelle, can you get out of the car?" I was smelling gasoline, and was terrified that the car would catch fire.

"I think so," but before she moved, she said, "Idelle? Odelle? Are you all right?"

"I'm fine," a weak voice said.

"She is not," another voice said. "Her head is bleeding."

I took Carlelle's arm and helped her out of the car. She moved normally, as far as I could tell. "Go over there by our car," I said to her, then helped the other triplets crawl out of the backseat. Funny things come into your mind at a time like that. All I could think of is that I would never, ever own a two-door car.

Idelle and Odelle helped themselves over to our car, and I went to see about Slim.

"He's still unconscious," Richard said. "I don't know if we should move him or not."

"I think we better. I smell gasoline." I found out later that cars rarely explode after an accident, but I still had those driver's education warning films playing in the back of my mind.

Richard nodded. "You get back, and I'll pull him out."

"Don't be silly," I said, knowing that he just wanted to get me away from danger. I reached in for Slim's feet before Richard could argue with me.

Somehow we managed to get Slim out of the car and started to carry him over to ours.

"He's not dead, is he?" Carlelle asked.

"No," I said, but didn't elaborate. His breathing sounded normal to me, and he hadn't grunted when we lifted him, so maybe there weren't any broken bones, but I would have felt better if he were awake.

"Where should we put him?" I asked Richard.

"Just lay him out in the grass," he said. "I'm afraid we'd hurt him if we tried to get him into the backseat."

We put him down, and the triplets gathered around.

"We better go for help," Richard said.

I said, "You go. I'll stay here with Slim and the triplets. Unless one of them wants to go with you?"

"No," one of them said quickly. "We're staying together."

Richard gave me a quick kiss. "I'll be back as soon as I can. Stay away from that car!"

"We will," I said.

After Richard drove away, I asked the triplets, "What happened?"

"The brakes went," Idelle said. At least I thought it was Idelle.

"Are you three okay?"

"My head hurts," Idelle said.

"It's bleeding," Odelle said, and ripped a piece off of her blouse to wipe her sister's forehead. "I don't think it's bad, but don't you move around any."

"What about you?" Carlelle said. "You were limping."

"Just twisted my ankle."

"Let me see." Carlelle leaned down, and felt Odelle's ankle. "It's swelling. Don't try to walk on it."

"What was that?" Idelle said.

"What?" Carlelle said.

"That sound you made when you bent over Odelle. You're hurt!"

"My chest is kind of sore, that's all. I think I bruised myself on the shoulder harness."

"It could be a broken rib!" Idelle said.

"Don't move around! You could poke a hole in your lung!" Odelle ordered.

The three of them went on that way, diagnosing each other's injuries while Slim slept on. I was afraid that he was in shock, but he didn't feel cold or clammy the way people in shock are supposed to. Then I wondered whether or not he had a concussion, and I didn't know how people with concussions were supposed to feel. I was awfully relieved when I saw headlights approaching us.

Chapter 31

Richard must have driven nearly as fast as Slim had, because he wasn't gone but fifteen minutes, and Junior's patrol car and the ambulances weren't far behind him.

The ambulance attendants quickly roused Slim, and though they said there was a chance of a concussion, they were fairly sure that he hadn't hit his head that hard. The triplets did have a bleeding forehead, a twisted ankle, and a cracked rib—as well as a bunch of bruises—but otherwise, they were fine. Since they refused to split up, they squeezed into one ambulance while Slim rode in the second.

Junior stayed to deal with Slim's car, while Richard and I followed the ambulances to the hospital. There were an awful lot of people who would have to be called, and the triplets were in no shape to do it.

It was nearly four when we got to the hospital in Hickory, but despite that, it didn't take long for most of the Burnettes to gather. Aunt Nellie and Uncle Ruben were the first we called, of course, and they didn't take long to get there and check on their daughters. Then Roger had to come check on Slim. Plus Aunt Daphine had to come to check on everybody, including me and Richard when we weren't even in the accident. Then Aunt Nora and Thaddeous came in with enough biscuits and coffee for all of us, and most of the people on duty in the emergency room besides.

After Idelle's head wound was stitched, Odelle's twisted ankle wrapped, and Carlelle's cracked rib strapped, they were released. Aunt Nellie and Uncle Ruben drove them back to their place, and said they'd get them settled.

It turned out that Slim didn't have a concussion after all, and he could go home, too. Aunt Nora announced that she'd take him home, and ignored his protests that he'd be all right by himself.

Richard and I were so tired by this point that Thaddeous refused to let us drive ourselves back to Aunt Maggie's. Instead he drove us over there in our car, and somehow got a ride back to the hospital to get his pickup truck. I say "somehow" because I fell asleep on the way to the house, and later found out that Thaddeous carried me upstairs to the bedroom. He'd have carried Richard, too, if Richard had let him.

After all that, we slept until well after one o'clock. If I had been awake to think about it, I would have wondered why we weren't woken by the phone long before that. After all, there were going to be an awful lot of Burnettes trying to find out all the gory details. Once we managed to get downstairs, we found a note from Aunt Maggie that told us why.

Laurie Anne and Richard,

Nora brought over something for y'all to eat and left it in the refrigerator. I figured you two needed your sleep, so I unplugged the phones from the wall before I left.

Aunt Maggie

I waited until after Richard and I had showered and eaten the ham, mashed potatoes, and biscuits from Aunt Nora before plugging the phone back in, and wasn't a bit surprised when it rang at once. I wasn't surprised by who it was calling, either.

"Burnette residence," I said.

"It's about time!"

"Hi, Vasti."

"Why haven't you been answering the phone?"

"We just got up." Not wanting to get Aunt Maggie in trouble, I decided not to mention the unplugged phone.

"What on Earth is happening to this family? Ilene in jail, the triplets in the hospital—"

"Are they back in the hospital?" I asked. "They left before I did, and I thought they were all right."

"Oh, I guess they're fine now. I just want to know how I'm supposed to put a wedding together in the midst of all this."

I wanted to know what she expected me to do about it all, but instead of saying so, I took a deep breath then said, "Vasti, I have the utmost confidence in your abilities to see this through."

There was a pause, then she said, "That's sweet, Laurie Anne," with just a hint of suspicion in her voice. "I don't suppose you've found out anything that will get Ilene out of jail, have you?"

"If I had, Vasti, do you really think I'd have been sleeping?"

"I suppose not." She sighed theatrically. "I guess I'll get through this somehow, even though I just found out that Roger has a road trip planned. He's leaving tomorrow morning and won't be back until Thursday afternoon. How can he leave town now when the wedding is on Saturday?"

I took another deep breath. "Maybe he realizes that it will be easier for you if he gets out of your way and lets you handle things."

Again she sounded suspicious when she said, "Maybe you're right. Anyway, this has been nice, but I don't have time to chat anymore. I have a million things to do. Bye now!"

She hung up before I could remind her that she had been the one to call me.

"Laura," Richard said, "you don't have to be polite all the time."

"I know," I said, "but Vasti means well. At least, I'm pretty sure that she does." I shook all thoughts of that particular cousin out of my head. "Anyway, what shall we do today?"

"Nothing," he said firmly.

"Nothing? We still haven't figured out who was supposed to get killed."

"And we're not going to, not today anyway."

"But—"

"But nothing. We're both tired—we've been going full steam ever since we got to Byerly, and it's time to take a breather. You know you think better when you've had a chance to relax."

"Yes, but—"

He hushed me up with a big kiss and said, "Every time you say something related to Ilene or Tom Honeywell, I'm going to kiss you."

"This is supposed to discourage me?"

"No, it's supposed to distract you."

And distract me he did. Thoroughly enough that we decided to unplug the phone again. After that, we sat and read, and then went out and got ice cream. Aunt Maggie showed up around dinnertime, and the three of us went out to Fork-in-the-Road for barbecue. We watched a little television that night, then went to bed early. After sleeping so late, Richard and I weren't quite ready for sleep yet, but we were ready to be distracted some more.

All in all, it was the best day we had had in Byerly that trip. Richard was right—we needed it.

Chapter 32

When I woke up the next morning, I really felt ready to get back to work. Richard and I were trying to decide who we could talk to about the Ramblers when the phone rang.

"Burnette residence," I said.

"Laurie Anne? This is Idelle."

"How are you feeling this morning?"

"Still stiff, but much better, thanks to you and Richard. I don't know what would have happened if y'all hadn't shown up."

"I'm just glad we were handy. How are Carlelle and Odelle?"

"Same as me. Stiff, but doing fine."

"I'm glad to hear it. What's the word on Slim?"

"I guess he's all right. I hear he went on that road trip with Roger."

I was surprised that she sounded so casual about Slim, considering how much she and her sisters had been fighting over him.

"The reason I'm calling, Laurie Anne, is that there's something we'd like to tell to you about the night Tom Honeywell was killed. What with Carlelle's rib and Odelle's ankle bothering them, could you come over here?"

"Of course. We'll be right over."

There was a pause from the other line. Then Idelle said, "No offense to Richard, but do you think you can come by yourself? This is kind of personal. Girl talk."

"No problem," I said. "I'll be right over." I hung up and explained the situation to Richard.

He said, "In that case, could you drop me at Aunt Nora's house? We've mined Junior, Roger, and the Ramblers themselves for information, but we haven't delved into the full depths of Byerly's gossip mill. For that, we need Aunt Nora."

That sounded like a good idea to me, so I grabbed my pocketbook, drove Richard to Aunt Nora's house, and reminded him to go to the back door and knock instead of ringing the front door bell like he was company. Then I drove to the triplets' place.

When Idelle opened the door to the small house they rented, the first thing I noticed was that the three sisters were wearing the same outfit, blue jeans and red gingham shirts. Their hair didn't exactly match, but that was because of the bandage on Idelle's forehead. The feud was definitely over.

Actually the triplets' house wasn't all that small. It couldn't be, not and hold all the clothes my cousins had. What with them being the same size, you would have thought that they could have fewer clothes than three mismatched sisters, but the opposite was true. Before their feud started, and now that it was over, they needed three of everything so they could dress alike.

"Hey, Laurie Anne," Idelle said, and gave me a hug. Then I had to go hug Odelle, who was folding clothes on the couch with her foot propped on a stack of pillows, and Carlelle, who was sewing buttons on a blouse while sitting carefully upright in a wing chair to protect her cracked rib.

"You just sit down here next to me," Odelle said, patting the couch.

"What would you like to drink?" Idelle said.

"Iced tea?" I said.

"You bet. How about you two?"

They both nodded, and Carlelle said, "Idelle, don't you want me to help?"

"Nope, you stay right where you're at. The doctor said you're not to move around any more than you have to, and you don't want anybody as cute as he is mad at you."

"All right," she said.

"Idelle has been waiting on us hand and foot," Carlelle said. "You'd think she hadn't been in an accident at all."

"How is her head?" I asked.

"Healing nicely," Odelle said. "The doctor said there won't be much of a scar at all, and there better not be, or I'm going to have words with him."

"Now don't you worry your head about that," Idelle said, coming back in with four glasses. "I'm going to be fine." She passed out the iced tea, making sure to leave glasses within her sisters' reaches.

"I see y'all are getting along together again," I said. The truth was, they were being so sweet to each other it was making me a little ill. The only thing that kept me from saying something sarcastic was remembering how they had been just a few days ago.

They nodded solemnly and in unison.

"You bet we are," Idelle said. "That accident set us back on our heels."

Odelle joined in, "Coming that close to meeting our

Maker made us realize just how silly we were being. I just
can't imagine how I'd have felt if Carlelle or Idelle had really
been hurt. Or even—"

"Don't even say it!" Carlelle said. "Just the idea gives me
nightmares." She shuddered, and the shudder was echoed
by her sisters.

"And to be fighting over a man!" Idelle said. "It all comes
from breaking our own rule."

"You see, Laurie Anne," Odelle said, "ever since we
started dating, we've had this rule. If more than one of us is
interested in the same fellow, we *all* give him up."

"And this is the first time you've broken that rule?" I
said.

"Lord, no!" Carlelle said with a laugh. "We've broken it
more times than I can count. There was Cameron when he
first came to work at the mill. Both Idelle and I had our eye
on him."

Idelle said, "And when Tucker started delivering our
mail, especially when he wears those shorts in the summer.
Odelle and I raced for the mailbox every day."

"And that dentist in Hickory," Odelle said. "Carlelle and
I had our teeth cleaned so many times that I'm surprised we
have any teeth left."

"The thing is, Slim was the first one all *three* of use were
interested in. The other sister could always bring the two of
us to our senses before now. I can't imagine why we were
being so silly. Men come and go, but sisters are forever."

I admit I felt a little defensive right then. I considered
my relationship with Richard more than a passing fancy.

Carlelle must have realized how that had sounded. "We
don't mean you and Richard, of course."

"Anybody can see that the two of you were meant for one

another," Idelle put in. "It was different with Slim. He was just a fling."

"Hardly more than a schoolgirl crush," Odelle said.

"An infatuation," Carlelle said. "He's nice enough, I guess, but not worth losing the love of my sisters."

The three of them looked at one another, nodding, and I swear that it was all I could do to keep a straight face. I knew that they were sincere, but sometimes even sincerity sounds pretty sappy. Not that Richard and I were any less sappy, but we did try to keep it to ourselves.

"I'm really glad that y'all have mended all your fences," I said. "So why was it Idelle called me? Something about Tom Honeywell?"

"That's right," Idelle said. "The three of us have been talking over everything since the accident, and we figured out something that might help you."

Odelle said, "You remember that night Tom was killed? We were there at that dance at the Jamboree, but we weren't talking to one another."

Carlelle said, "We were too busy chasing after Slim, each of us trying to get him alone long enough to hook him. Well, I was getting something to drink when that Tom Honeywell came up. I thought that he was going to say something ugly like he usually did, but what he said was that he had heard one of my sisters making a date with Slim for later that night. He said he wasn't sure which sister it was, but that they were supposed to meet at the Ramblers' bus, and he didn't have to draw me a picture about what they were going to be doing out there. I wasn't about to let that happen, so I figured that if I stuck with Slim like glue, he wouldn't be able to slip out with Idelle or Odelle. What I didn't know was that—"

"Was that Tom had told me the exact same tale," Odelle said. "And I did the same thing that she did. I wouldn't let Slim out of my sight that whole night."

I turned to Idelle. "I suppose he told you the same thing."

She nodded. "So I was right there with Slim and the other two."

Carlelle giggled. "Poor fellow. We didn't hardly give him a chance to go pee by himself that night."

"At first we figured it was just Tom having a joke at our expense," Idelle said. "But then we got to thinking. A couple of times that night Slim said something about checking on the bus, that he wanted to make sure it was locked up and all."

"Really?" I said, starting to realize the implications.

Odelle said, "Of course, every time he said that, we thought he was meaning to sneak out and meet one of us, so we'd drag him off or start to tell him something or do anything so he wouldn't go. And he never did. The only place he went that night was to his car, and we watched him drive off."

"So he never checked the bus," I said slowly.

The triplets nodded enthusiastically.

"So Tom *knew* he had a clear shot at getting to the bus so he could steal some of the equipment."

The triplets nodded again, and Idelle asked, "Does this mean anything to you?"

"You bet it does. It means that the killer thought he was shooting Slim!" I wasn't sure how Tom had known Slim was planning to go out to the bus, but it was reasonable to think that he had overheard it at the dance. That was a detail I could track down later.

"But why would anybody want to shoot Slim?" Carlelle wanted to know.

"I don't know," I said, "but I'm going to find out." I finished my iced tea, thanked them profusely, and headed for the Byerly Police Station. Now that I knew who the real target was, surely I could figure out who wanted Slim dead. Then we could get Ilene out of jail, with two days to spare before the wedding!

Chapter 33

I burst into the police station and called out, "Junior!" before I saw she was talking to a woman I didn't know.

"Is it an emergency?" Junior asked.

"No."

"Then would you mind waiting out back with your cousin for a minute?"

"Of course not. Sorry."

Ilene's cell looked even less like a cell than it had before. The carpet remnant Trey had found even matched Ilene's bedspread. This time, Ilene was by herself.

"How are you doing?" she asked.

"I just got back from seeing the triplets," I said.

"I heard about the accident. Are they all right?"

"Bruised a bit, but fine. And they've finally stopped fighting."

"It's about time."

"They told me something interesting," I said, and told her what the triplets had said.

Ilene shook her head. "That sounds like Tom, all right, setting people at each other's throats. The more I find out about him, the more I realize what a mean son of a bitch he was. I cannot believe what a fool I was to run around with him."

"Ilene, I don't know a woman on Earth who hasn't dated the wrong man at least once. I should tell you about one fellow Vasti dated." Just then, I heard the door to the police station open and close, and Junior called out my name. "I've got to go see Junior. I'll tell you about him later."

Junior was at her desk, leaned back in her chair with her feet up. I knew her well enough to know that her position meant that she had just found out something interesting.

"Well?" I said.

"Well, yourself," she said. "You're the one who came rushing in here like your house was on fire."

"I know, but you've got something, too."

"Maybe I do, but I don't know that it's connected with what you're doing."

"Junior!"

"You just go ahead and tell me your news."

"Be that way. I think I've figured out who the intended victim was." I told her how Tom had engineered it so that Slim wouldn't go out to the bus. "What do you think?"

"I think you've got a pretty good idea there. And it just so happens that your idea and my new information have something in common."

"What's that?"

"That woman who just left is with the company that insured Slim Grady's car."

"She got moving quickly."

"They do move quickly sometimes. Like when it looks like an accident wasn't an accident at all."

"Are you serious?"

She nodded. "I had a hunch, so I got my mechanic to take

a look at Slim's car. The reason his brakes failed is that
somebody cut the brake line. No brake fluid."

"Which means that somebody has tried to kill Slim twice.
Junior, we've got to warn him!"

"I already thought of that, but he and the other Ramblers left yesterday to play a club in South Carolina."

"Doesn't Aunt Ruby Lee know how to get in touch with
them?"

"She does, but there was no answer at the hotel. Either
they're still in bed with the phone off the hook, or they're
already on the way back. If I don't get in touch with him
before he gets back to Byerly, I'll catch him this evening.
Truth is, I think he'd be better off if he stayed away. The
first attempt on his life was in Rocky Shoals, and the second
was here in Byerly. I imagine that our killer is local."

"Unless it was one of the other Ramblers," I said, realizing that I had only considered them as victims.

"Do you have any reason to think it was?"

I thought about it. "Not really. I don't know about the
night Tom was shot, but all of them were together the night
of the accident, and I was there, too. Slim drove to Roger's
that evening, and his brakes were fine then. There's no way
anybody could have slipped away from the bar in Statesville
and driven back to cut the brake line without it being noticed."

"Then I'm guessing that Slim is safe enough for now, and
we might find out who the murderer is before he gets back."

"Have you called Chief Monroe yet?"

"Not yet. Would you like to sit in?"

"You know I would."

"All right, but be quiet. This is official police business."

"Yes, Junior," I said meekly.

She reached for the phone to dial the number of the police station in Rocky Shoals. "Hey, Lloyd, this is Junior over in Byerly. How are you doing over there? . . . I'm doing all right. . . . Daddy's fine, too. I'll be sure and tell him you asked after him. . . . Well, no, this isn't strictly a social call. I found out something that might help you out with that Honeywell case. Did you hear about that car accident we had over here the night before last? . . . That's right. That accident just didn't sound right to me, so I had a mechanic check out the car. It looks like that brake line was cut. . . . Yes, I'm pretty sure it happened before the accident, not during. For one thing, it looks like a clean cut, and for another, Slim Grady says the brakes went out. The passengers confirm his story. . . . No, he hadn't been drinking. He'd had a beer or two earlier that evening, but his blood alcohol level was way below the limit. . . . Of course I checked for priors—Lloyd, you're not trying to teach your grandmama how to suck eggs, are you?"

Junior rolled her eyes at me, then went on. "Anyway, the reason I'm telling you all of this is that it looks like somebody was trying to put Slim Grady away. And since there was already some doubt about whether Tom Honeywell was the one who was supposed to get shot, I thought you might want to take another look at your case. I've found out that Slim Grady was supposed to be on that bus that night. . . . Laurie Anne Fleming tracked it down for me. . . . She found it out from her cousins the Holt sisters. . . . Of course they're Ilene Bailey's cousins, too. . . . Yes, I think the information is reliable."

It took every bit of self-control I had to keep from saying something at that point, but I had promised Junior.

Junior took a deep breath. "No, I can't *prove* that the car crash is connected to the shooting, but it stands to reason, doesn't it? How many murders do we have in a given year, especially involving the same group of people? . . . No, I can't *prove* that Slim was the one who was supposed to be shot, but I've got a hunch— . . . I know hunches aren't formal police procedure, but I'll put my hunches against your procedure any day of the week. . . . I know that's not how you run your department, Lloyd. . . . Of course I'll continue to keep Ilene Bailey in custody, unless you're saying you don't trust me to. . . . I'm glad to hear that, Lloyd. I'll be sure to let you know if I learn anything more *definite.*"

She hung up the phone and took several deep breaths. "That man has got a *bad* case of blindness."

"He's not going to let Ilene go, is he?" I asked, though I didn't need to.

Junior shook her head. "He said he'd tell the district attorney on the case about my theory, but he's satisfied that he has the right person for the crime. He doesn't doubt that somebody tried to kill Slim, but he won't accept that the two are connected."

"Damn!"

"What does he need, a dadblasted diagram? What is the matter with that man? A new idea would bust his head wide open."

"You told me that he wasn't stupid," I couldn't resist saying.

"That was before he talked like I was a moron for thinking that the shooting and the car accident just might be connected. He's going to be laughing out of the other side of his face when this is all over."

I had to grin at her indignation. "Forget about Monroe. Now that we know Slim was the target, all we have to do is figure out who wants him dead. So I guess the next step is to check into Slim's background." I noticed that Junior was looking at me funny, and realized why. "Sorry, Junior. I didn't mean to step on your toes. This is your case now."

"Yes it is," she said sternly "So you're going to let me take over, right?"

"Um . . ."

"You do trust me to do it on my own, don't you?"

It was like pulling teeth to say it, but I said, "Of course I do, Junior. I'll stay out of the way."

Junior was looking at me speculatively for a minute, then grinned. "I'm impressed. I didn't think you'd ever agree to that."

"Don't you want me to?" I asked, a little confused.

"It's what I *should* want. Letting an amateur investigate a murder attempt isn't exactly in the book. But like I said, I don't play by the book. You've helped me out before, and I don't think it would be fair to make you back out now. Besides, I didn't say one word when you were interfering in Lloyd's case, so it wouldn't be right if I made you stay out of mine."

"Thank you, Junior. So where do we start?"

"With a background check on Slim."

"I've spoken to Roger already, and he didn't help. Richard is talking to Aunt Nora now, so we can call and see if he's found anything out."

"No offense, Laurie Anne, but there are official channels I can go through. They might not be as efficient as your Aunt Nora—"

"All right, all right, I get the hint. I thought you had already told me everything you had."

"I told you what I've got in the files, but that's a long way from all the information available to us professionals. First off, I think I'll call that insurance lady who was here. You have to fill out all kinds of paperwork to get insured these days, and under the circumstances, I'll bet she'll share."

What followed was a long series of phone calls, mostly Junior talking to people and asking them to send her information. After the insurance company, she called Social Security, the registry of motor vehicles, the clerk in charge of local taxes, Slim's landlady, and Aunt Ruby Lee to see what job records Roger kept on the band members. Pretty much everybody said they'd check their files and then get back to her.

"There," she said after the last phone call. "The wheels are in motion. Isn't police work exciting?"

I yawned an exaggerated yawn. "You bet. How do you stand the pressure?"

"I do have to pace myself."

"I'll bet. What's next?"

"More routine, of course."

I remembered the lecture she had given me the other day. "Let me guess. Since Slim drove his car to Roger's apartment with no problem, the car was probably tampered with there. So the next step is for us to interview the people around there to see if they saw anything unusual the night before last. Right?"

"Almost. *I'm* going to talk to Roger's neighbors. *You're* going to stay here and listen to the phones, and wait for information about Slim."

"Junior!"

"I'm serious, Laurie Anne. I cannot have you riding around in the squad car acting like a police officer. For one, the city council would pitch a fortified fit if they found out, especially Big Bill Walters."

"Arthur's on the city council—he could take of them," I said. Especially if Vasti told him to.

Junior went on as if I hadn't spoken. "For another, I don't need your help asking questions. What I need is for you to stay here." Before I could argue, she said, "You know we don't have the staff in Byerly like they do in Boston. It's only me, Mark Pope, and Trey in the summers. Well, Mark is on vacation and Trey and I are working overtime to make sure that there's somebody here with Ilene all the time so she can be here in Byerly, like you Burnettes wanted. I can't leave her here alone, and I can't take her with me, because if I did either and Lloyd found out, he'd take her right back to Rocky Shoals."

"Don't you think he'd be a mite upset if he found out you let Ilene's own cousin guard her?" I shot back.

"Not if I deputize you."

I opened my mouth to argue some more, but what came out was, "All right, Junior."

"Moreover . . ." she started to say, then said, "All right?"

"All right. You've convinced me." She looked suspicious, so I added, "I mean it." It would have been more fun to ride with her, but Junior had cut me an awful lot of slack in the past, including deputizing me once before. This was the least I could do. Besides which, I didn't really have any ideas for my next step anyway. If I did think of something, I could always send Richard.

Junior swore me in as a Byerly deputy, then spent a few minutes telling me what to do and showing me how to use the radio and the fax machine. Basically, I was supposed to call her on the radio if any important phone calls came in, and not go anywhere. It was only ten o'clock, and she said that Trey would be in by twelve-thirty and he could either get me lunch or spell me while I got my own. Then she left.

After Junior was gone, I went into the back to tell Ilene what was going on. I had thought I'd stay with her to keep her company, but she was in the middle of writing a new song, and though she was polite, she really didn't want me around.

So I went back to Junior's desk to sit and wait. Well, I did call Richard over at Aunt Nora's to catch him up. He said that Aunt Nora said there wasn't much gossip about Slim, other than speculation on why there wasn't much gossip.

Since I had the car, he said he'd stay with Aunt Nora until he could get a ride to the police station. He assured me that this decision had nothing to do with the cookies Aunt Nora was baking or the lunch she had promised to make for him. We traded a volley of Shakespeare versus Southern-ism, which I won, and hung up. Then I sat and waited.

Chapter 34

It didn't take long for me to realize that I never wanted to be a police officer. Hanging around the station waiting for somebody to do something illegal just didn't appeal to me. Oh, I did get to sign for some envelopes from messengers and make sure there was enough paper when faxes came in, but since Junior hadn't told me to look at anything, I thought I better not. That meant that all there was for me to do was to sit and *not* look at potentially useful information.

It's a sign of how bored I was that when Vasti walked in, I was actually glad to see her.

"Laurie Anne, what on Earth are you doing here? I thought you were trying to get Ilene out of jail in time for the wedding."

I was a little offended, both because of the implied criticism and because it seemed to me that there were other reasons to get Ilene out of jail than for her to go to a wedding. "Junior is out tracking down some leads, and she deputized me to keep an eye on things here. Are you here to visit Ilene?"

"Visit? Some of us don't have time to visit. Aunt Ruby Lee and the seamstress are meeting me here for Ilene's final fitting." She looked at her watch and sighed theatrically. "They should be here now."

Aunt Ruby Lee and a woman I didn't recognize came in just then, but before Aunt Ruby Lee could introduce the woman to me or even say hello, Vasti whisked them to Ilene's cell. I decided that the better part of valor was to stay out of their way. Maybe thirty minutes later, Vasti rushed the seamstress out the door again, but Aunt Ruby Lee stopped to drop off the information Roger had about Slim and find out why I was there.

I told Aunt Ruby Lee what we had found out, and though she seemed happy at the news, she seemed a little distracted. "Aunt Ruby Lee," I finally said, "are you all right?"

"I guess so," she said.

"You better put a smile on that face," Vasti said. "What kind of wedding pictures are you going to take with a frown like that?"

Aunt Ruby Lee didn't answer her, just stared out the window for a little while. Then she said, "Girls, am I doing the right thing? Marrying Roger again, I mean?"

Vasti gasped. "Aunt Ruby Lee, how can you ask such a thing two days before the wedding? All the arrangements have been made! Laurie Anne will get Ilene out of jail in time!"

"I'm not talking about Ilene," Aunt Ruby Lee said. "I'm talking about me and Roger. It didn't work the first time. What business do I have thinking that it will work this time?"

"Well," I said, both to cut Vasti off and give myself time to think, "you and Roger have both changed, and for the better, I think. Y'all know the mistakes you've made in the past."

Aunt Ruby Lee snorted. "All too well. What I don't know is whether or not we'll make them again."

"I don't know, Aunt Ruby Lee. You're the only one who can answer that question."

She nodded. "Lord knows that I don't want to put me and the kids through another divorce. Maybe this stuff with Ilene was a sign. Maybe Roger and I aren't meant to get married."

"But—" Vasti started to say.

I jumped in with, "I don't think God plays games like that, Aunt Ruby Lee, I really don't. But if you're not sure about this, then maybe you should put it off for a while."

She nodded.

"But—" Vasti started to say.

I said, "Why don't you take some time to be alone for a while and think. Ilene is all right here."

"You're right, Laurie Anne," Aunt Ruby Lee said. "Things have been moving so fast that I haven't had any time to myself. I think I'll go—"

"Don't tell us," I said, more to keep Vasti from finding out than anything else. "Just go and be by yourself."

"I'll do just that," she said, and headed purposely out the door.

"But we have to go to the florist," Vasti said in a stunned tone and started toward the door.

"Vasti!" I said, and stepped in her path. "Did it not *once* ever occur to you that Aunt Ruby Lee might have other things to worry about right now? Her daughter is in jail for murder, for heaven's sake!"

"But you're going to find the real murderer, aren't you?"

"I'm trying as hard as I can, but that's not the point. Be-

sides which, maybe Aunt Ruby Lee is right. Maybe marrying Roger again would be a mistake."

"What about the wedding arrangements?"

"This is Aunt Ruby Lee's life we're talking about! If she
decides she doesn't want to marry Roger, then I don't want
to hear one word from you. Not one!"

"But—" I saw her swallow. "It's just that—" Again she
swallowed whatever it was she had been about to say. "All
right. I see what you're saying. Aunt Ruby Lee being happy
is the most important thing."

"Good."

"I didn't mean to push her."

"I know you didn't," even though I wasn't all that sure.

"People usually seem to like it when I'm in charge, so I
guess I've just gotten into the habit."

She was right. She took over automatically these days,
but it hadn't always been that way, and it wouldn't be that
way now if we hadn't let her get away with it before.

She went on, "It just seems like people have come to expect it of me, and I hate to disappoint them."

"I know what you mean," I had to say. "We *have* kind of
assumed that you would take care of the parties and organizing. Easier than doing it ourselves, I guess. Which isn't really fair to you." I shrugged. "This detective stuff has been
the same for me."

"The only thing is, I like running parties and things. I really do." She cocked her head. "Do you not like detecting?"

"I guess I do," I said. I thought back over the frustra-
tions involved in trying to get Ilene out of jail, and even so, I
had enjoyed much of it. "Oh, who am I trying to fool? You
know I do. I don't know why, but I do."

"That's how I am with parties. They're an awful lot of

work, and sometimes I think I'm going to just go crazy, but I keep doing it." Then she added in a diffident tone, "I thought I had done a pretty good job before."

"No, Vasti," I said. "You don't do a pretty good job. You do an excellent job. The garden party you threw when I was in town last summer, and that party at the nursing home the Christmas before last, and Aunt Ruby Lee's bridal shower—they were all great. You throw wonderful parties. It's just that sometimes you get carried away."

"I suppose you're right. Do you really think she's going to call off the wedding?"

"I don't know. It could go either way at this point. I'll tell you one thing. I'm going to do my darnedest to make sure Ilene is out of jail in time for the wedding, because I don't want something like that making Aunt Ruby Lee's decision for her."

"And I'll have the wedding ready if she wants one. I swear I don't know what we're going to do with all that punch if she doesn't. I wonder if Clifford and Liz are ready to tie the knot yet? Or maybe Aunt Edna and Caleb?" Her voice trailed off, and then she looked at me with a grin. "Well, we have to have a party of some kind with all that food."

"I know you'll think of something, Vasti."

"I always do."

"Yes, you do. And I respect you for that." She looked surprised that I had said it, but it was true, even though I hadn't thought of it that way before. That seemed like a good time for a hug, and I guess Vasti thought so, too, because she hugged me right back.

Chapter 35

Junior came in carrying several Hardee's bags about then, and Trey was right on her heels. Vasti remembered a couple dozen things she had to get people to do, and left.

Junior handed one bag of food to Trey and said, "Why don't you keep Ilene company while she eats?" Somehow he kept from running in his eagerness to obey her. To me she said, "I hope you've got something here," she said. "I have got to get your cousin out of my jail."

"I take it you didn't have much luck?" I said.

"Well, I wouldn't say that. I found a dog somebody had reported missing, which had been found by somebody else. And I think I talked a woman who's being abused into getting some help. That last part is just between you, me, and the gatepost."

"Absolutely," I said. She hadn't named any names, but I could easily have figured it out from the neighborhood she had been visiting.

She went on. "Unfortunately, I didn't find anybody who saw anything suspicious around the parking lot when Slim's car was tampered with."

"Don't you get frustrated?"

She shrugged. "All part of the game. Daddy taught me a

long time ago that patience counts for a lot in this job. What information did you get?"

I pointed to the stack of faxes and messenger envelopes. "There it is."

"Didn't you look at any of it?"

"I didn't think I was supposed to."

"Then I think you've got me beat in the patience department." She handed me one of the other Hardee's bags. "Help yourself to a hamburger, and we'll see what we've got."

She grabbed a burger of her own, and then picked up the first sheet on the stack. "This is the application Slim filled out when he got his apartment. Only his real name isn't Slim, of course, but I knew that already."

"What is his real name?"

"Horatio."

"No wonder he likes 'Slim.' "

"According to this, before he moved to Byerly, he lived in Atlanta for six years. He used to be a mechanic before turning musician."

"That's right," I said. "He mentioned that."

"I've got a friend in the Atlanta police force we can call if we don't come up with anything else." The next sheet. "According to the form he filled out for Roger, he played with a couple of country music bands in Atlanta before joining the Ramblers."

"Maybe somebody was mad about him leaving their group?" I speculated. "Were any of his former bands at the Jamboree?"

"None of the names look familiar, but band names tend to change a lot. We can check on that later if we need to." The next sheet. "A list of his previous jobs and employers, going back to his getting out of high school." She skimmed the page. "This is interesting. He used to work in Rocky Shoals."

"Really? I didn't think Slim was from around here."

"He's not. He went to high school in Georgia, but ended up working for the county maintaining school buses."

That rang a disquieting bell. "When was that?"

"When he was right out of high school. About fifteen years ago." Junior looked at me, and I knew she had caught the same thing I had.

"You don't suppose?" I said.

"Could be." She scrambled around in the papers. "The insurance people must have checked on previous accidents." She read silently for a minute or two.

"Well?" I said, not at all patiently.

"It's not here, but it might be beyond the time limit. Or maybe he didn't report it to them since it wasn't his fault and it wasn't his vehicle."

"How can we find out for sure?"

"Hank Parker at the *Gazette* would know. I'll call him." Junior dialed his number. "Hank, this is Junior Norton, and I need a favor.... Yes, I know what quid pro quo means, but I seem to recall that you owe me a couple of quids already. Do you remember that party I saw you at? ... I know you were just on an assignment, but it would look bad if folks in town found out." I was hoping she'd say more, but instead she said, "But we won't talk about that now, Hank. I need some information about the Rocky Shoals bus crash. Have you got any files on it? ... Good. I'll just wait, if that's all right." There was a long pause. "I'm still here.... Does it give the name of the fellow who was driving the bus? ... That's what I thought.... No, I don't have any comment on why I want to know. Remember that party? . . . I have now forgotten all about it. Bye, Hank."

"Party?" I had to ask when Junior hung up the phone.

"I don't remember any party," she said with a grin.

I turned back to the business at hand. "So who was the driver?"

"The driver was Ray Grady. Ray was short for Horatio. AKA, Slim Grady."

Neither of us said anything for a long time, but then I said, "That's it. That's got to be it. Somebody must have recognized Slim at the Jamboree, somebody who has been blaming him all these years."

"Maybe," Junior said.

"Come on, Junior. Are you saying that you don't have a hunch about this? That bus wreck *has* to be why somebody has been trying to kill Slim."

"I'll admit that it looks like a good bet," she said, and before I could object further, she added, "All right, I think that's probably our motive. Of course, that gives us an awful lot of suspects."

"True," I admitted. "What was it, twenty or thirty kids who died on that bus? So we have to consider any of their friends or relatives."

"Which means most of the people in Rocky Shoals."

I nodded, thinking of all of them I already knew about. "Homer Caldwell mentioned losing a nephew he lost, and there was a bereaved mother and father, too. Forrest Jefferson's best friend and her boyfriend were killed."

"That Maureen Shula who won the novice competition at the Jamboree had a cousin who died," Junior added. "They said something about that in the *Gazette* story about her winning. Florence Easterly used to live in Rocky Shoals, and I think she lost somebody, too."

Having Ilene's lawyer as a suspect bothered me, but not as much as another person that came to mind. "What about Lloyd Monroe?" I said.

"Laurie Anne, I know you don't like the man, but isn't this carrying it a bit too far?"

"I'm serious. If he was as upset about that accident as you said, why couldn't he be holding a grudge against Slim Grady?"

"Because he knew it wasn't Slim's fault, and besides which, it was himself he blamed, not Slim."

"Maybe," I said, "but Monroe had access to the dressing rooms at the Jamboree, and if he was guilty, it would explain why he hasn't been more reasonable about Ilene. Do you know where he was the night Tom was shot, or the night of Slim's accident?"

"I don't usually ask other police officers for their alibis," Junior said dryly.

"Then you don't know that it wasn't him." Before she could object further, I added, "I'm not saying it was either, but I think we ought to consider him a possibility."

"A very slim possibility," she said, but she didn't argue any further. "I think that the families of the victims would be more likely candidates."

"Granted. Who do we start with?"

"With Mr. Grady himself. The Ramblers are due back in town this evening, and I don't see any reason to go traipsing around Rocky Shoals until we talk to him. He was there— he'd know if anybody blamed him."

I checked my watch. It was only one o'clock. "That's

hours away. Isn't there something we can do between now and then?"

"Patience, remember?"

I nodded. "I know, but it's Thursday, and if I don't get Ilene out of jail soon enough to keep from canceling the wedding, I'm never going to hear the end of it." If Aunt Ruby Lee didn't call it off anyway, I thought to myself.

She thought for a minute, then said, "I suppose you could go to the *Gazette* office, and see if that quid pro quo I just collected extends to Hank giving you copies of the articles about the crash. And maybe the following weeks, to see if anybody wrote letters to the editor suggesting that they lynch Slim."

"Okay," I said, even though I knew Junior was just trying to keep me busy. It might give us something to go on. "I'll take Richard with me. He and Hank get along pretty well."

"Good enough," Junior said. "Just remember that you're still a deputy, which means that you have to tell me anything you find out."

"Aye, aye," I said, and faked a salute.

"Watch it," she said, wagging a warning finger. "I'll dock your paycheck if you don't behave."

Chapter 36

Even though Junior's methods had meant finding out something I never would have guessed, I was glad to be out of the station and back on my own. Having to hurry up and wait had never come easily to me. Besides, I knew that the cookies Aunt Nora was going to give me would be a lot tastier than the hamburger Junior had supplied.

Despite the cookies, I wasted little time in picking up Richard and getting back in the car to head for the *Gazette*. For dramatic reasons, I let him report on the gossip on Slim first. Despite several phone calls from Aunt Nora to Byerly's best gossips, there wasn't anything useful.

After he was done, I said, "It's a shame that you didn't check around Rocky Shoals instead."

"Oh?"

"Slim used to live there."

"What am I missing?"

"You remember how he told us he used to be a mechanic? He forgot to mention that he worked on the school buses in Rocky Shoals."

"The bus crash?"

"Got it in one."

Instead of a Shakespeare quote, he let out a low whistle,

which showed how surprised he was. "I'm surprised he went to the Jamboree."

"He didn't know what it was for. Remember him reading that awful poem in the Jamboree program."

"And he didn't say anything."

"Would you? Under those circumstances? I can't imagine living with something like that. I bet he was scared to death that somebody was going to recognize him. Do you remember that girl who screamed when she saw him, and how he jumped? I bet he thought she recognized him as the bus driver, not as a Rambler."

" 'Suspicion always haunts the guilty mind; the thief doth fear each bush an officer.' *Henry VI, Part Three*, Act V, Scene 6."

"He was as jumpy as a long-tailed cat in a room full of rocking chairs." I looked at him. "I think I win that one."

He nodded, and adjusted my score. "So why didn't anybody recognize him?"

"I imagine he looks different after fifteen years, but I'm guessing that one person did recognize him, and that's the one who's been trying to kill him."

We got to the *Gazette* office, and between Junior's threat, Richard's friendship, and my veiled offer of a big story real soon, Hank was convinced to pull out the files from around the bus crash. Rocky Shoals had not had a newspaper at the time, so the main coverage had been in the *Gazette*.

The story was even more chilling than I had remembered. So many young people killed, and several terribly injured. One was crippled, and two others probably still had scars. When it happened, I was so young that it just seemed kind of exciting, the biggest thing to happen around Byerly. Now, I was shaken by the pain of the people involved.

There were descriptions of how Homer Caldwell had found his nephew's crumpled body, of one woman's total collapse when she found out both of her twin boys had been killed, of how one girl had survived the crash only to die in the hospital a week later. There were pictures from the funerals, and a heart-breaking photo of Forrest Jefferson leading her pitifully small class into the graduation ceremony.

At first I tried to write down the name of anybody mentioned as having lost a loved one, but I had to give up. There were just too many. As Junior had said, we had to consider almost everybody in Rocky Shoals a suspect.

"I'm surprised that nobody has picked up this story for a movie of the week," I said to Richard, trying to lighten the mood.

He wasn't fooled by my flippancy, and reached out for my hand. "It doesn't look like Slim was at fault at all. He was minding his own business when that Volkswagen passed him and made the truck swerve. He's even praised here for helping to pull survivors out of the bus."

"Some of these letters to the editor seem pretty angry."

"True," Richard admitted, "but they aren't really aimed at Slim. They're mostly talking about the bad roads."

I said, "People aren't always rational when somebody dies. Or about holding a grudge. What about in Othello? Iago never did have a good reason for hating Othello and getting him to murder his wife."

"Actually there is some textual evidence suggesting various motives."

"The point is that he blamed something on Othello and

took it out on him, the same way somebody must have blamed the bus crash on Slim."

"I guess," he said.

"That *must* be it," I said, but I wasn't convinced either. "Unless this is another dead end. I just can't think of anything else to try." Then I did think of something, but I didn't like it. "Richard, what if Tom Honeywell was the intended victim all along?"

"You've got to be kidding. Slim was supposed to be on the bus, not Tom."

"What if Slim is the murderer? What if Tom recognized him as the infamous bus driver, and tried to blackmail him. And Slim arranged to meet him on the bus to give him some of the Ramblers' equipment as the first payment. But Slim shot him instead."

Richard opened his mouth, but I'm not sure if he was going to agree with me or argue with me, because I quickly figured out half a dozen holes in that theory. "Never mind. Tom was younger than me, so I can't see how he could have recognized Slim, and the triplets kept Slim so busy he couldn't have gotten to the bus. Plus, if Slim had cut his own brake line, he'd have come up with some way to 'notice' it without running into a tree." I sighed and rubbed my head. "My ideas are getting more and more improbable."

" 'When you have eliminated the impossible, whatever remains, however improbable, must be the truth.' "

"Shakespeare?"

"Sherlock Holmes."

I nodded, glad that I didn't have to try to come up with a Southernism to match that, and started putting the newspapers back in order. "I better call the boss and see what she wants me to do next."

I told Junior what little we had found out, and she told me that I was off-duty until seven-thirty, at which time I was to meet her at the office so we could go see Slim. I relayed the message to Richard. "It's only four now, and I'm not hungry yet," I said.

"Then perhaps we should adjourn to our boudoir for a short time."

"For what possible reason?" I asked with a grin.

"Because I've never been intimate with an officer of the law."

"Is this an attraction?"

"It is."

"Then let's make like a tree and leave."

"That's not a Southernism."

We argued the point while we gave an understandably curious Hank Parker back his newspapers, and drove to Aunt Maggie's house. Somehow, once we got inside, we got distracted and never did get around to deciding the winner of that round.

Chapter 37

Richard and I got to the police station at seven-thirty on the dot. Junior hadn't actually said that Richard could come with us, but she hadn't said that he couldn't either. As it turned out, he did come and she didn't.

"Hi, boss," I said when I walked in the door. "Deputy Fleming reporting for duty." I expected a smart remark in return.

Instead Junior was frowning.

"What's the matter?" I asked. "Has anything happened to Slim?"

"No, Slim's fine. I talked to him about the brake line, and warned him to watch out. It's one of my deputies that's the problem." Seeing my expression, she said, "Not you. I just got off the phone with Mark Pope. He was supposed to be back from vacation tonight, and I was planning for him to stay with Ilene while we go talk to Slim. Only his car broke down in Myrtle Beach, and he can't get it fixed until sometime tomorrow. So he gets to lay on the beach another day while I'm stuck here by myself."

"What about Trey?" I asked.

"He promised to take my sister Pamela's three boys to the movies. If he disappoints Derek, Michael, and Kyle, they're going to tell Pamela, and Pamela is going to tell my Mama, and Mama is going to tell me. I could get away with it if it was an emergency, but Mama was a police chief's wife long enough to know the difference between a real emergency and something that could wait until tomorrow morning. And talking to Slim is going to have to wait until then."

I hated to say it, but at this point Aunt Ruby Lee's wedding was more important than my curiosity. "Couldn't I stay with Ilene, Junior? Like I did this afternoon."

"I've thought of that, Laurie Anne, but I can't get away with it this time. Big Bill Walters is coming over this evening to check over our accounts, and if he finds anybody other than an official Byerly police officer in charge, there'll be hell to pay. I'm stuck here, and that's all there is to it."

"Couldn't Richard and I go talk to Slim?" I asked, still worrying about time.

"Not as a deputy," she said. "Like I said this afternoon, if you went around asking police questions, they'd hang me up to dry."

"Then un-deputize me," I said, "and I can go talk to whoever I want."

She assumed a stern expression. "Laurie Anne Fleming, I'll have you know that law enforcement is a serious calling and not to be put on and off like a hat." Then she spoiled the effect by breaking out in a grin. "All right, I officially un-deputize you, but that doesn't mean that you don't have to tell me what you find out."

I said, "Since when do private citizens have to report their private conversations?"

"Since I'm threatening to kick their butts if they don't."

"No need for violence," Richard said in mock alarm. "We'll talk."

"All right, then," Junior said. "Get going."

It only took a few minutes to get to Slim's place. He rented half of a duplex in a part of town where a lot of single folks live. I saw that his light was on when we came up the walk, but could also hear loud country music coming from the open window, so I wasn't surprised when it took a few rings on the doorbell to get his attention. The music was turned down, and a second later, Slim opened the door.

"Hey there." He sounded friendly, but surprised.

"Hi, Slim. Can we come in?"

"Of course you can." He let us in, and waved us to a sagging but still comfortable couch. "Hope you weren't out there long. I had the music up kind of loud."

"We just rang the once," I lied politely.

"What can I do for you folks?"

I said, "I know Junior told you what she found out about your car wreck, and what she suspects about Tom Honeywell's shooting."

"She did, but I told her just like I told y'all that I don't think anybody is trying to kill me."

"But Slim, your brake line was cut."

"How can we be sure it wasn't cut in the accident?"

"Junior was pretty sure," I said. "And what about the night Tom Honeywell was shot? You were supposed to be on the bus, weren't you?"

"I had told Cotton and Al that I'd check to make sure the bus was locked," he admitted, "and I think that Tom was around when I said it, so I guess he really was trying to keep me away. But you're saying that one of the other people around us killed Tom, thinking it was me. That's crazy."

"Do you know who was around then?"

He shrugged. "It was a dance. Anybody could have heard."

That didn't sound very definite to me.

"Besides," he went on, "I can't imagine why anybody would want to hurt me."

"What about somebody from Rocky Shoals?" I said. "Somebody who remembers you?"

Slim was completely still for a long moment, not even breathing. Then he said, "I guess I shouldn't be surprised that you found that out. Roger's told me about some of the things you've done before."

"Actually, it was Junior who found out," I said.

He nodded. "I thought long and hard about moving back so close to Rocky Shoals, and I sure wish Roger had never agreed for us to go to the Jamboree. I was just glad that nobody remembered me."

"I think somebody did remember."

He cocked his head. "You think somebody is trying to kill me because of the bus wreck?"

"Don't you?"

He shook his head vigorously. "No, you're barking up the wrong tree. The people in Rocky Shoals never blamed me, not for a minute."

"Then why were you worried about somebody recognizing you?" Richard asked.

"Because I didn't want to dredge up bad memories. Rocky Shoals was a small place. For them to lose so many at once took the heart out of them. People were nice enough, but I know that every time one of them saw me, they were wondering why I was alive when their son or daughter wasn't."

"Was it them wondering," I asked, "or you?"

"Some of both, I guess. They say people who live through something awful, like concentration camps or a disaster, often feel bad about being alive. Survivor guilt. I think I've got some of that."

"But it wasn't your fault," Richard said. "Witnesses confirmed that. They said you were a hero for saving some of those who did make it."

Slim half smiled. "I've tried to tell myself that, time and time again. It's just hard. People don't always make sense, you know that."

"And that's why we think somebody blames you for the wreck," I said. "People don't always make sense."

He shook his head again. "I just can't accept that."

"Somebody *is* trying to kill you, Slim," I said. "If it isn't because of the bus crash, then why?"

Just for a second, I saw him hesitate. But then he said, "No, you must have it wrong. There's no reason for anybody to want me dead."

That was all he would say. He was very polite, even offered us something to drink, but Slim would not admit that anybody could have a reason to hurt him. He kept denying that anybody in Rocky Shoals would blame him for the bus wreck.

Finally Richard nudged me to let me know that it was time to give up and leave.

Chapter 38

"Slim's not telling us everything," I said to Richard as soon as we were back in the car.

"I know," he said. "Any ideas of what?"

"No." Then I started thinking about the articles about the bus crash we had read. "Richard, maybe we've been going about this the wrong way."

"Meaning that Slim wasn't the target? Or meaning that the bus crash wasn't the reason?"

"Neither. We've been assuming that somebody wants to kill Slim for revenge because he crashed the bus."

"Right."

"But as far as we can tell, nobody blamed Slim for the accident."

"Surely the murderer would hide his feelings."

"He or she could be faking it now, but why would he have faked it fifteen years ago? Even then, the only person who blamed Slim was Slim himself. Look at the way he's never let anybody get close to him. I think he's been punishing himself all these years."

"Could Honeywell's death have been a botched suicide?" Richard asked. "Maybe coming back to Rocky Shoals made Slim remember his guilt, and he went to the Ramblers' bus to kill himself. The bus would have been appropriate because the others died in a bus. Only when he found Tom there, they got into a fight and Slim accidentally shot Tom."

I thought about it, because I was ready to consider *any* possibility, but it sounded unlikely to me. "No, it doesn't fit with Slim's personality. Unless he's been faking it for the past year, he's a pretty nice guy. I suppose he might be willing to let Ilene stay in jail for his crime, hoping that she'd be found not guilty, but why would he cut his own brake line?"

"Another suicide attempt?"

"Maybe, but when did he do it? And what about the triplets? Even if he doesn't want to date one of them, I don't think he'd have risked their lives."

Richard shrugged. "I didn't think it made much sense, but it's the only thing we haven't considered."

"Nope, I had one other thought. If the killer doesn't blame Slim, then he must be trying to kill him for another reason, and that reason must have something to do with the bus crash."

"Like what?"

"Like maybe Slim knows who was driving the blue Volkswagen that caused the accident."

"What?"

"Junior told me that one of the survivors saw the Volkswagen, but couldn't make out the driver because she wasn't wearing her glasses. And the truck driver didn't have a chance to see the driver."

"Okay."

"But why couldn't Slim have seen him? When a car passes me on the highway, I usually have time to take a look, and it would take more time to pass a bus, because the bus is longer. Slim *should* have been able to see the driver, but he said that he didn't."

"So maybe he didn't. It was nighttime, and a bus is taller than a car. All he would have been able to see was the top of the Volkswagen."

"The Volkswagen was a convertible with the top down. He'd have been able to look right into it. When the truck came around the curve, the headlights would have lit it up bright as day."

"It's possible," Richard said, "but if he did see the driver, why didn't he tell anybody?"

"What if he knew the person? Maybe he didn't want to get anybody in trouble?" I shrugged my shoulders. "The only one who can answer that question is Slim."

We were passing a gas station, so I pulled into the parking lot and turned back in the direction from which we came.

"I take it that we're going to go ask him right now," Richard said.

"No time like the present. The wedding is supposed to be the day after tomorrow."

We were in sight of Slim's house, when a car pulled out of his driveway.

"Isn't that Slim now?" Richard asked.

"I think it is." I turned onto a side street to let him go by. "Did he see us?"

"I don't think so. Why?"

"I want to know where he's going at this time of night." I made a three-point road turn and went after him. "Let's find out, shall we?"

Following Slim through Byerly wasn't all that difficult, and if he ever noticed us, he never gave any indication of it.

It didn't take long for him to reach the road to Rocky Shoals, and we followed him there, too.

"What's the plan?" Richard asked.

"What makes you think that I've got a plan? I'm just following him. Once he gets to where he's going, we'll figure out what to do."

"I was afraid of that."

"I'm open to suggestions."

"I was afraid of that, too."

So we kept following him.

"This looks familiar," Richard said. "We're headed for the high school, aren't we?"

"I think we are," I said.

A minute or two later, I was sure of it. Slim turned down the same back road I had used to avoid the crowds on the first day of the Jamboree, and there wasn't much else down that way.

"We're not going to keep following him, are we?" Richard asked.

"Of course not," I said, pulling into the parking lot of the Hardee's where we had found Ilene. "We're going to call Chief Monroe and let him know what's going on."

The only problem was, Chief Monroe wasn't at the station or in his patrol car. "Is there something I can do for you?" said a voice that I thought belonged to Wade, the young officer who we had seen at the police station.

I said, "You're familiar with the Honeywell shooting, aren't you?"

"Yes, ma'am."

"I'm Laura Fleming, and it's my cousin who's in jail for the shooting, but she didn't do it."

"She didn't?"

"We're pretty sure the killer didn't mean to kill Honeywell, anyway. We think he was trying to kill Slim Grady."

"Slim Grady?"

"He's one of the Ramblers, and somebody tried to kill him by cutting his brake line earlier this week."

"Is that a fact?"

The tone of his voice told me that he wasn't following all of this, and maybe not any of it. "Look, I've spoken to Chief Monroe about this, so he'll know what I'm talking about. The reason I'm calling is that Slim Grady has just driven to the Rocky Shoals High School and we think he's going to meet the killer."

"Why would he do that?"

"I'm not sure," I had to admit, "but I'm sure that he's in danger."

"Ma'am, I'm not sure what it is you're asking me to do."

I hesitated long enough to count to ten in binary. "What I want you to do is to get in touch with Chief Monroe and tell him that Slim Grady has gone to the high school. Tell him that he needs to go down there and check it out. Have you got that?"

"Yes, ma'am, I've got it."

I didn't much believe him, but I said, "Fine. My husband and I are at the pay phone at the Hardee's near the high school, so you can reach us there." I read out the number, and he dutifully repeated it after me before hanging up.

"Did that sound as foolish to you as it did to that police officer?" I asked Richard.

"It was a bit hard to follow," he said tactfully. "I take it that Chief Monroe wasn't available."

"You take it correctly."

"He's probably holed up in a doughnut shop somewhere."

I grinned, but then had an awful thought. "Unless it was him that Slim went to meet. The fellow at the station sounded surprised that Monroe wasn't answering his radio, and that would explain why."

"I thought we had eliminated him as a suspect."

"Not really. It's just that Junior was so convinced. She's usually right about people, but what if she's wrong this time? Monroe could finish off Slim, and then claim he had gone there in response to our call and found him dead. We may have helped him create an alibi!"

I stuck another quarter into the phone.

"Junior?" Richard asked.

"Junior," I said. She answered on the first ring, and I explained to her what Slim had said, what we thought we had figured out, and where Slim was now.

"Did you call Lloyd?" Junior asked.

"I tried, but he's not available. What if it's Monroe that Slim's gone to see?"

"You don't believe that, do you?"

"Junior, I just don't know. All I know is that Slim has gone to the school, and I can't think of any other reason he'd have than to meet the person who's been trying to kill him."

"Well, it's not my town, but maybe I won't get in too much trouble if I ride over there and see what's going on." Then she said, "Damn! I'm not thinking. I can't come out there! I've got to stay with Ilene."

"Is Trey still at the movies?"

"Yes, but even Mama would have to admit that this is an emergency. The problem is that I don't know which theater they went to, and it would take me awhile to track them down."

"Can't you leave Ilene alone for a while?" I asked. "You know she won't go anywhere."

"I wish I could." There was a pause. "Look, I'll think of something and I'll be there just as soon as I can. Where are y'all now?"

I told her, and she hung up. "She's going to try to get here," I said to Richard, and explained the problems involved.

We didn't say anything as we stood by the phone and waited for five endless minutes before Richard called the Rocky Shoals station again. Chief Monroe still hadn't reported in, and Wade still thought we were crazy as loons.

Another five minutes crept by, and still there was no call from Monroe or Junior.

"I can't stand this," I said. "Slim could be dead by now!"

I was halfway expecting Richard to try to reassure me, but what he said was, "And the murderer could be back at home by the time Junior or Monroe show up, so we'll never prove who it was."

"What are you thinking?" I asked.

"That it wouldn't hurt to drive down there," he said. "All we have to do is look for the cars and get the license number of the one that's not Slim's."

"Let's go," I said, and we jumped back into the car. I drove safely down that back road, but I have to admit that I didn't pay any mind to the speed limit.

Chapter 39

As we approached the parking lot, I turned off the headlights. With the parking lot lights Homer Caldwell took so much care with, there was enough light to drive by, and maybe this way, nobody would notice us. If there was a light on inside the school, it was away from any window.

"There's a car," Richard said, and I drove toward the only car in the back lot.

"It's Slim's," I said. "Let's try the front lot." We drove all through it, but the only car there was ours. "Rats, rats, rats!" I said. There was still no sign of Chief Monroe or Junior. "Now what?"

"I don't know," Richard said. "Maybe the person Slim came to meet hasn't gotten here yet."

"Or maybe he's already left." I didn't have the heart to say what I was thinking. Maybe Slim was already dead, or in there dying while we dithered around.

Richard asked, "Do you think we should go in?"

"Do *you* think so?"

He looked at the dark building. "I don't suppose I could talk you into staying out here while I investigate."

"Not hardly."

We both thought about it for a minute or two, or at least

I think he was thinking the same thing I was. If Slim died because we didn't go in, would I ever be able to look myself in the mirror again?

"Let's go in," we said at the same time.

We left our car parked next to Slim's, and went to the nearest door. It was unlocked, which probably meant that Slim had gone in that way. I winced at the noise it made when we opened and shut it, but there was no reaction from inside the building.

It was awfully quiet inside, so we just went to the main hall and walked down it as quietly as we could. The only light was from outside, the reflections from the light poles streaming across the waxed squares of linoleum.

Richard was the first to hear something, probably because I was trying to sort out the suspects who could have had keys to the school. I'd like to say that I figured out who it was then, but the truth was, all I could do was narrow it to Chief Monroe, who might have a key for security reasons, and Homer Caldwell, whom I had seen with a set.

It was only when Richard pulled me in the direction from which he heard people that I remembered who else might have a key. Even then, I wasn't sure until we got close enough to hear the voices.

The door to the office was open, and the light made a sharp diamond shape on the floor. Richard and I stopped a few feet away, close enough to hear what was being said, but not close enough to see inside.

"I just don't understand what you were afraid of," Slim was saying. "If I was going to say anything, I'd have done it right after the accident. What would I have to gain by telling anybody now?"

"Surely you don't think I'm that naive?" a voice answered him. Richard's tiny intake of breath told me he was as surprised as I was. I should have realized when we went down this corridor that Forrest Jefferson's office was at the end, and I should have known that Forrest had to have her own key to run the Jamboree.

Forrest went on, "You see, I was never sure if you had seen me that night, but when I saw your face that day at the Jamboree, I knew that you had. I could see it when you looked at me."

"But why would I tell now, when I didn't fifteen years ago?"

"Fifteen years ago I was a child. Now I'm a woman of wealth and position. I had nothing you would want then, but now I do, and I'll be damned if I'll lose it to you!"

"Forrest, I swear that I never had any intention of blackmailing you."

What was it Richard quoted earlier? Something about suspicion haunting the guilty mind? Only Slim wasn't the only one guilt had haunted. Forrest had been haunted, too, and for better reason.

She laughed. "You would say that now, with a gun aimed at your belly."

Richard grabbed my hand hard enough to hurt.

"You don't want to shoot me, do you, Forrest?" Slim asked softly.

"What I want has nothing to do with it. Now that you know that I killed Tom Honeywell, you have to go. It's a shame that your car accident wasn't more serious."

"That accident could have killed three innocent people," Slim said, and for the first time he sounded angry.

"It would have been their own fault," Forrest said. "They had no business chasing after you like that."

Up until that point, I might have had a little sympathy for Forrest. Allowing for the fact that she thought Slim was going to ruin her, I could almost see her trying to protect herself. What I couldn't accept was the way she casually condemned my cousins. Not to mention the fact that Ilene was in jail for her crime.

"It would have been much simpler if you hadn't come back to Rocky Shoals," Forrest said. "That mistake has caused a lot of trouble." I heard a chair scrape against the floor, and Forrest said, "Don't try to get away from me. I'm an excellent shot."

Richard started shoving me back. I didn't want to go, but I didn't want to spoil his plan either, so I backed to the next hallway, ducked into it, and leaned against the wall.

"I wouldn't do that, Miss Jefferson," Richard said clearly. "The police are on the way."

There were noises from the office, and I heard footsteps. I prayed that Richard knew what he was doing.

"Good Lord," Forrest said in a tone of supreme annoyance. "What are you doing here?"

"Keeping you from killing anybody else," Richard said calmly. "My wife has already gone to get help."

There was a pause, then Forrest decisively said, "You're lying. Your wife would never have allowed you to stay here alone."

I had to admit that she had our number.

"Mrs. Fleming," she called out. "Either come out now, or I'll shoot your husband. I can assure you that I'm not bluffing."

Not moving was the hardest thing I've ever done in my life. Reason told me that if I went out where she could see me, I would be signing all of our death warrants. The tension caused painful knots in my back, and I realized later that I had left marks in my palm from clenching my fists.

"Very well," Forrest said, and I could just picture her aiming at Richard.

Tears ran down my cheeks, but I didn't move as I waited for the shot.

"Mrs. Fleming?" Forrest called again, and again I didn't respond. "You're stronger than I thought," she said, and damned if there wasn't a hint of admiration in her voice.

"It's over, Forrest," Slim said. "You can't kill everybody."

"Perhaps not," Forrest said, "but I can kill you two. If I'm right and Mrs. Fleming is in the building, she'll come running at the gunshot. If I'm wrong and she's gone for the police, I'll be done with you and gone before they get here. Then it will be her word against mine, and my word is not without value in this town."

I was screaming inside, not knowing if she was really going to go through with it. It was only then that I realized the worst pain in my back wasn't a knotted muscle at all, but a bank of light switches. There wasn't time to try to hope that one of them was for the hall they were in, I just flipped them all and started running. Lights came on all around me.

I heard a shot from behind me, and what I thought was a struggle, and then running footsteps. I must have aged a year in the next few seconds, trying to guess who was running after me, but then I turned just enough to see Slim and Richard. I kept going, knowing that Forrest must be behind them.

Another gunshot echoed through the halls, and I turned down the first hall I came to, this one still dark. Richard and Slim followed, then Slim passed me to lead us down another hall. I was completely lost now, disoriented by running in the darkness.

Slim stopped in front of a closed door, opened it, then pulled us into a classroom after him. We moved away from the door, and put our backs against the wall. Without speaking, Richard found my hand and brought it to his lips. I wanted to grab hold of him, but was afraid it would make a noise that would bring Forrest down on us.

It was only then, while we stood there listening for Forrest, that I realized Slim was breathing funny. I reached out to touch him just as he started to sag to the floor, and held him long enough for Richard to see what was happening and help pull him up.

"You've been shot," I whispered.

Slim nodded. "I don't think it's too bad, but it's slowing me down. You two ought to hotfoot it on out of here. Forrest isn't going to stop until she finds me."

"She's not going to stop until she finds all of us," I said. "We've got to get to the car."

Slim shook his head. "I can't make it."

"We'll carry you," Richard said.

Slim started to say something else when the light came on in the hall outside the door. "I know y'all are in here," Forrest said. "There's nowhere for y'all to go." She passed by the door, her shadow brushing against the translucent glass on the door.

I hardly dared breathe. Then she went on past, still calling for us.

"The window," Richard said.

"I'll check." I left him supporting Slim, and tiptoed to the row of windows along the side of the room, but when I got to them, I saw that they would be no help. They were louvered glass, opened with a crank. Even if we managed to open them without Forrest hearing us, we'd never be able to squeeze out. I imagine that we could have broken them down eventually, but not before Forrest got there.

I went back, and took Slim's other arm. "No way."

"Weapons?" Richard asked.

I looked around, and he did the same, but apparently they had cleaned the rooms thoroughly. The only thing smaller than a desk was a plastic trash can, and I didn't think that it would do us any good.

Slim hadn't responded to any of this, and I didn't think he was completely conscious. Running from Forrest had taken everything out of him.

As if he had been listening to my thoughts, Richard said, "You go for help, and I'll stay here with Slim."

"You run faster than I do," I countered. "You go."

Though neither of us spoke, and we couldn't very well kiss over Slim, I don't think I had ever been so sure of us as a couple as I was at that moment. We wouldn't leave Slim, and we couldn't leave each other. If we hadn't already been married for four and a half years, I'd have considered us married that minute.

"Can't we wait for Junior?" I asked.

Richard shook his head. "Forrest is going to start opening doors soon."

Sure enough, I thought I heard a door open in another corridor. I looked around the room again, but there was nowhere for three people to hide.

Richard nodded at the door, and I left him holding Slim again. I think we were both afraid that if we let Slim sit down, we'd never get him back up.

I listened for a second, but didn't hear anything. Then I

opened it as slowly as I could manage, and waited for a reaction. Again nothing, so I stuck my head out enough to look down the hall both ways. I didn't see Forrest, though I could hear her footsteps. I waved at Richard, and he threw one of Slim's arms around his shoulders and half carried, half dragged him to the door.

That's how we got as far as we did. At each corner, I'd check for Forrest, and Richard would follow along with Slim, both of us trying to be as quiet as we could be. Slim never did make a sound, and I never found out if it was because he was completely out of it or if he knew what we were doing.

We were trying to get back to the door we had come in because it was the only one we were sure we could open. It seemed like it took us hours to get within sight of it, and when I saw it, I thought sure that we were going to make it. Then Forrest stepped out from a doorway and aimed her gun at us.

She said, "I was wondering where y'all had got to. I do appreciate your not splitting up—it makes this much easier for me."

Richard pulled me back toward him, and Slim roused himself. "You don't have to shoot them, Forrest. I'm the only one who knows your secret."

"They know far too much, whether they know about the bus crash or not."

"She's right, Slim," I said. "We do know too much. In fact, I know more than Forrest realizes."

"Is that so?" she said, trying to sound like she wasn't interested.

I nodded. "I figured out a long time ago that you were the one driving the blue Volkswagen because of that picture of you and your friend Mary and your boyfriend Archie leaning against it." That was a lie, of course, but it did get her attention. "What I never could figure out was why you went to the concert when you were supposed to be at the library?"

She didn't answer, and I went on. "Even though your best friend and your boyfriend were going, I know you weren't the type to sneak out, so why did you disobey your parents?" I was venturing into pure speculation at this point, but I had to stall, and it did make more and more sense as I spoke. "Was it because of your best friend and your boyfriend? Or should I say your best friend and *her* boyfriend?"

She stiffened in anger, even after all those years.

I said, "You must have started to realize that Archie was more interested in Mary than he was in you, but you weren't sure, were you? Following them to the concert to spy on them was the only way you could find out."

"You're talking crazy," Forrest said. "Mary would never have betrayed me, and Archie was crazy about me. Everybody in town knew that he wanted to marry me."

"They know you said he wanted to marry you," I countered. "Did anybody ever hear *him* say it? Were Archie and Mary holding hands at the concert, Forrest? Were they dancing together?"

Her reddening face was enough answer for me. I said, "That must have made you crazy. Here you thought you had all three of your lives planned out, and then they had to go and start making their own decisions. You must have meant to leave ahead of the bus so you could get back to Rocky Shoals before they did, but you must have been so angry that you stayed longer than you had intended to and got stuck in traffic. So you ended up behind them, and didn't catch up until they were nearly home. Were you that much in a hurry to get ahead of them, or did you try to pass them just so you could see if Archie and Mary were sitting together? Did you see them? Were they kissing?"

"*Stop it!*" Forrest raised her gun and aimed it straight at me.

Richard told me later that he thought I was trying to draw Forrest's fire, and he was tensing to push me down and jump her when my real reason for stalling appeared. Junior came tearing around a corner and threw herself at Forrest, pushing her to the floor with a heavy thud and knocking the gun from her hand. The gun slid across the floor, and came to a stop at the foot of Chief Monroe, who leaned down and picked it up while Junior got Forrest in a headlock.

Chapter 40

"Hey, Lloyd, can I borrow your cuffs?" Junior asked as she struggled with Forrest.

"Regulations say you should carry a set at all times," he replied.

"I've got a set, but my hands are full right now."

Monroe obliged, and between the two of them, they got Forrest cuffed and stood her up. She was sputtering for breath from Junior's tackle, but still managed to let loose a stream of foul language.

"Regulations also say that you shouldn't engage an armed suspect in hand-to-hand combat if you can avoid it. Why didn't you use your weapon?" Monroe said.

"Because the only way to have stopped her from shooting back would have been to kill her with the first shot," Junior retorted. "Don't regulations say something about not killing suspects if you don't have to?"

"They might," Monroe admitted.

"Do regulations say anything about getting an ambulance for Slim?" I asked in some irritation.

"I thought I got her before she fired," Junior said, and she hurried to help us lay Slim down while Monroe called for an ambulance and kept an eye on Forrest.

"She shot him before you got here," I explained as Junior examined the wound.

"I've seen a few gun shots in my time," she said, "and this one doesn't look too bad." Then she looked at Richard. "You, on the other hand, look like thirty miles of bad road."

Just from looking at him, you would have thought Richard had been the one to get shot, because he had more blood on him than Slim did. Blood or no blood, this was the first chance I had had to hug and kiss my husband in an eternity, and I took full advantage of it.

The ambulance showed up in record time, and Monroe and Junior got Forrest out to Monroe's patrol car while the ambulance attendants took care of Slim. Off to the side, one of the attendants told me that it looked like he would be fine. Then we walked Slim to the ambulance, me on one side of the stretcher and Richard on the other.

Slim was weaving in and out of consciousness, but he did wake up long enough to say, "Thank you."

The ambulance roared off, and Junior said, "Would you go speak to my prisoner for a minute? She's bound to be worried about you."

"Forrest is worried about us?" I said.

"I said, 'my prisoner.' Forrest is Lloyd's prisoner. My prisoner is in my patrol car, which is parked on the other side of the school."

I wasn't sure who Junior was talking about until we got to her patrol car, and there in the backseat, with Junior's handcuffs on, was Ilene.

"Are you two all right?" Ilene asked as soon as she saw us.

"We're fine," I said. "What are you doing here?"

"Junior didn't have anybody to guard me, so she made

me promise to stay here in the car. When I saw the ambulance drive up, I thought sure that one of you had been hurt."

My cousin had better self-control than I did. If I had been in her place, I'd never have been able to stay in the car, promise or no promise.

Richard said, "Slim's been shot, but he's going to be all right."

"What happened in there?" Ilene asked, and I explained it to her.

When I got to the part where Forrest caught us, Richard said, "Laura, please tell me that you knew Junior was in the building."

I grinned. "Just before Forrest stepped out, I thought I saw some movement outside, and while Slim was trying to talk Forrest out of killing us, a hand flashed me an Okay sign in the window. I figured it had to be either Junior or Chief Monroe, so I stalled until whoever it was could get there."

"We got there right about the same time, as a matter of fact," said Monroe, who had joined us. "Sorry that you couldn't get in touch with me sooner, but my radio was out of whack. I hear that I was one of your suspects."

I suppose I should have been embarrassed about that, but I wasn't. "If you can suspect my cousin of murder, I don't think it's so awful for me to suspect you."

To my surprise, he just nodded. "You should always keep an open mind during an investigation." To Ilene, he said, "I was wrong about you, young lady, but I hope you understand why."

I could tell it was a strain for her, but she said, "I guess I did make myself look pretty guilty."

"That's nice of you to say. I'll be glad to set you loose after I get the paperwork squared away."

That was Chief Monroe, all right. By the book to the last.

"Could you at least take the cuffs off of her?" I said.

He nodded. "I got the keys from Chief Norton so I could do that very thing." He unlocked the cuffs, then said to me and Richard, "As soon as Wade gets here to seal off the scene, I'll be taking Miss Jefferson over to the jail. Could you two meet me over there so I can get your statements while the incident is fresh in your mind?"

I was exhausted and covered in blood, and for some reason I was starving, and he wanted me to go fill out forms? I was about to say something really rude but Richard said, "Yes, sir. We'll see you there."

"I appreciate that," Monroe said, then went back to his squad car.

"We better get going," I said to Ilene. "I don't want to give him an excuse for arresting us, too."

Ilene reached out through the open window for my hand and Richard's. "Thank y'all so much," was all she said.

Ilene's and Slim's thank-you's would have been plenty for me, but that was just the beginning. We stopped at the Hardee's again, and while I grabbed food and Cokes, Richard called Aunt Ruby Lee and told her to meet us at the Rocky Shoals police station. He almost couldn't get off the phone for her thanking him. Then I made a quick call to Hank Parker, so he could get the story into the next edition of the *Byerly Gazette,* and he thanked me for the scoop.

We got to the police station and had just barely finished our hamburgers when the first family members arrived. Aunt Ruby Lee, Roger, Clifford, and Earl got there first, and each one had to hug us separately, even if we were still covered in blood. I thought Roger was going to squeeze the life right out of me. Then Vasti rushed in, bubbling over with new ideas for the wedding that she had been saving, just in case. Aunt Maggie, Aunt Nora, and Aunt Daphine showed up next and got their hugs in before Aunt Edna and her boyfriend Caleb came. I lost track after that, but I'm fairly sure that most of my aunts, uncles, and cousins were there.

They weren't all Burnettes, either. Florence Easterly came, too, not at all disappointed to be losing a client. She limited her exuberance to a light handclasp and a peck on the cheek. Hank Parker came to get quotes from everybody, and Vasti made sure he got pictures, too. Trey Norton must have gotten out of the movies, because he was there standing in a corner, not saying anything, just waiting for Ilene.

I'm quite sure that if nobody ever thanks me for anything again, I'm covered after that night.

When Junior brought Ilene in, the hugs began all over again because everybody wanted to thank Junior for saving me and Richard. Junior is a warm person, but she's not the hugging type, and I've always been convinced that she invented that urgent call from Byerly just so she could get out of that crowd of hugging Burnettes. She did give me a thumbs-up as she escaped, which is the equal to a twenty-one-gun salute from anybody else.

Ilene got hugged the most of all, but then she burst out crying and laughing at the same time. We all tried to quiet down after that, and Aunt Ruby Lee took her back into Chief Monroe's office, with Trey running back and forth with wet washcloths and cold drinks.

Junior must have warned Chief Monroe about what was waiting for him, because he snuck Forrest Jefferson in the back door and had her locked up in a cell before we knew he was there. I'll give him credit for taking care of Ilene's paperwork in mere minutes, so everybody could head for Aunt Nora's for coffee and the cookies she just happened to have ready. I'd like to think he wanted to free Ilene as soon as possible because she was innocent, but I suspect it had as much to do with getting the family out of there as anything else. Trey happily led the cavalcade of Burnettes to Byerly, blue lights flashing.

Richard and I had to stay awhile longer to give our statements, but I think Monroe went easy on us. It was a good thing, too, because I was worn slap out by that point. Once we had initialed the last photocopy, Chief Monroe said, "I think that covers it. Y'all will be in the area for a few more days if I need anything else, won't you?"

"Yes, sir," Richard said.

Official duties over, Monroe leaned back in his chair. "I never would have guessed that it was Forrest Jefferson in that car. I knew she had a blue Volkswagen, of course, but it just didn't occur to me. Not so much the wreck itself, but her speeding the way she did when she came through here. As many times as I've been caught behind her on a two-lane road and wished to God that she'd speed a little, I wouldn't have thought it." He looked at us. "I don't know that I'd have figured any of it out without you two."

"You're not going to thank us, are you?" I said, not meaning to sound ungracious.

He smiled a little, and said, "It wouldn't be proper to thank private citizens for interfering in police business, even if they did do a bang-up job."

"Of course not," I said, feeling a little let down, despite what I had just said.

Monroe went on. "It would be all right to shake your

hands, if you're willing." And he stood and did just that, first Richard and then me.

"You're welcome," I said, even if it wasn't proper. For a by-the-book man, he wasn't all that bad.

Chapter 41

I called Aunt Nora before Richard and I left the police station, and she assured me that everybody was still at her house celebrating. "After all," she told me, "it's only a little after midnight." I thought she was nuts until I checked my watch, but she was right. It just seemed later. We drove over there and joined the crowd who had been at the police station, plus a few that hadn't been.

Of course, they wanted to hear the whole story again, but Richard is an excellent storyteller and rarely gets a chance to show off like that. He did such a good job of it that I was starting to wonder how it would turn out myself.

After he finished, there was a pause while people got more coffee and grabbed more of Aunt Nora's sugar cookies. Then Roger said, "Well, Ilene, I hope you've learned your lesson. Laurie Anne and Richard could have been killed. If you had minded me and your mama, none of this would have happened."

Ilene nodded, and looked down.

I was furious! It was Forrest who did the killing, not Ilene. And it was Aunt Ruby Lee who asked me and Richard to investigate. And it was Roger himself who had said that he was afraid the marriage wouldn't take place if we didn't find the murderer. How dare he blame Ilene for all of that!

But I didn't say anything, not one word. It wasn't my business, I kept saying to myself. If I had learned *anything* during this mess, surely I had learned to keep my nose out of things that don't concern me. Even so, I'm not sure how long I'd have been able to hold out if somebody else hadn't spoken up.

It was Aunt Ruby Lee who said, "You hold on there, buddy! It's not Ilene who should be apologizing to Laurie Anne, Roger Bailey! It's you!"

"But honey—" Roger said, clearly astonished.

"But nothing! I've been thinking a lot about things, and the way I figure it, if you had helped Ilene out when she wanted to learn about the music business, she wouldn't have taken up with somebody like Tom Honeywell and she wouldn't have gotten into trouble. But not you! You knew what was best for her, no matter what anybody else said, and you must be more stubborn than any mule ever born or you'd admit it. I'm not saying it's your fault either, because it wasn't you who shot people, but if there's anybody in this room who should take some blame, it's you. And maybe me, too, for not speaking my mind. Well, it's not going to be that way anymore. I'm telling you right here and now, if you don't straighten up and fly right, you can just forget about this wedding."

"But Ruby Lee—"

"Me and the kids have been doing fine without you in the house, and I don't see why I should let you come in and change how we're doing everything because you think you know better. I'm not saying we won't change if it's a good idea, but I am saying that we aren't going to change things just on your say-so. That means Ilene is going to keep dressing the way she does and she's going to keep working on her music. You don't have to help her, but I'll be damned if I'll let you hinder her. And when *I* make a decision, you are *not* going to come along behind me and say anything different. Now what do you have to say to that?"

I saw the absolute horror on Vasti's face as she realized that all her plans might have just gone out the window, and I have to give my cousin a lot of credit. She didn't say one word. Her knuckles turned white, but she waited for Roger's response along with the rest of us.

It was a long time coming. From the expressions that came and went on Roger's face, he made up and changed his mind any number of times. Finally he said, "Ruby Lee, I've always said that you were the prettiest woman on Earth and the sweetest, but damned if you aren't the smartest, too."

Aunt Ruby Lee didn't back off, not yet.

Now Roger was shaking his head. "I've been pure out-and-out blind not to see what I've been doing. You're absolutely right, Ruby Lee, one hundred percent."

Still Aunt Ruby Lee wasn't ready to let go. "And?"

"And I'm going to change. I won't say that it's going to happen right this minute, because you're right about my being stubborn, but I'll do it if that's what it takes to keep you, and be the father these kids deserve."

He got down on one knee in front of her. "Ruby Lee, I've asked you this twice before, and I'm going to ask you again. Will you marry me?"

Her stern look dissolved as if it had never been, and she smiled the way only a woman in love can. Then she said, "Yes, Roger. I will." She threw her arms around him, and they kissed long enough to make me right jealous.

Then Roger stood up, lifting Aunt Ruby Lee with him, and just whooped for joy. The two of them spread their arms out, and Clifford, Earl, and Ilene all joined in. It wasn't long before everybody was hugging everybody within reach, and of course, Aunt Nora started crying. I got weepy myself.

Chapter 42

Eventually we all settled down again, and Aunt Maggie said that it was getting late and that we all looked like we had been rid hard and put away wet. Richard was so tired that he didn't even try to come up with a Shakespearean way to say the same thing, so I knew it was time for us to get to bed. As the two of us argued over who was the more tired, Aunt Maggie plucked the keys from my hand and announced that she was driving us home.

A good long rest was just what we needed the next day, but it wasn't what we got. With the wedding definitely on, Vasti had errands for us to run all day long. When I protested, she reminded me that I had told her that she didn't have to run all the events anymore, and it was time for me to do my share. This wasn't quite the way I remembered the conversation, but I put up with it anyway.

When all was said and done, it was a lovely wedding. Aunt Ruby Lee and Ilene looked beautiful, and Roger, Clifford, and Earl looked so handsome. Even Aunt Maggie looked wonderful, in a very nice dress and high heels. Alton Brown may have looked the happiest of all, which meant that he had won his bet.

If there was a dry eye in the church during the ceremony, I didn't see it because I was too busy trying to find a tissue to wipe my own eyes. We all cried the hardest at the music. The Ramblers had planned to sing, but with Slim in the hospital, it was Ilene and Clifford who sang to Earl's accompaniment. Best of all, I think it was one of the songs Ilene had written.

Afterward at the reception, Vasti even complimented me on my dress, without any hidden meanings that I could find.

I smiled and said, "It's not too pretty for nice, but it's great for good." Then I turned to Richard. "Richard? Your turn."

"That's not fair. I don't even know what that one means."

"Then give me the point."

He did so, but only grudgingly.

"Didn't Ilene and the boys sound wonderful?" I said.

"They sure did," Vasti said. "I can't wait until they perform at the Jamboree next year."

"I didn't think there'd be one next year. Forrest Jefferson was the driving force behind it."

"Somebody has already volunteered to take over, and this time it's going to be done right."

I had a suspicion, but I said, "Who?"

"Me, of course."

"Of course." I made a mental note to avoid North Carolina next June. "If this wedding is any indication, you're going to do a wonderful job. You must be awfully glad that it went off as scheduled."

"I suppose so," she said.

"You don't sound very glad."

"I'm glad they got married and all, and it does look like things are going to work out for them. It's just that I had an idea for what to do with all the wedding stuff, just in case, and I'm kind of disappointed that I didn't get to use it."

I had to ask. "What did you have in mind?"

"I thought all of us Burnettes who are married could renew our vows. Me and Arthur, and you and Richard, and Aunt Nora and Uncle Buddy, and Linwood and Sue, and Aunt Nellie and Uncle Ruben."

I was touched. "Vasti, that's really sweet."

"And wouldn't it have made a wonderful photo opportunity for Hank Parker? A big picture of all of us in the *Gazette* would have been a great way to get Arthur back in the news before we get started on his reelection campaign."

Now that was the Vasti I knew. "Maybe next time," was all I said.

As we watched the newlyweds ducking through the shower of rice to leave for their honeymoon, Richard took my hand, leaned over to kiss me, and whispered, " 'The sight of lovers feedeth those in love.' *As You Like It*, Act II, Scene 4."

"You win," I whispered back to him, without even adding up the score, but funny, I didn't feel like I had lost a thing.

Please turn the page for
an exciting sneak peek of
Toni L.P. Kelner's
next Laura Fleming mystery
COUNTRY COMES TO TOWN
to be published in hardcover
by Kensington Books in
September 1996

Chapter 23

Chapter 1

The doorbell rang while I was in the middle of writing to my husband Richard. He had only been gone since the night before, but overseas mail is slow, and I kept telling myself that I wanted him to get a letter right away so he wouldn't be lonely. Of course, the real reason I was writing was because it would make *me* feel less lonely.

I pushed the intercom button. "Who is it?"

"Laura? Is that you?"

The voice sounded familiar, but I couldn't quite place it. "Yes, this is Laura."

"Laura, it's Philip. Can I come in?"

I hesitated, more out of shock than anything else. I hadn't seen Philip Dennis for at least two years, and I really wouldn't have minded if it had stretched to three or four.

"Laura?"

I pushed the buzzer so he could come in, then started to wonder if I should have. Philip always had that effect on me, making me question every action.

I opened the door to my apartment, and watched as Philip came up the stairs to the second floor. He looked almost the same as he had the last time I had seen him. Maybe his hair was a bit thinner, I thought meanly, but surely that

was the same ratty blue jean jacket he always used to wear.
When he saw me watching him, he grinned that grin I used
to find so attractive. I hadn't known what "insouciant"
meant until I met Philip.

As soon as he got to the landing, he said, "You look great!
Better than ever."

"Thanks," I said, though I knew I didn't look all that
great. I hadn't intended to go out that evening, so I was
wearing my most faded jeans and a stretched-out red
sweater. With anybody else, I'd have thought they were just
being polite. With Philip, I was suspicious. "This is a surprise."

"I guess it is. Can I come in?"

I stepped back to let him in the door, and closed it behind
him.

"What a great place!" he said, turning around and looking at everything—the furniture, the pictures on the wall,
even Richard's sword hanging above the couch. Philip pulled
off his jacket and sat down, instinctively picking out Richard's favorite chair. I tried not to wince.

I sat down on the couch, a safe distance away. "I didn't
realize you knew our address."

"I got it from Jessie. So how's Rich?"

Nobody ever calls Richard by anything but his full name.
"Richard's fine. How's Colleen?"

He shrugged his shoulders, which always was his favorite way to change the subject. I wondered if he could read
me as easily as I could read him. Probably not. I hadn't ever
been as important to him as he had been to me.

"So what brings you out this way?" I asked. Snow was
predicted for later that night, and though he had been born

in Massachusetts, Philip never had been fond of winter weather.

"Actually, I need a favor."

"What's that?" I said, halfway expecting to be asked for a loan. Most people wouldn't have looked up an old girlfriend to borrow money, but Philip wouldn't hesitate.

"Do you think I can crash here for a while? I know Rich is out of town, so this way you'd have a man around. I'll sleep on the couch, of course."

That got me mad, and I wasn't sure what I was madder about: that he would ask such a thing after all this time, the idea that I needed a man around the house, or his thinking that I would even consider letting him sleep anywhere but on the couch. "I don't think so, Philip," was all I trusted myself to say.

"Look, Laura, I know it's asking a lot, but I really need someplace to crash."

"What happened to your house?"

"Colleen and I haven't been getting along, so I decided to split."

In other words, she had thrown him out. "Why don't you sleep at the office?"

"I can't. Vinnie and Inez are on the warpath about me doing anything that might 'reflect badly on the company.' They want to fire me already, so I don't dare sleep there."

"You're kidding." Philip had co-founded Statistical Software, Inc. right out of college, and had been the author of StatSys, their mainstay software package. Though Vinnie and Inez were officially in charge, I couldn't imagine them actually firing Philip. In fact, I would have thought that he'd have set up the company so they couldn't fire him.

He looked disgusted. "Vinnie got the bright idea that we

should sell stock and let a bunch of ignoramus investors run the company. Now he and Inez want me to be Mr. Corporate, and you know that's not me."

"Not hardly," I said. In fact, I had always suspected that Philip founded his own company so he wouldn't have to put on a suit to interview elsewhere. "But there must be somebody from SSI who can put you up."

"You'd think so, wouldn't you? As much as I've done for them, and now they're all ganging up against me. They're a bunch of losers anyway." He did his best to look forlorn. "You're all I've got."

A few years back, maybe I'd have fallen for it, but not now. "No, Philip."

"Come on, Laura, it'll be like old times. I'll eat whatever you've got handy, and I don't make much of a mess."

I translated that to mean that he'd allow me to cook and clean up for him. "No."

"It won't be for long. A few weeks, a month or two at most."

"No."

"All I've got to do is to rattle a few cages at SSI and they'll get off my back. Once I've got my job settled, I know I'll be able to convince Colleen to let me go back home. They need me, all of them. How long can it take for them to realize that?"

"I'm sorry, Philip. No."

"Look, I know it's going to be awkward, after all we've meant to one another, but I swear that I won't come between you and Rich."

As if he could! I was getting tired of being polite. "Forget it, Philip. You're not staying."

"Why not?"

"Because it's my house and I said so. I'm not going to argue with you, Philip." My grandfather taught me a long time ago that it's never a good idea to get into a pissing contest with a skunk.

"At least let me stay the night. You know it's supposed to snow."

"Then you better get moving and find someplace to stay." It sounded callous, but I knew that once I let him into my home, I'd never get him out again without the help of the police. And he had to have enough money to get himself a hotel room, if not with cash than with a credit card. He'd just rather mooch if he could. And his next plea made me so mad I wished I had said something meaner.

"What about that Southern hospitality y'all used to tell me about, like in Byerly, North Carolina," he said in a Southern accent so patently false that it hurt my ears. Though we had dated for two and a half years, he never had bothered to figure out that "y'all" is plural.

"Since you used to refer to Byerly as the armpit of the universe, I don't think you should be invoking its name now."

"I was kidding, Laura. You know that."

"Well, I'm not kidding, Philip. You cannot stay here. Not a month, not a week, not a night. In fact, I think you ought to leave now."

"But Laura . . ."

I went to the door, opened it, and held it open.

For a minute he just sat there, as if daring me to throw him out. But I guess that he could tell that I would if I had to, because he finally got up.

"Jesus, Laura, what a bitch you've turned into."

I didn't answer, just kept holding the door.

"This is your revenge for my breaking up with you, isn't it? I can't believe you'd be small enough to hold that against me." With the word "small," he stretched to his full height, which was nearly a foot taller than my own. "I guess you can take the girl out of the country, but you can't take the country out of the girl."

"That may be," I said, "but I sure can take the asshole out of my apartment." I shut the door firmly behind him, and loudly rattled the locks and dead bolt to make sure he knew that he couldn't get back in.

I didn't have a chance to brood about Philip because the phone rang right after I heard him stomp down the stairs. "Hello?"

"Laurie Anne?"

"Vasti? What's up?" My cousin rarely spent money on long distance charges from North Carolina to Boston, and it wasn't even weekend rates yet.

"I just wanted to make sure he got there all right. Mama was watching the Weather Channel and she said that y'all were having a snow storm up there."

"Richard left last night, and the storm hasn't started yet, so everything's fine," I said, touched by her concern. I should have known better.

"Richard? I'm talking about Thaddeous."

"What about Thaddeous?"

"Did he not make it in?"

"In where? What are you talking about?"

"Aunt Nora said he was leaving first thing Saturday morning, and even with changing planes in Charlotte, I thought sure he'd be there by now."

"It's Friday, Vasti."

"Oh dear!" she said unconvincingly. "I've gone and spoiled the surprise."

"What surprise?"

"I better not say another word. Bye now!"

"Vasti!" It was too late. She had already hung up. Of course, I thought I knew what was going on by now, but I called Aunt Nora, Thaddeous's mother, to make sure.

"Hello?"

"Aunt Nora? This is Laura."

"Why, Laurie Anne," she said in a theatrical voice that would have told me that something was up even if I hadn't already known it. "This is such a surprise."

"Aunt Nora, is Thaddeous coming up here?"

There was a short silence. "How did you find out?"

"How do you think?"

"Vasti?"

"She just called."

"I knew I shouldn't have told her, but it slipped out. And Thaddeous wanted it to be a surprise."

Looking at the mess in my living room, and remembering that the kitchen was even worse, I was pretty sure that it was Thaddeous who would have been surprised. "How was he planning on getting to my apartment?"

"He figured he could take the subway, like you do." As I was trying to imagine my cousin making his way on the Boston subway all by his lonesome, Aunt Nora added, "He figured he could stop and ask directions if he needed to."

"It'll probably be better if I meet him at the airport," I said diplomatically. Knowing how much Aunt Nora liked surprises, even vicarious ones, I said, "Tell you what, don't tell him I know, and I'll surprise *him* instead."

"That's a good idea." She paused. "Then you don't mind him coming?"

"Mind? I've been wanting him to come up to visit for I don't know how long." I would have preferred more notice, but that was neither here nor there.

"That's good. He hasn't taken any time off from the mill in a coon's age, and he's got so much vacation stored up that they were going to take it away from him. Besides, I thought maybe you could use the company with Richard being gone."

I knew which of those reasons was the real one, of course. Though Aunt Nora tries to be a nineties woman, she just hates the idea of my being in a big city without my family around. But she meant well, and I really was looking forward to seeing Thaddeous. I got his flight information, and just before I hung up, warned her, "Now don't let him talk to Vasti before he leaves."

So much for my plans to mope about Richard, pig out on sour cream and onion potato chips, and watch the snow come down. I looked out the window. No snow yet, but I could tell from the grey glow in the sky that it was coming. Then I went into the kitchen and sighed. I knew Thaddeous wouldn't expect my place to be as clean as his mama's, but he wasn't going to be expecting dirty dishes on every available surface either.

I was pushing up the sleeves of my sweater to start washing up when I realized something else, and opened the refrigerator. It wasn't empty, but I didn't have enough food to feed my cousin for even one meal. Thaddeous was a big fellow, and he had an appetite to match. That meant I was going to have to go out to the store. Normally that wouldn't have been a big deal, but since it was right before a storm, the stores would be filled with people buying enough milk and bread to last in case this storm turned out to be as bad as the legendary Blizzard of 1978.

I wasn't happy about it, but there was nothing else I could do. So I pulled on my coat, grabbed my pocketbook, and left. I did check to make sure Philip wasn't hanging around when I left the building, but the coast was clear. I just wish it had been that empty in the grocery store.

By the time I got to the airport the next day, I had finished my shopping, washed all the dishes and most of the laundry, mopped the kitchen and bathroom, vacuumed and dusted the living room and bedroom, and neatly stacked everything I didn't actually put away. I didn't think Thaddeous would write home about my housekeeping, but he wouldn't decide to stay at a hotel, either.

Boston's Logan Airport maintains what they call sterile concourses, meaning that I couldn't go down to the gate to meet Thaddeous as he came in. Instead I waited at the end of the concourse, hoping to catch sight of my cousin before he headed for baggage claim.

I needn't have worried about missing him. Thaddeous towers over most crowds, unless the Boston Celtics are around, and I spotted him long before he got to me.

"Thaddeous!" I yelled. "Over here!"

He peered over heads until he saw my wildly flailing arms and grinned. "What in the Sam Hill are you doing here?"

"I live here. What's your excuse?"

By now, he had made his way to me, and nearly lifted me off my feet in a great big hug I did my best to return.

He said, "Just thought you might like some company for a few days."

"A few days? If you try to get back on that airplane in

less than a week, I'm going to knock a knot on your noggin. And two weeks would be better than one!"

"How did you find out I was coming?" Then, before I could say anything, he answered his own question, "Never mind. I knew Mama shouldn't have told Vasti."

I saw we were blocking traffic, so I said, "Come on, and we'll go get your luggage."

I've flown in and out of Logan enough that it took me no time at all to find the right baggage carousel, meaning that we had that much more time to wait for his suitcase to arrive. Actually, unless I missed my guess, it was Aunt Daphine's suitcase. I guess Thaddeous had never needed one before.

"I thought we'd take a cab into town," I said.

"What about that subway you keep telling me about?"

"There's time for that later. This way you'll get to see a little bit of the city on our ride in."

Fortunately the cabbie knew my neighborhood, so I didn't have to spend the whole trip directing him. Instead I could show off for Thaddeous. "That building with the clock is the Custom House Building," I said. "Just wait until you see it lit up at night. And that's Faneuil Hall and Quincy Market. It's just filled with funky shops and places to eat. The Aquarium is right by there, and I know you'll like that."

"I thought y'all had snow last night," he said, "but it looks like everything's open."

"We got about six inches, but Lord, Thaddeous, Boston can't close down every time it snows like Byerly does. They get the streets cleared pretty quick, so about the only real difference snow makes is messing up the sidewalks and making it even harder to find a place to park." I pointed to a snowbank that was filling up two car lengths along a side street. "See what I mean? Makes me glad I don't have a car."

"I'm right surprised that there's so much traffic," Thaddeous said. "I though I'd miss most of it, coming in on the weekend."

"This isn't much traffic, Thaddeous. Wait until you live through rush hour." I kept on pointing things out for him until I decided he was on overload. Then I leaned back and watched him. Seeing his face made me remember how I had felt when I first came up North to go to college. Until then, the biggest city I had ever seen was Charlotte, and Boston had seemed magical to me. I kind of envied Thaddeous, seeing it all for the first time.

When we got to the street where Richard and I live, the end was blocked with police cars, so I paid off the cab there and we walked the half-block that remained.

My upstairs neighbor, a man I knew just enough to speak to, was standing on the steps to our building.

"Hi, John," I said. "This is my cousin Thaddeous from North Carolina." The two men shook hands. "What's going on?"

"The police found a body in the alley behind the building," he said.

"Are you serious?"

He nodded. "Some bum froze to death back there." A car pulled up and honked its horn. "There's my ride. See you later."

Thaddeous looked at me, but all I could say was, "Welcome to Boston."

YOU WON'T WANT TO READ
JUST ONE—KATHERINE STONE

ROOMMATES   (0-8217-5206-5, $6.99/$7.99)
No one could have prepared Carrie for the monumental changes she would face when she met her new circle of friends at Stanford University. Once their lives intertwined and became woven into the tapestry of the times, they would never be the same.

TWINS   (0-8217-5207-3, $6.99/$7.99)
Brook and Melanie Chandler were so different, it was hard to believe they were sisters. One was a dark, serious, ambitious New York attorney; the other, a golden, glamourous, sophisticated supermodel. But they were more than sisters—they were twins and more alike than even they knew . . .

THE CARLTON CLUB   (0-8217-5204-9, $6.99/$7.99)
It was the place to see and be seen, the only place to be. And for those who frequented the playground of the very rich, it was a way of life. Mark, Kathleen, Leslie and Janet—they worked together, played together, and loved together, all behind exclusive gates of the *Carlton Club*.

TODAY'S HOTTEST READS
ARE TOMORROW'S SUPERSTARS

VICTORY'S WOMAN   (4484, $4.50)
by Gretchen Genet
Andrew — the carefree soldier who sought glory on the battlefield,
and returned a shattered man . . . Niall — the legandary frontiers-
man and a former Shawnee captive, tormented by his past . . .
Roger — the troubled youth, who would rise up to claim a shock-
ing legacy . . . and Clarice — the passionate beauty bound by one
man, and hopelessly in love with another. Set against the back-
drop of the American revolution, three men fight for their
heritage — and one woman is destined to change all their lives forever!

FORBIDDEN   (4488, $4.99)
by Jo Beverley
While fleeing from her brothers, who are attempting to sell her
into a loveless marriage, Serena Riverton accepts a carriage ride
from a stranger — who is the handsomest man she has ever seen.
Lord Middlethorpe, himself, is actually contemplating marriage
to a dull daughter of the aristocracy, when he encounters the
breathtaking Serena. She arouses him as no woman ever has. And
after a night of thrilling intimacy — a forbidden liaison — Serena
must choose between a lady's place and a woman's passion!

WINDS OF DESTINY   (4489, $4.99)
by Victoria Thompson
Becky Tate is a half-breed outcast — branded by her Comanche
heritage. Then she meets a rugged stranger who awakens her
heart to the magic and mystery of passion. Hiding a desperate
past, Texas Ranger Clint Masterson has ridden into cattle country
to bring peace to a divided land. But a greater battle rages inside
him when he dares to desire the beautiful Becky!

WILDEST HEART   (4456, $4.99)
by Virginia Brown
Maggie Malone had come to cattle country to forge her future as
a healer. Now she was faced by Devon Conrad, an outlaw
wounded body and soul by his shadowy past . . . whose eyes
blazed with fury even as his burning caress sent her spiraling with
desire. They came together in a Texas town about to explode in sin
and scandal. Danger was their destiny — and there was nothing
they wouldn't dare for love!

*Available wherever paperbacks are sold, or order direct from the
Publisher. Send cover price plus 50¢ per copy for mailing and
handling to Penguin USA, P.O. Box 999, c/o Dept. 17109,
Bergenfield, NJ 07621. Residents of New York and Tennessee
must include sales tax. DO NOT SEND CASH.*